A Ro[...]

First published in Great [...]
Derbysh[...]

Copyright @ Rob Wyllie 2024

The right of Rob Wyllie to be identified as the author of this work has been asserted by him in accordance with the Copyright, Design and Patents Act 1988

All rights reserved. No part of this publication may be reproduced, stored in a retrieval system, or transmitted. in any form or by any means, electronic, mechanical, photocopying, recording or otherwise, without the prior permission of the copyright owner.

All the characters in this book are fictitious and any resemblance to actual persons, living or dead, is purely coincidental.

RobWyllie.com

MURDER AT CHRISTMAS LODGE

Rob Wyllie

Chapter 1

As a rule, Maggie didn't like dressing up in her glad rags, and right now, the dislike was further intensified by the fact that she was now some fourteen weeks into her pregnancy. Accordingly, squeezing into that little black dress – the only one she owned, and a fixture in her wardrobe for nearly ten years – had presented somewhat of a challenge. But squeeze into it she had, and in the event, it wasn't as uncomfortable as she'd feared, a benefit of the stretchy fabric from which it was constructed. Designed to be figure-hugging, it seemed it was equally forgiving if its wearer had added an unwelcome pound or two since its last outing. Her extra pound or two was far from unwelcome of course, and she smiled as Frank stretched out a hand and patted her gently on the tummy.

'You look amazing, by the way,' he said, smiling warmly. 'Almost worth me having to truss myself up in this bloody penguin suit.'

She laughed. 'Actually darling, there's a bit of the James Bond about you tonight. And I've heard there's going to be a vacancy soon, when Mister Craig hands in his notice. You should apply for the job. You'd be a natural.'

His brother Jimmy, seated just behind them, had evidently overheard the conversation and was struggling to suppress a guffaw. He leant over and said, 'I wouldn't give up the day job right now Frankie-boy. Just saying. Not until you've lost a pound or five.'

'*You* would be a dead good Bond, so you would,' Maggie's assistant Lori Logan said, giving Jimmy, sitting alongside her, a look that could only be described as drooling. 'No offence Frank, but he would,' she added hastily.

He laughed. 'Aye, none taken wee Lori. But anyway, when's this damn shindig going to be over and done with? We've had about a hundred awards already by my calculation and it's nearly ten o'clock. Surely there can't be much more of it? My arse is number than a numb thing that's lost all feeling.'

Jimmy grinned. 'Just the big one to go now I think.' As he spoke, the screen at the back of the stage changed to display the title of the upcoming and final award. *Scotland's Woman of the Year, Sponsored by the Scottish Chronicle.* 'Look,' he continued, prodding Frank on the shoulder, 'our mate Yash's got the golden envelope out and I think he's just about to read the nominations.' He nodded towards the stage, where the star reporter was now standing behind a lectern bearing the newspaper's logo and was evidently about to speak.

'I think you should win it Maggie, so I do,' Lori whispered earnestly. 'After all the big crimes you've solved since you moved to Scotland. You should be a shoo-in.'

Maggie shrugged. 'We did it together Lori, as a team. You, me and Jimmy. With a *little* bit of help from the police,' she added, shooting Frank a cheeky smile. 'But, no, I don't think they would want a Yorkshirewoman running away with the big prize. It was nice of them to ask us all to attend, but I don't think Bainbridge Associates will be taking anything home tonight. Scotland's Woman of the Year needs to be Scottish and obviously I'm not.'

'It's a crappy wee trophy anyway,' Frank said, pointing towards the lectern. 'Look at it. You wouldn't want that on your mantelpiece.'

'Shh,' Maggie interrupted. 'Here's Yash now.'

Up on the stage, the young reporter raised his hands and waited for the gentle hum of conversation to fade, then said, 'So ladies and gentlemen, we come to the highlight of our evening, when we all get to find out the identity of Scotland's Woman of the Year, as voted for by the readers of the Scottish edition of the Chronicle. But before that, can I just ask you to put your hands together for the brilliant team here at the Princes Street Grampian hotel, who have looked after us so wonderfully this evening. It's always a great pleasure for me to be back in Scotland's amazing capital city, and like so many others, I wouldn't stay anywhere else when I visit.'

Maggie reflected wryly that the eye-watering room rates of the upmarket Edinburgh hotel meant that only those with a fat expense account like Patel could afford to stay here. But at least the award ceremony wasn't being held at the hotel's sister establishment, the Royal Mile Grampian, a place that nurtured anything but fond memories for her.

'And haven't they done a fantastic job of decorating this room?' Patel continued. 'With this *magnificent* tree and all these beautiful garlands and bobbles? I don't know about all of you, but I wasn't feeling very Christmassy before, but now I'm *really* in the spirit. It's incredible, isn't it? So beautiful.'

A huge round of applause reverberated round the room, but anyone catching sight of Maggie or Frank would have observed a less than enthusiastic response from the pair.

'Bloody hell,' he grumbled. 'By my calculation there are just about twenty-two sleeps until Santa pops down the chimney, and we haven't bloody got one yet. And not a sniff either. We've been to every bloody toy shop and supermarket in a fifty-mile radius and we're online twenty-four by seven. In fact, I got up in the middle of the night last night and had another look on the auction sites, but nothing. A big fat zero.'

Maggie shook her head and gave him a sad look. 'He'll be devastated. And this is probably the last year he'll believe in Santa too.' She paused for a moment. 'In fact, I'm not sure he still *does* believe. But I want to preserve the magic for as long as I can.'

Frank squeezed her hand. 'Don't worry, we'll solve this one, nae bother. I'm a Detective Chief Inspector, remember? I might even go on *Crimewatch* and make an appeal if we get desperate.' That made her laugh, but further discussion on the subject was curtailed by Patel speaking again into his microphone.

'Thank you, thank you,' he boomed, nodding and beaming a broad smile at the audience as he waited for the applause to fade. 'So finally, to our premier award.' He was silent for a moment then grinned. 'That is, if I can get this envelope opened.' Eventually managing to tear it apart, he again paused as he feigned to read the names on the gold-braided card that he had succeeded in extracting. 'So, the nominations *are*....' This time, the pause was theatrical, in a misguided attempt to build tension amongst the audience, who, to a man and woman, had long since lost patience with the extended proceedings.

'Bloody get on with it,' a disgruntled Glaswegian voice shouted from the back of the room.

Patel gave a weak smile and continued, picking up pace. '... the nominations are Sheila McClelland, Scotland's revered former First Minister, nominated for services to the governance of this fine country, and Eilish Macbeth, author of the multi-million selling children's book *My Daddy's Dead But He Still Loves Me*. So please, bear with me whilst we show you this excellent little film.'

To a collective if subdued grumble from the audience, the screen began running a short film highlighting the achievements of the two nominees. Maggie knew all about the politician Sheila McClelland of course, having not long ago helped solve the mystery surrounding the disappearance of her daughter Juliet, but of Eilish Macbeth, she knew less, other than she was the younger sister of the renowned Scottish actress Kirsty Bonnar. Until just two days ago, all she knew was the little she had read in the press, the tragic fact that Macbeth's husband had committed suicide on Christmas Eve almost one year ago, leaving a wife, a daughter and a step-daughter behind. In an attempt to help other families who had suffered the same devastating loss, Eilish had written an illustrated children's book, which had become an instant success, being swiftly translated into a dozen languages and hitting the bestseller charts around the globe. Some cynical commentators attributed the success of the book to the author's famous sister, but others were less unkind. The book pulled no punches, it being as much an attempt to persuade any mother or father thinking of taking their own life to think again as being a support for the bereaved children. A staple on the Morning TV couches, the photogenic Eilish continually made it clear that she would gladly give away all her recently acquired fame and fortune to have her husband back. She was as convincing as she was beautiful, every media appearance amplifying the huge wave of sympathy that her family's tragic loss had engendered in the public consciousness. And Maggie would have felt that same sympathy if it were not for one rather awkward fact.

The fact that two days earlier, a woman called Agnes Napier had rung Maggie's office and told her that Alasdair Macbeth hadn't killed himself.

Chapter 2

'Right then team, how have we got on? Any leads or lines of enquiry yet? Because this is a matter of national importance, I'm sure I don't have to tell you that again.'

DCI Frank Stewart's question was directed at his laptop, the sound slightly distorted by him speaking through a mouthful of sausage sandwich purchased a few minutes earlier from the canteen at New Gorbals police station, where he was occupying a corner table. On the video call from London were his colleagues Detective Constable Ronnie French and Principal Forensic Officer Eleanor Campbell, both recently recruited to the embryonic National Independent Cold-Case Investigations Agency, the organisation of which he was the nominal head. But with the recent change of government and the removal of the former minister whose brainchild it had been – one Katherine Collins, formerly Minister of State for Crime and Policing, now a defiant figure carving out a new role as an opposition disrupter – the future of the department was uncertain. Still, nearly five grand continued to pop into his bank account every month, courtesy of his elevated status as Investigations Director of the unit, and that would cover their expenses very nicely indeed during Maggie's maternity leave. As for his colleagues, they had the safety net of returning to their old jobs at any time, which was a source of great comfort to him, because he didn't want them to suffer should the unit suddenly be closed down, which he thought was a definite risk. That safety net encompassed the super-smart DC Lexy McDonald too, currently sitting alongside him and enjoying an americano and the second of the three rounds of toast and marmalade she had ordered.

It was, characteristically, Eleanor Campbell, who spoke first. 'This isn't police business. You can't like *order* me to do this kind of stuff. You just want one for your little boy's Christmas, and I don't think that's within the terms of my employment contract, even if you are my boss now.'

Frank laughed. 'All I did was ask you to see if there were any for sale online, including on the dark web. And didn't you see there were questions asked about it in the House the other day? Some muppet MP asked the Business Secretary what she was going to do about the shortage, and another one asked the Home Secretary if he thought there might be riots on the streets if the supply situation continued. If that's not proof of the matter's importance, I don't know what is.'

'Did you hear that Suffolk police are arranging a motorcycle escort for the next shipment?' Ronnie asked. 'And they're saying that their boys and girls will definitely be armed.'

'That's smart after what happened last time,' Lexy said. 'And Eleanor, I hate to disagree with you, but this is very much police business. That poor lorry driver was severely beaten up during that hijack two weeks ago and he's in hospital now in a very bad way. We need to find who did that and it starts with tracking down who's selling the stolen stock. Which is almost certainly being advertised on the dark web. Which is why we asked for your help.'

'But it's not like *our* responsibility,' the Forensic Officer protested. 'We're supposed to be cold cases and police corruption and stuff like that. We don't do robberies. There's another team for that.'

'This is a bit more than just a robbery,' Frank said. 'This one's got organised crime written all over it. Anyway, back to my original question. Any leads or lines of enquiry to report?'

'I spoke to a DI in the Northamptonshire force,' French said. 'That's where the hijack happened, at Newport Pagnell services and it's them that's running with the case. The thing is, the heist happened at midday or there or thereabouts, right in the middle of the day. As you can imagine, there were hundreds and hundreds of vehicles going in and out of the place, and besides that, the bad guys could have arrived at the service station hours before. The Northamptonshire boys have got hold of the CCTV from the traffic cameras, but it's like looking for a needle in a haystack.'

'Nothing from the toilets then?' Frank asked.

'They don't have cameras in there,' Eleanor interjected. 'It's like a privacy thing.'

He struggled to suppress a laugh. 'Aye, I think I knew that, but thanks for pointing it out for us Eleanor. So, what happened in there Ronnie, do you know?'

'A cleaner found the driver slumped in a cubical. We're guessing that would have been a couple of hours after it happened. The bad guys must have followed the poor guy in and knocked him out cold. It was a pretty vicious assault according to my DI contact.'

'Aye, poor guy right enough' Frank agreed. 'And nobody saw anything?'

French shrugged. 'Seems not guv. They've had posters up all around the place asking for witnesses to the incident, but nothing so far.'

'And what about you, wee Eleanor?' Frank asked, smiling. 'Anything to report from the big bad dark web?'

She gave him a sullen stare. 'I didn't think it was police business, like I told you. So I haven't looked yet.'

He laughed. 'What, disobeying a direct order Campbell? I could have you court-martialled and shot for this. And before you say anything, I know they only do that in the army, worst luck.' He paused for a moment then gave her a fond look. 'But no, I do appreciate your moral scruples, but hopefully your esteemed colleagues here have now convinced you that this really is a matter for us cops.'

'I suppose,' she mumbled, staring at the floor.

'Good to know,' he responded, his voice a jaunty lilt. 'Anyway, as far as this matter being outside our remit is concerned, there's something I haven't told you lot yet.' He hesitated then said, 'You see, the shipping company had been worried about a couple of previous attempted break-ins when their lorries were parked up in service stations, and so they had asked the Suffolk plod if they would provide an escort for the next shipment, even if it was only for the first thirty or so miles after it had left the Felixstowe container port.'

'But the plod said no,' French supplied. 'That's right guv, ain't it?'

Frank nodded. 'Exactly right Ronnie, they said no, spouting the usual guff about it being a poor use of scarce resources etcetera etcetera. But the thing is, before they got that big *no*, the shipping boys had supplied the cops with the full details of both the truck *and* the route it was going to take to the warehouse in the West Midlands. For security reasons the wagon was going to carry no logos or any form of identification, but the criminals somehow knew everything about it - including the registration number - and were able to track it to the service area on the M1 where, as you know, they coshed the driver when he went for a poo, then nicked the keys and made off with his truck.'

'Are you thinking the details might have been leaked by a bent cop sir?' Lexy asked, sounding sceptical. 'That seems a bit far-fetched if you don't mind me saying so. Surely it's more likely that it was somebody in the shipping company itself or someone working at the port? Or maybe it was an inside job.'

'Aye maybe,' Frank conceded. 'But you see, it's not me that's saying it. It's our old boss, former minister of state Katherine Collins. Not that she was our boss for long, poor woman,' he added. 'But now that she's on the opposition benches, it seems she's set herself up as the scourge of police incompetence. It gets her into the papers nearly every day, which I think she quite likes. Anyway, she's singled out the Suffolk force for particular attention. Someone from there obviously leaked it to her that they'd been asked to escort the last shipment, and that they turned it down. So now she's saying that the Chief Constable has some questions to answer, and she's saying it very publicly.' He paused for a moment then smiled. 'Which is where we come in.'

'Bloody hell,' French said, shaking his head as he anticipated what was coming next. 'I hate these bloody internal investigations. Count me out guv, count me out.'

Frank laughed 'So the beleaguered Chief Constable didn't have much choice other than to give me a wee call. The upshot is, he wants us to do a quick but discreet investigation over at Felixstowe nick to see if he's got anything to be worried about. And funnily enough Frenchie, it was you that immediately sprung to mind when I heard the words *quick* and *discreet* in the same sentence.'

'Aw come on guv,' the DC protested again. 'Can't you get someone else to do it? Just this once?

'We haven't got anyone else except Lexy,' Frank replied, giving a shrug, 'and we don't really want to be jetting someone down from Glasgow when you're just an hour's drive away. That doesn't make logistical sense.'

'I'd be quite happy to do it sir,' Lexy said brightly. 'And they might open up to me if I put on my silly wee lassie from Scotland act.'

Ronnie French looked up at the ceiling and sighed. 'No, I can't let you do that Lexy.' He sounded guilty, exactly as Frank had intended. 'The guv's right, it's only five minutes up the road for me.' He sighed again then said. 'All right, I'll do it.'

'But it's like only a *toy*,' Eleanor interrupted, evidently unwilling to give up her protest without a final token struggle.

'It's more than just a toy,' Frank said. 'It's an Aquanaut Island, and it's what every bloody kid in the country between five and fifteen wants for Christmas this year. And yes, I admit that includes our wee Ollie.' He paused for a moment. 'But the fact is, these toys are fetching nearly a thousand quid online and if one comes up for sale on the auction sites, literally thousands of folks are after it. That level of demand is like catnip to these hoods. Nab a thousand of them and you're looking at a million quid, cash. You can see the attraction, can't you?'

Lexy laughed. 'It just looks like a big lump of plastic to me. And what is this Aquanaut thing all about anyway?'

'It's a kids' TV programme,' Frank explained, 'and it's the biggest show in town at the moment, one of those fancy CGI animation jobs. A girl called Captain Aquanaut is the hero or heroine, whatever you call her, and she's a squid or an octopus or something like that. Oh aye, and they live on an underwater island with lots of flashing lights and computer screens and they whizz about on jet submarines rescuing people whilst saving the ocean from evil polluters.'

'You seem to know a lot about it sir,' she said, raising an amused eyebrow.

He gave a wry smile. 'My knowledge of the subject is beyond encyclopaedic, even if I say so myself. That's because Ollie watches it twenty-four by seven, and I now know every episode off by heart.'

'And they sell for a thousand pounds?' Eleanor said. 'That's like *weird.*'

Frank smiled. 'Weird or not, that's what they're going for right now.' And then he remembered that Eleanor too was expecting a baby, due to arrive about a month before Maggie's. 'And if I were you, I'd put a deposit down on one right now. Your wee bundle of joy will definitely want one, and knowing how clever the bairn is bound to be given the brainpower of its mother, I predict he or she will be firing up the Aqua-Sub in about eighteen months' time.'

To his surprise, Eleanor responded with a coy smile. 'We've found out it's a girl actually. We're going to call her Lulu.'

'Oh that's *lovely*,' Lexy said. 'And what a nice name.'

'*Boom-bang-a-bang*,' Frank was about to quip, before thinking better of it, realising that his younger colleagues probably wouldn't get the cultural reference to the iconic Scottish *chanteuse* anyway. Instead he said, 'Well that's really great Eleanor and aye, it's a lovely name right enough.' He paused for a moment before continuing. 'So, just to make it clear, *your* mission is to scan the dark web thingy and see if you can find any Aquanaut Islands for sale. And naturally, anything you can do to trace the actual physical location of the thieves will be amazingly helpful.'

'They'll be hidden behind military-strength firewalls and using gigabyte encryption,' Eleanor said, her face breaking into that superior expression she often adopted, the one he'd seen so many times before. The one that said *I know lots of stuff that you wouldn't understand.*

'Naturally,' he said. 'But I'm sure you'll be able to crack it with a wee app or some of that clever but secret MI5 beta software that you talk about so much. And before you protest, I know it'll be *really* difficult. Just do your best.'

'You mean like I always do,' she said with a mild scowl.

'Exactly that. So Ronnie, I want you to get up there tomorrow if you can. The Big Chief wants to meet and greet you, then he's allocated one of the duty sergeants who'll look after you at Felixstowe nick, a guy by the name of Pete Dudley. We have to assume he's a bloke that the Chief Constable trusts.'

'What, I've got to meet the bloody brass?' French protested. 'Well thanks a bunch guv, that's all I can say. And I hope that bloody sergeant is kosher if you're going to drop me into the lion's den,' he added gloomily. 'And how long do I need to stay?'

Frank shrugged. 'As long as it takes. But I guess it'll be a few days up there, then back to base for a bit of thinking about whatever you find out.'

The DC gave a reluctant thumbs up. 'Right you are guv, I'll do my best.'

'Good, so it seems like we've got a plan. Now finally, don't forget it's our Christmas lunch in a couple of weeks, and just to let you know, we'll be splashing out, because our government accounting wonk Mister Trevor Park says it's important that we spend all of our budget before the financial year end. That means it's first-class tickets for you two, that is Eleanor if you're still okay to travel to Glasgow and have a wee overnight stay afterwards.'

She gave him a look. 'I'm pregnant, I'm not like *ill*.'

He laughed. 'No, of course you're not. It's settled then. And I should mention, we'll be joined by Maggie's team too, a kind of joint celebration of all the work we've done together. She's booked a nice restaurant in the West End and the mulled wine will no doubt be flowing. It should be a hoot.'

'Just one thing guv, ' French interjected. 'If our budget is so healthy and we're being urged to spend it, couldn't you come down to Felixstowe too? Because I don't fancy talking to that Chief Constable geezer on my own. Way above my pay grade. Maybe you could just come for the day.'

Frank thought for a moment then gave a reluctant nod. 'Aye, I think that would be okay I suppose.' Glancing at his laptop, he saw French was beaming what looked like a relieved smile. 'And I know it's a cliché, but they do say two heads are better than one. Even our two. ' He paused then said. 'That's it then. Off we all go, and we'll meet again in a couple of weeks' time in this fair city of Glasgow to attack the turkey and stuffing, or in your case Eleanor, a nut roast plus cranberries.'

By which time, he hoped very much to have got his hands on one of those bloody Aquanaut Islands.

Chapter 3

'Don't you think it's a bit strange that it was that Agnes Napier woman who phoned you?' Lori asked Maggie. 'And isn't it strange that she waited a year after that terrible thing happened before she said anything?'

'Yes, I was thinking that too,' Maggie agreed, reaching out to pick up her cup and taking a sip of her coffee. It was mid-morning, and as was their custom, they were camped up in the Bikini Barista Cafe, the cozy eating establishment located just two doors down from the Byres Road office of Bainbridge Associates, her little private investigations firm. Not for the first time, she reflected she could save herself the not inconsiderable rent by closing down her office and moving here on a permanent basis, given how much of their time they spent in the place. Certainly, she was confident she could come to a suitable financial arrangement with Stevie, the cafe's amiable proprietor and former employer of her young associate Lorilynn (Lori) Logan. But no, they needed an office if the firm was going to be taken seriously, and indeed in just thirty minutes' time they would be sitting down in those self-same premises to hear Agnes Napier tell her story.

'Is Jimmy going to be dialling in?' Lori asked, a hint of wistfulness in her tone.

Maggie shook her head. 'No, not today. He's up in the Cairngorms leading one of his crazy outdoor leadership courses. This is the hardcore winter one that he and his partner Stew run a few times a year. The weather is mental up there at this time of year, but that seems to add to the attraction. In fact, they had nearly a foot of snow yesterday. He texted me a picture of Braemar, it looked amazing.'

Lori smiled. 'I hope the snow gets down here soon. I'd love a white Christmas, so I would.'

'Well, it's forecast to arrive in a couple of days if the cold front keeps creeping down from the Arctic.' She laughed. 'I sound like a weather girl, don't I? But yes, I'd like a white Christmas too and Ollie's desperate to get out on his sledge.'

Lori gave her boss an enquiring look. 'Talking of Ollie, any luck on the Aqua- thingy front?'

'Nope, nothing. But Frank's still hopeful. Anyway, time to focus on the Macbeth matter. And just so you know, I haven't made up my mind whether to take on the case yet. Because from what I can see, it looks like a very difficult one.'

Lori gave her boss an enquiring look. 'Really? Well to be fair, there is something that's got me scratching my head already. Do you know why this Napier woman came to us and not the police? Because if she's saying Alasdair Macbeth didn't kill himself, that must mean she thinks the guy was murdered, doesn't it?'

Maggie nodded. 'Yes, and I did ask her that when she called. But she didn't exactly answer that question, just mumbled something about her not being sure that she wasn't just imagining things.'

'So she came to us instead.'

'Exactly. But to be fair, I can see why she might not want to go to the police. Because all she seemed to be offering in way of explanation was that Alasdair Macbeth was a lovely chap and that he would never have killed himself. Vague to say the least.'

'That was all?' Lori asked, unimpressed.

Her boss nodded again. 'Pretty much. Although she did say that she'd been thinking about the terrible incident a lot as Christmas was approaching again, and that was what persuaded her to finally do something about her concerns. Which, she says, she'd had right from the start. It sounded like perhaps she always had suspicions but didn't have any evidence to back it up. That's my opening assumption at least.'

'But who is this woman anyway?' Lori asked.

'She says she was the housekeeper at the lodge Eilish Macbeth's family rented over Christmas. The one where Alasdair Macbeth was found hanged.'

Lori looked at her wide-eyed. 'So she would have been there on that awful day, and seen the body dangling there? That must have been horrible, especially on Christmas day. But how come she's waited until now before coming forward? Do you think something specific has happened or something's changed? Something that's made her do something now?'

Maggie shrugged. 'Like I said, she didn't mention anything specific on the phone, but maybe she'll be a bit more forthcoming when we meet her face to face. Speaking of which, look at the time. We'd better get back, because we don't want to keep her waiting.'

Agnes Napier arrived on schedule just a few minutes after their return. She was in her fifties, Maggie estimated, grey-haired and sturdily built, dressed in a purple woollen skirt, grey blouse and olive-green gilet.

Maggie smiled. 'Agnes, thank you for coming in to see us. I'm Maggie Bainbridge, and this is my associate, Lori Logan.' She paused for a moment. 'So Agnes, I only know a little of the matter you want us to look at from our brief conversation the other day, so perhaps you could start from the beginning, and give us as much background as possible.'

Napier looked at them nervously, then glanced at her watch before replying. 'Sorry, I said I'd meet my sister at twelve o'clock. She lives here in Glasgow. She calls it Dowanhill, but it's actually Partick.' She paused for a moment. 'Actually, it was Maisie that said I should come and see you. She knows all about the cases you worked on in the last twelve months or so. She's followed them all and she says you've become really famous.'

Maggie smiled again. 'I'd hardly say that. But yes, I can't deny we've been very busy recently. Anyway, how can we help you?'

Agnes Napier hesitated before answering. 'I'm not sure exactly where to start. But as I said on the phone, it's to do with the death of poor Alasdair Macbeth.'

'Which you now don't think was a suicide, is that right?'

Napier gave her an uncertain look. 'Yes, I'm beginning to think so, but to tell the truth, I'm far from sure. That's why I thought I should speak to you. Or at least, that's what Maisie said I should do.'

'Well, let's hear your story, shall we?' Maggie said in a kindly tone. 'Then perhaps between us we can decide what we should do next. Would that be okay?'

The woman gave a shy nod. 'Aye, that's fine. Can I just start by saying I work for the Glengarry estate? The Laird of Glengarry is the biggest landowner around where I stay in Nethy Bridge, and a very nice gentleman too. I don't know if you've heard of him? Mr Chambers. James Chambers'

'No, I can't say I have,' Maggie said, 'but I do know of Nethy Bridge, because one of our cases took us up there not so long ago. It's a beautiful place, and I imagine it's magical in winter.'

She smiled. 'I've lived there all my life, so I'm biased, but aye, it is beautiful. And I've worked for the laird for nearly thirty years, as did my mother and father for his father. A few years ago, he developed some very posh holiday lodges on the edge of Abernethy Forest, and I'm employed as a housekeeper at the biggest one. It's called Christmas Lodge, and it's got six bedrooms and a huge kitchen and a lounge with a big log fire. It's the fanciest one on the development, and his lairdship always insists that it's me who looks after the guests there.' She paused for a moment. 'And that's where Mr. Macbeth died that Christmas morning.'

'And what a terrible thing that must have been,' Lori said.

Napier nodded. 'Aye, it was. And Mr. Macbeth was such a lovely man too. It gave me such a terrible shock when I saw him hanging there dead. Not just me of course,' she added hastily. 'It was awful for the whole family. I was just thankful that the wee kiddies didn't see it.'

'Yes, it would have been horrible for them to have witnessed that,' Maggie agreed. 'So perhaps it would be good if you brought Lori and me up to speed with who was at the lodge that Christmas. Could you do that please? Maybe start with the adults if you would.'

'Aye, okay, I can do that. Well obviously, there was poor Alasdair, he was there with his wife Eilish, and their two children. Then there were Eilish's two sisters - Kirsty, who's the eldest, and who I'm sure you know.'

'That's Kirsty Bonnar, the actress,' Maggie said. 'I know who she is of course. She's been amazing in everything I've seen her in.'

'That's right. She was there with her husband Tom, who's English and some sort of fancy lawyer in London. The youngest one, that's Isla, was there with her partner Drew and their two little kids. And then there was Nan of course, Nan Bonnar. She's the sisters' old mother.' She paused for a moment then said, 'Actually, I've got a photograph, if you'd like to see it?'

'Yes, that would be good,' Maggie said.

The woman fiddled with her phone for a few seconds then turned it so that Maggie and Lori could see it. She said, 'I'll send it to you, but we can have a look at it now. This is all of them, in front of the big Christmas tree, on Christmas Eve. I took the picture myself of course.'

'So that's the three sisters and the mother in front I guess, with the kids,' Maggie said. 'Kirsty I know of course, and Eilish, I recognise from her TV appearances. And that's her daughter Christabelle, isn't it?'

'Aye, that's right. She was going to be sixteen on that Christmas day. That's how she got her name, because of the day she was born on obviously.' The woman pointed to the picture again. 'That's Isla and that's Drew behind her, and next to her is Tom, Kirsty's man. Then there's the three wee ones. Daniel and Hope are Isla's two, and they were four and six I think, and then there's Eilish's wee one Mirabelle. She's six as well.'

'Mirabelle and Christabelle?' Lori said. 'They're dead nice names for two sisters.'

Napier shrugged but made no comment, before pointing at the photograph again. 'And that's Alasdair.'

'He looks happy,' Maggie said, observing the man's wide smile, 'but photographs don't always tell the truth, do they? It's so sad.'

'I've seen that Christabelle on telly too,' Lori said. 'She's been on with her mother, and she sounds right full of herself, so she does.'

'I never took to the girl,' the woman said. 'And the way she dresses too, I don't know what her mother is thinking of, allowing her to go about like that. Well, you can see it in the picture, can't you? Mind you, the mother's not much better, is she? Like mother like daughter, that's what they say, isn't it?'

'There were girls like that at my school,' Lori said. 'Dead popular with the boys and horrible to all the other girls and they bullied all the weaker kids too. I hated them.' Maggie gave her assistant an affectionate look, wondering whether she had been one of those weaker kids too. But whatever the case, no-one would think of bullying Lorilynn Logan now, that was for sure.

'And by the way, Christabelle isn't actually Alasdair's daughter,' Napier said. 'Eilish had her before they got married. She never said who the father was. But then she probably doesn't know, seeing what she was like back then,' she added, giving the two detectives a look that shouted disapproval.

'And how long had the family been up there?' Maggie asked. 'Because Christmas Day was a Tuesday that year, wasn't it?'

'Yes, it was,' Napier said. 'They all arrived on the Saturday afternoon before. It was the third or fourth time they'd taken Christmas Lodge as a family, and they always tried to get up a few days before the big day. This time, Tom and Kirsty had flown up to Inverness from London then hired a car, and the others drove up from Glasgow. I think the old witch came up with Isla and her man.' She shot the detectives an apologetic look. 'Sorry, I shouldn't have said that. But Nan Bonnar isn't a very nice woman. She always looks down her nose at me, as if I was dirt, and she's never happy with anything I do for her. But then she looks down on just about everyone. A right old lady muck.'

'And what exactly are your duties as housekeeper?' Maggie asked, prompted by the direction of the conversation.

'Housemaid, cook and general dogsbody,' Napier replied with a hint of sourness. 'Mind you, the laird pays me very well, so I've no reason to complain.'

'And do you live in?' Lori asked. 'Do you have your own room in the lodge?'

'Aye, sometimes,' the housekeeper said. 'I do have a tiny room with a single bed upstairs, but I'll only stay there if I've been working late. My own wee cottage is only a few minutes away in the village and I prefer to go home when I can. Although I did stay over that Christmas Eve with all the work that had to be done, you know, setting the big table for dinner and whatnot.'

Lori nodded. 'And were you having to cook the Christmas dinner for *all* of those people? That sounds like hard work.'

The woman shook her head. 'Och no, they were having caterers in for that. Kirsty arranged it all as usual, but I would be helping with the serving up. And doing all the washing-up afterwards,' she added, this time not attempting to hide her displeasure. 'But of course, we never got to have that lovely dinner,' she said. 'Not with the police and the paramedics swarming around and everything else. It was an awful day.'

'Who discovered the body?' Maggie asked, 'and when was that, timewise I mean?'

'It was poor Kirsty who found him,' Napier said. 'And I think it was about eight or maybe nearer to quarter past. She'd got up at that time so she could watch the wee ones opening their presents and found him just hanging there. She screamed her head off and of course everyone jumped out of bed and ran downstairs to see what had happened. Somebody decided to cut him down to see if they could give him the kiss of life, but it was too late by then. Then someone dialled nine-nine-nine, and then the police and an ambulance arrived and gave him more CPR, but everybody knew it was pointless. They took the body away to the hospital in Inverness and then everyone just sat around either crying their eyes out or too stunned to do anything.'

Maggie nodded. 'Yes, it must have been absolutely awful. But now, twelve months on, you think Alasdair Macbeth didn't kill himself, which leaves me to assume that at the time, you did. Is that right?'

The woman gave her an uncertain look. 'Aye I did. You see, at the time there was an atmosphere in that house, a right *poisonous* atmosphere. It was dreadful.'

'How do you mean?' Maggie asked.

'Well, for a start, there was Kirsty boasting about her Oscar nomination and about some massive film role she'd just been offered. I think everybody was sick of hearing about it after the first day. And to make matters worse, she'd done an interview a week or two back with one of the tabloids and the subject matter had strayed on to how her family had fallen apart when she was just a child. Eilish and Isla were livid about that, as you can imagine. And so was the old mother. Her more than anyone in fact.'

'Sorry, I'm not sure I quite understand what you're getting at,' Maggie said, curious.

'Oh, didn't you know?' the housekeeper said. 'You see, the girl's father left them when they were young. Kirsty was twelve, which I suppose is quite old, but Eilish was just six and Isla only four. It's never been talked about when I've been in earshot, but I've always assumed that their father couldn't take any more of being married to Nan, and to be honest, who could blame him, knowing what she's like. But the thing is, Kirsty adored her father and insisted that she wanted to live with him, and after a bitter custody battle, the children's court eventually ruled in his favour.'

'The sisters were brought up separately then?' Maggie asked, surprised. 'How did that work out?'

'Kirsty grew up to be a kind and loving and capable woman, and Eilish and Isla grew up to be bitter, twisted and needy. That's how it worked out. I know it's a horrible thing to say, but unfortunately, it's the truth.'

Hearing the last sentence, Maggie shot Lori a surreptitious look that plainly said *bloody hell*.

'And all of this appeared in a newspaper recently then?' she asked, thinking if that was the case, then Kirsty Bonnar wasn't exactly being kind and loving to her sisters, or her mother either for that matter.

'Yes, it did,' Napier said, her expression making it clear she was enjoying this immensely. 'Although as to the bitterness, I suppose it's truer with respect to Eilish than Isla. Isla's always been an enigma to me. Quiet, but you're never quite sure what's going on in her head, if you know what I'm saying? And she's always been a bit in her older sister's shadow. That's Eilish I mean.'

'So they must all hate one another then?' Lori asked.

Napier gave a snort. 'I don't know if I'd call it hate. But despite all the history, Kirsty seems to have a compulsion to keep the family together through thick and thin, and she feels a responsibility as the big sister to support them through all their self-inflicted traumas. Despite them not giving a damn when she was going through her own troubles,' she added.

'I'm sorry, but is there something else you're not telling us?' Maggie said, struggling to hide her incredulity.

'Kirsty and her husband haven't been able to have children. They tried for years but it just didn't happen, and they had rounds and rounds of IVF and that didn't work either.'

'That's dead sad,' Lori said. 'Poor things.'

'Well, if you want to know my opinion, I don't agree with all that nonsense, using science to do what God and nature never intended. And she was far too old in any case, nearly forty-five. As I said, it's a nonsense.'

Lori looked as if she was going to comment but stopped as she caught Maggie giving her a sharp look.

'And of course they looked into adoption,' Napier went on, 'but the fact is, local authorities don't want to place children with couples like *them,* do they?' She paused and shook her head sadly. 'Too privileged, that's what they say, which is more nonsense. Two *white*, that's what I say, and I don't care who hears it either. Any child living with that couple would have a wonderful life, but the councils don't care about the child, only about reinforcing their own stupid prejudices.' *So says one of the most bigoted women I've ever had the misfortune to have to listen to*, Maggie thought, whilst recognising that what she was being told might be vital to the case. 'Of course, Kirsty has everything,' Agnes Napier continued, 'so she hasn't really got anything to complain about. And she is *so* devoted to her nieces and nephews. But it's not the same as having your own, is it?' she added, leaving the question hanging in the air.

'Is she jealous of her sisters then?' Lori asked. 'Even although she's dead rich and famous?'

'She's got *class*, so she wouldn't show it,' the housekeeper said in a knowing tone, 'but, aye, I expect she is, a bit. Who wouldn't be if you were so desperate to have your own wee ones?'

Maggie nodded. 'Well, thank you for sharing this with us Agnes. It's very useful background.'

'Aye, but all of that wasn't the only thing, not by a long shot,' Napier interjected. 'Because it was the Macbeth family troubles that were causing even more ructions.' She hesitated for a moment then said, 'They thought that they were all going to be rich you see, and then they found out they weren't,' she replied, her voice dropping to a conspiratorial whisper. 'They were being horrible to Alasdair, especially that little madam Christabelle. As if it was his fault. I mean, I ask you? Everybody knew that old Macbeth was hopeless at business.' She paused. 'Mind you, no-one knew quite how hopeless he was until he died, leaving all that debt for his poor son to deal with.'

'I take it's Alasdair's father you're referring to? And that he had died recently?'

The woman nodded. 'Aye, just four months earlier. Alasdair really loved his father, but it didn't take him long to realise what a state the family estate was in. I think old Robert Macbeth had lost the will to live when Lady Macbeth died a few years previously, and he'd let the place go to wrack and ruin.'

'Sorry, did you say Lady Macbeth?' Maggie asked, surprised.

'Aye, that's right,' Napier said. 'Robert Macbeth was the Laird of Invermore estate, and his wife had the right to use the honorary title.' She paused again. 'Anyway, the upshot was, there were mortgages and loans on everything, and the farm equipment was all old and in bad condition, and all the feeders for the game birds and such like had been left to rust away. Alasdair tried to arrange an estate sale, but the auctioneers said there was barely anything worth selling. The poor man was distraught about his dad's death, and then he had all the business problems to deal with. And all his family problems too, on top of it,' she added.

'And you thought all of this might have been enough to make him take his own life?' Maggie asked.

'Aye, I did at the time. Because they'd all been getting at him over dinner that night, you know, wee sly digs about him being a failure and all that kind of thing, and he'd been getting through a lot of wine and was quite drunk. He looked so unhappy, but he just sat there and took it. So I was shocked but not surprised when he killed himself.'

'But now you don't think he did,' Lori said. 'Can you tell us why that is?'

Napier hesitated before answering. 'It's just that I've been thinking about it a lot recently, now that we're coming up to Christmas again. And I've been talking to Maisie about it too. She'd been reading an article in the paper about how selfish suicide is, especially the ones where the person doesn't leave a note or anything. And that's when it struck me.' She paused again before continuing. 'You see, Alasdair was such a gentle, kind and considerate man, and even if he had been driven to despair, he would still have been thinking about his family. He would have left a note, definitely. But he didn't, you see. He didn't leave a note. Nothing at all.'

'Okay,' Maggie said slowly. 'I can see where you're coming from. And there's undoubtedly some logic in what you're saying,' she added, although feeling far from convinced. 'But perhaps you should speak to the police about your concerns?'

'No no,' she said, visibly alarmed. 'I don't want the police involved. I don't think his lairdship would want that, with all that bad publicity. Especially if I turn out to be wrong.'

'But you do understand that if we were to take on this investigation you would have to pay us, and it could turn out to be quite expensive?'

'I've got money,' she shot back. 'That wouldn't be a problem.'

Maggie gave her chin a pensive stroke. 'Well okay Agnes, I'll give it some consideration. But it might be a very difficult matter to pursue. Because it's quite likely that the family will refuse to talk to us, whereas of course the police have powers to compel them to do so. You do understand that, don't you?'

'They'll talk to you all right,' she said as she got up to leave, her tone conveying a mixture of self-satisfaction and cunning. 'Once they see their names all over the Grampian Times.'

Chapter 4

It was the next day, and it seemed Maggie and Lori weren't feeling any more positive about the Macbeth case than they had been when Agnes Napier left their office sixteen hours earlier.

'See, I looked it up on Google,' Lori was saying, 'and it says it's actually a minority of suicides who leave notes. So that's Agnes's theory shot down in flames before we even get started.'

Maggie looked at her uncertainly. 'That's true, but remember, she was talking about someone she'd got to know quite well, and she obviously feels strongly that Alasdair Macbeth wouldn't have taken his own life without leaving an explanation. I know it sounds a bit far-fetched, but I can see why a man like Alasdair would have felt as if it was his duty to explain. Even in his final despair, it would have been something he just had to do.'

Lori raised an eyebrow. 'But it's a *bit* of a stretch, don't you think? This Agnes woman's clutching at straws in my opinion. Definitely.'

'Yes, well perhaps. But it is *something* at least.'

'Aye, that's what she said. Me, I think it's a big fat nothing. And I'll tell you what else is weird. Why is she prepared to shell out her own cash to a firm of private investigators? If she has her suspicions, why doesn't she go straight to the police?'

Maggie shrugged. 'Well yes, I share your doubts about that. Her explanation is that she's worried that it might affect the Laird's lodge rental business, and she obviously holds the man in great esteem. It's a bit muddle-headed I agree, but I do kind of see her logic.'

'But isn't she a right piece of work?' Lori said, making a face. 'She really was determined to stick the knife into all of them.'

'She's a horrible woman all right. But she does seem to have this so-called murder business firmly between her teeth.'

'But using her own money?' Lori said, evidently not satisfied. 'And what about that throwaway remark right at the end, about them seeing their names in the papers? What's that all about?'

'Yes, that threw me a bit,' Maggie admitted. 'It sounds as if she has been talking to a journalist, which might not have been the smartest idea.' She paused for a moment. 'The more I think about it, the more I think we've got to say no to this case. The fact is, everything about it would be bloody awkward, wouldn't it? I mean, I just can't see how we could interview everyone who was in that lodge over Christmas without causing an almighty stink. *Eilish, the housekeeper thinks your husband might have been murdered, and so I have to ask, where were you between the hours of 10pm on Christmas Eve and 6am on Christmas morning?*' She paused again. 'Do you see what I mean Lori? Bloody awkward.'

Her colleague nodded in agreement. 'Aye, you're not wrong Maggie. And what you've just said highlights the fact that we don't know even the most basic stuff like who might have a motive and when Alasdair was last seen, and other things like that. If we *are* going to take this case on, there's a ton of stuff we'd have to find out. And it would be great to meet Kirsty Bonnar, wouldn't it? We might get tickets for one of her plays or get to go behind the scenes and see her filming.'

Maggie laughed. 'Yes perhaps, but I don't think that in itself is *quite* a big enough reason for us to take on the case.' Just then, her phone rang. She glanced down then smiled as she saw it was Frank.

'Darling,' she said brightly. 'This is an unexpected pleasure. A slow day on the front line of crime-fighting I take it? Murderers and bank-robbers having a day off?'

He gave a short laugh before answering. *'You seen the news? About the Suez canal?'*

'No,' she said, puzzled. 'I'm not a great follower of international events as you know.'

'Well this is a bloody catastrophe. Another one of these giant container ships has only gone and got itself stuck in there, and now they're saying it'll be eight days or more before they manage to unblock it.'

'That does sound serious,' she agreed, 'but I'm not exactly sure why you had to break off from chasing bank-robbers and murderers to tell me this.'

'The bloody Chinese ship is stuck behind it, and I mean the ship that's supposed to be speeding seventy-five thousand Aquanaut Islands to these fair shores. They're saying it won't make it into Felixstowe until the twenty-seventh at the earliest. It's a bloody disaster. In fact, it wouldn't surprise me if there's a question in the House of Commons about getting Christmas moved back a few days. But that's why I called. Because I think we need to come up

with a Plan B for wee Ollie's Christmas. Just in case I can't find one anywhere else, although obviously I'll be trying everything,' he added, sounding anything but confident.

'Oh dear, he'll be devastated when he opens his presents on Christmas morning,' Maggie said, 'and I really don't know what we could give him instead. He's really set his heart on it.'

'Maybe you could get him a Scotland football shirt,' Lori piped up, having evidently got the gist of the conversation.

Frank laughed. *'What, and sentence him to a lifetime of agony and disappointment like I've suffered? No way, we'd have the child protection agencies onto us before we know it.'*

'I'll think of something, don't worry,' Maggie said, 'and thanks for letting me know. But just make sure your team knows how serious this is,' she added, suppressing a laugh. 'You *need* to find one.'

'Message understood. See you tonight,' he said, before hanging up.

'Bad news, eh?' Lori said sadly. 'No Aquanaut Island for wee Ollie then? But listen, my dad said there was a similar kind of thing that happened when he was a kid with a Thunderbirds toy, and all the mums and dads made them out of cardboard and old washing-up liquid bottles instead and they were dead good. Maybe we could do that.'

Maggie gave a rueful smile. 'It's a nice thought, but this thing is packed with electronics, with loads of flashing lights and stuff, and it's connected to the internet, and it can even talk to you. I don't think you can do that with a couple of old cereal boxes. No, I'm afraid it's the real thing or nothing.'

'Ah well, I'm sure Frank will track one down. But I was thinking about our Macbeth case whilst you were talking, and I've come up with a dead brilliant idea. Even if I do say so myself.'

'Dead brilliant you say?' Maggie said, laughing. 'Okay then Miss Logan, let's hear it.'

The girl took a breath then said, 'Aye, well you're dead right about the awkwardness of the case. We know that it must have been one of the people who were at that family gathering that killed him – if he was killed, I mean – but are any of them going to be willing to speak to us? No way, and we're not the police, so we can't force them to say anything, can we?'

Maggie nodded. 'Yep, we told her that already, and I agree with you one hundred percent.'

'And she herself has already contacted the media, or so she says. So what if it's Yash Patel of the *Chronicle* who's running with this story, rather than the poxy wee Grampian Times? We get him to take it on, but we then get him to commission us to help him with the investigation. And that way, we don't have to take any money off of Agnes Napier, and then it can be a proper independent investigation.'

'He won't do it,' Maggie said, shaking her head. 'It won't be a big enough thing for him.'

'Not big enough?' Lori shot back. 'That Eilish Macbeth is a right babe and she's *everywhere* in the public eye right now. And there's that wee tart of a daughter too, not to mention that Eilish is Kirsty Bonnar's sister. This is pure tabloid gold, he'll be biting our hands off.'

'I have my doubts,' Maggie said, but somehow, she found herself reaching for her phone. She swiped down her contacts until she came to the reporter's number. He answered within a few seconds, his tone friendly but businesslike.

'Maggie, good to hear from you. What can I do for you?'

She grinned. 'Quite a lot, I think. Yash, have you heard of Eilish Macbeth? And by the way, I've got you on speaker phone. My assistant Lori's with me.'

'Hi Lori. And as to Macbeth, of course I've heard of her, who hasn't? She's quite a babe. And she's Kirsty Bonnar's sister too.'

'Funny, that's exactly the words Miss Logan here used,' Maggie grinned. 'The thing is, we might have a story for you. A big story.' Succinctly, she explained how they had been approached by Agnes Napier and the woman's doubts about Alasdair Macbeth's death. But when he heard the reasons for the housekeeper's suspicions, it seemed Yash shared Maggie's own reservations.

'Sounds very flimsy,' he said. *'Just because there was no suicide note. That was it?'*

'I know, I know, it's not exactly compelling,' Maggie admitted. 'But I think you would agree I'm a pretty good judge of people, and when this woman says Alasdair Macbeth would definitely have left a note, I'm inclined to believe her.' She paused for a moment and then added, 'And just think how sensational it would be if you broke the story. Especially if it turned out that Eilish herself was the murderer.'

'Is that what this housekeeper woman thinks? That Eilish was the murderer?' Patel asked, his curiosity evidently growing.

'No, she hasn't said that, but in a lot of murder cases it turns out to be the spouse, doesn't it? And even if it's not her, think what a web of suspicion and intrigue you would be able to spin. I'm sure it would sell a lot of papers.'

She heard him laugh. *'We don't sell many papers these days, it's subscribers to the online edition we're interested in. But you're right, it would be an interesting story, although there's not very much to go on, is there?'* There was silence at the end of the line, Maggie assuming he was thinking through the pros and cons of the matter. Finally, he said, *'No I'm sorry, it is very interesting, but there's not enough for me. I think I'm going to have to say no on this occasion.'*

'That's disappointing,' Maggie said truthfully, 'but I understand. And anyway, the Grampian Times is already running with it. You probably haven't heard of it,' she added, laughing. 'They're the local rag up in Inverness.'

'And they'll probably win an award for it,' Lori interjected, wearing a sly expression. 'Well I'm sorry you can't take it on Yash. And that probably means we'll have to take the other big story to another paper too.'

'What story's that?' Patel shot back.

'Nah, don't worry about it,' she said brightly. 'We'll speak to the Globe about that one. But it's been good to talk to you again. See you soon. Bye.'

'*No, wait,*' he barked out.

All through the discourse, Maggie had been looking at her colleague with a growing sense of bewilderment. But now it seemed Lori was ready to explain.

'See, we're chasing this *massive* story about a plot to steal *millions* of those Aquanaut Island thingies, and there's international criminal gangs involved and possible police corruption and maritime sabotage too. It's sensational, and the story's going to explode just in time for Christmas. I'll tell you what Yash, the Globe are going to *completely* love it. Anyway, as I said, no time to talk. Speak soon. Bye.'

'Wait,' he shouted again, then laughed. '*You're a little devil Lori Logan, and you too Maggie flipping Bainbridge. And I suppose I'll only get to know about this amazing scoop if I agree to help you with the Macbeth investigation.*'

Lori smirked. 'Yeah, pretty much. But they're both fantastic stories, so they are. The Grampian Times are salivating at the thought.'

They heard him swear under his breath. '*Okay, but I'm only going to commit a few days to it, and if nothing comes out of the Macbeth investigation by then, then you're on your own.*'

'That's perfectly reasonable Yash, and thank you so much,' Maggie said. 'And I'll give you a call in the next couple of days on the other story too.' *If Frank doesn't go mental when he hears what we've done*, she thought. With that, she ended the call.

Lori, correctly anticipating that a difficult conversation with her boss was about to begin, had evidently decided to get her defence in first. Speaking at about a thousand miles an hour she said, 'But Maggie, you always say you appreciate initiative, and you can't deny I was using my initiative there. And it worked out well, didn't it? Yash is going to take on the Macbeth story, and it'll be tons easier for us too because we can just say we're working on behalf of the Chronicle. And I'm sure your Frank will *massively* appreciate Yash's help in trying to track down these Island toys.'

Maggie gave her assistant a stern look. 'That, I think, is highly unlikely.' But then, involuntarily, she found herself breaking into a smile. 'But yes, you certainly used your initiative, I can't deny that.' She paused for a moment. *'Over*-used it, if I'm being frank. However, in this instance, it does seem to have worked out rather well.'

***

True to his word, Patel had run the story in the paper's Friday edition, crafting a piece that was equally lavish in its praise of *My Daddy's Dead but He Still Loves Me* and of its author Eilish Macbeth. However, anyone reading to the end of the article would have been pulled up short by the sensational sting in the tail. *However, despite her great success, there are still questions to be answered about the tragic and mysterious death of her husband Alasdair on Christmas Day one year ago. The official verdict was that he took his own life, but now, twelve months on, that verdict is being challenged by a source close to the family.*

'It's a cracking story that Yash has written, isn't it?' Lori said. 'It'll be as if he's thrown a grenade into the heart of that family, because every single one of them will now be wondering who's been speaking to the Chronicle. I'd love to be a fly on every one of these walls to hear what they're all saying about each other, so I would.'

Maggie laughed. 'Yes, Yash has taken a big risk for us, so fair play to him. But now there's one thing I've just thought about. Do you think the sisters and their families are getting together *this* year for Christmas? I never thought to ask Agnes that.'

'I hadn't thought about that either,' Lori said. 'But I'd be bloody surprised if they are, given what might have happened back then. Because if Alasdair really was murdered, it must have been by one of them.'

Maggie nodded. 'You're absolutely right. Six adults and four kids, and amongst them there's a murderer. The big question is, who?'

Chapter 5

Frank's trip to deepest Suffolk to meet with Chief Constable Ed Springer had gone pretty much as expected, the senior officer being in turn defensive, aggressive, evasive and finally downright threatening in response to their mild questioning. Admittedly, most of Springer's ire was reserved for politicians in general and former minister Katherine Collins in particular, the MP whose very public condemnations had forced him into accepting an investigation into his force's role in the recent hijacking of a shipment of Aquanaut Island toys, but he had plenty of it left over to give Frank and Ronnie French an uncomfortable hour. Glad to be out of it but with mild feelings of guilt about leaving French behind in Felixstowe, he'd jumped on a train back to London, took a cross-city tube to Euston station and was soon speeding happily northwards. Partly in self-indulgence but mostly because he was conscious of the 'use it or lose it' nature of his organisation's budget, he had booked a first-class ticket. Glancing up and down the aisle, it appeared he was the only occupant of this coach on his mid-afternoon train. Satisfied that he wasn't going to be overheard, he grabbed his phone and called Eleanor Campbell.

'Hi Eleanor,' he said brightly as she picked up, 'and before we start, do you know how to patch Lexy onto this call?'

'You know I do, and I've shown you how to do it too, like a million times,' the Forensic Officer answered. She sounded grumpy, but then again, Eleanor always sounded grumpy when she spoke to him, so he wasn't bothered.

'Okay, I'll pay attention next time,' he lied. 'But just see if you can get her, will you?'

She didn't answer, but a few seconds later, he heard DC Lexy McDonald's voice on the line.

'Afternoon sir,' she said. *'I thought you were in Suffolk?'*

He laughed. 'I was, but the natives weren't exactly friendly, so I made my excuses and left as soon as I could.'

'Leaving DC French behind?'

'Exactly. Anyway, excuse the old-school audio call, but I'm on a train.'

'They've got wi-fi on trains now,' Eleanor said sourly. *'Since like the nineteenth century.'*

'Have they? Well, never mind, we're here now, and I was up at five o'clock this morning so I'm not exactly looking my finest so best to avoid the old video call. Anyway Miss Campbell, I'm hoping for an update on how you're getting on with your dark web explorations. Any luck with the undercover Googling?'

He heard her give an exasperated sigh. *'There's no Google on the dark web. That's the whole point. It's all hidden and unindexed. Everybody knows that.'*

'Well how the hell do you find anything then?' he asked, genuinely curious.

'That's like a state secret,' she said. *'If I told you...'*

'Aye, I know, you'd have to kill me,' he interrupted. 'Anyway, I don't care how it's done, I just need to know if you've managed to find anything.' And then he had another thought. 'But if Google or whatever doesn't work on this dark web thingy, how can ordinary punters hope to find out if any gangsters are selling dodgy knocked-off Aquanaut Islands?'

'I'm not an expert by any means sir,' Lexy interjected. *'But I was on a cyber-crime case a few months ago and our geeks told me about something called DarkScan. That's what the bad guys were using in our investigation. Apparently it's a bit like Google, but works on the dark web.'*

'It's nothing like Google,' Eleanor said, evidently unwilling to let her position as the team's tech authority be usurped by this amateur. *'Google uses a mega-server indexed database whereas DarkScan is a multi-node web-crawler.'*

'And do I need to understand the difference?' Frank asked.

'No, and you wouldn't be able to understand it anyway,' she responded, her tone matter-of-fact. *'No offence, but you wouldn't.'*

'You're dead right there, and none taken,' he conceded, grinning. 'But is that what punters in the know might be using to do their searching? This DarkScan app or program or whatever it is?'

'Like, probably,' she said. *'But we have way better tools.'*

'By *we*, I assume you're referring to the spooks and geeks of our security services?' He continued before she could answer. 'And so I can assume you've already done a scan of the dark web, using this piece of spook magic? To search for Aquanaut Islands?'

'Yeah, naturally. But I didn't find anything.'

'Nothing?' Frank said, surprised.

'You won't,' Lexy said. *'They'll be using an alias.'*

He gave his phone a puzzled look. 'Sorry Lexy, I don't understand. I mean, I know what an alias is, but not in this context.'

'It came up in that cyber case I told you about,' the DC explained. *'When the criminals are selling high-value stolen goods online, the word goes out on various dodgy WhatsApp forums that if you want to do a search, here's the term you should use.'*

'But who's on these dodgy WhatsApp forums of which you speak?' he asked, still puzzled.

'Loads of people,' Lexy said. *'Football hooligans, far right groups, far left groups, groups of traders in fake goods, dodgy car dealers, you name it. There's a massive underground network of them, with a couple of million subscribers at least. That's what drives the black economy nowadays, and it's highly sophisticated. And that means there's more than enough potential customers to shift those stolen Aquanaut Islands in a week, no problem.'*

'Well, isn't every day a school day?' Frank said. 'Because I didn't know any of this stuff before. But I think what you're saying is that there's a magic word or phrase you need to know if you're searching for this stuff – say 'roast chicken' or something equally daft – and that'll take you to where you need to go?'

'Basically, yes,' Lexy confirmed.

'So how do we crack these dodgy WhatsApp groups to find this magic word or phrase?' he asked. 'I guess that's a question I should direct at you Eleanor?'

The forensic officer's response was instant and authoritative. *'We won't need to,'* she said. *'I can hack the trending search term history using an awesome piece of software I downloaded from GCHQ. It's seriously cool.'*

Frank laughed. 'Awesome *and* seriously cool? That's something I'd really like to see. And before you say it, I know I would be bamboozled by it. So can you explain in words of one syllable or less what it is you're proposing?'

'If this weird toy is as popular as you say it is,' Eleanor said, with a hint of scepticism, *'then it will be trending at the top of the search charts on the dark web. I checked on Google, and 'Aquanaut Island' is getting over three hundred thousand searches a day on the regular web. It's the most popular search by miles.'*

'Okay,' he said, stretching out the word, 'but how exactly does this help us?'

'I can write some code. I can hack the web-crawler history database and find out what's the top search phrase on the dark web. And whatever it is, that will be the alias for Aquanaut Island. It'll be super-complicated, but I think I know how to do it.'

'That's brilliant,' he said, not bothering to hide his rising excitement. 'And how long will that take you, do you think?'

There was a pause on the line as she evidently worked out how to respond. Finally, she said, *'I'm not exactly sure. Three or four days. Maybe five. It's complicated code. Super-complicated.'*

'Aye, you said that,' he said, his tone harsher than he meant. 'But, no, I understand it'll be hard. Just do your best Eleanor, and anything you can do to speed things up will obviously be greatly appreciated. Because I don't need to remind you that Christmas day is drawing ever closer and we're running out of time.'

After the call had ended, he consoled himself with a complimentary shortbread and coffee from the catering trolley, and then followed it up, on a whim, by purchasing two ready-mixed cans of gin and tonic. Thus fortified, he idly picked up his phone, opened up Google and on another whim, typed in *'Dark Web alias for Aquanaut Island.'* Two seconds later, the astonishing result was providing further proof of something he had long known.

That nowadays, you can't keep *anything* a secret for long.

Chapter 6

Unsurprisingly, Maggie's conversation with Agnes Napier, updating her with the latest developments, had gone well. The news that the Chronicle was now running with her story had greatly thrilled the housekeeper, and with the added benefit of saving her the several thousand pounds in fees that would have been due to Maggie's firm. Now the two private detectives were back at the Bikini Barista cafe, awaiting Jimmy to join them on a video call from his office in Braemar. Whilst they waited, they mused over the unexpected condition that Yash Patel had imposed on their impending investigation.

'We've got just *two* weeks?' her assistant said incredulously. 'That's going to make this case bloody impossible if it wasn't already, surely?'

'Yes, it's not ideal,' Maggie agreed. 'But Yash's editor would only authorise a few thousand pounds to be spent on the story, which I can understand. And it's not just that. You see, the paper is sponsoring the British version of the Woman of the Year awards, and Eilish Macbeth has been nominated for that one too. The ceremony's on telly the Sunday before Christmas, and Yash would like it all done with by them.'

Lori raised an eyebrow. 'Aye, I suppose it would be awkward if she won it and then she turned out to be a murderer. Yash wouldn't want that at all, would he?'

Maggie laughed. 'You are such a sweet girl Lori. Actually, that's exactly what Yash *does* want. Think how sensational that story would be, especially if she won. And Eilish is the bookies' favourite, according to the papers.'

'So, he wants her to win that award and then the next day they run a story that says, *'woman of the year exposed as murderer'* or something like that.'

'You got it. But now our challenge is what to do in the two weeks we've got, because to be brutally honest, I haven't the faintest clue where to start.'

'We could start with visiting the crime scene,' Lori suggested, 'and there's loads more information and background we could get from Agnes Napier too, so we could do with meeting up with her again. And I'd love to go up there at this time of year. It'll be beautiful, with all that snow and everything.'

'Yes, it will,' Maggie agreed, 'and funnily enough, I'd been thinking along the same lines. In fact, that's one of the things I wanted to raise with Jimmy on our call. He's not that far away from Nethy Bridge, so I was going to ask him to drive across and take a look.'

Lori gave a disappointed sigh. 'Aye, I suppose that makes sense.'

'But don't worry, I was thinking you should go up there too,' Maggie said. 'You've already met Agnes, and it would be good for continuity.'

'Brilliant,' her assistant responded, her delight self-evident. 'And maybe I'll get a chance to see Frida again. She's dead beautiful, isn't she?'

'Very,' Maggie agreed. To her relief, it seemed that Lori, who once held a fiercely-burning candle for Captain Jimmy Stewart, had now accepted that her relationship with her handsome colleague would be one of affectionate but platonic friendship. 'Anyway, this looks like Jimmy on the line now.' She adjusted her laptop to get a better view of the screen then clicked the green 'accept' button.

'Hi you two,' he said brightly, then nodded behind him. *'Sorry for the background noise, but I thought I would camp up in Frida's cafe for the call. We've got a foot of snow up here and her place is nice and cosy and my wee office is bloody freezing.'* As he spoke, his girlfriend slid into view, nestling her chin on his shoulder. *'Hi both of you,'* she said. *'And Maggie, how have you been feeling? I take it your lovely little bump is growing nicely?'*

Maggie gave a proud smile. 'Yes, it is Frida, and what about yours?'

'Getting bigger by the day. And Jimmy swears he can feel the little mite kicking already. As soon as we go to bed, he rests his ear against my tummy. Honestly, I expect him to produce a stethoscope soon.'

'Got one on order as it happens,' he said, grinning. Frida gave him a lingering kiss on the cheek before disappearing out of view.

'I didn't expect you back from your expedition yet,' Maggie said, 'but you obviously are.'

He shot her a rueful look. *'Aye, conditions were brutal up there and you don't want to be taking any risks with a bunch of unfit and overweight middle managers. But we did a nice out-and-back hike up the pass from Braemar, about fifteen miles in all, and I'll tell you what, that was more than enough in this weather. Anyway, enough about me. You said in your text that we've got a new case.'*

She nodded. 'We have, and a bloody difficult one too. It's a proper country house mystery, a real-life Agatha Christie, and almost certainly someone who was staying at that house at the time is the killer. Although the place isn't a country house exactly, it's a big fancy wooden lodge on the Glengarry estate. And it's called Christmas Lodge, would you believe?'

'It's not that suicide, is it? The one they're saying might be murder? That Alasdair Macbeth guy?'

Maggie nodded again. 'That's the one. I guess you've been reading the Chronicle then?'

'Well actually, no,' he said. *'There was a story in yesterday's Grampian Times and everyone in this cafe's talking about it. The Laird of Glengarry owns quite a bit of land and property in this neck of the woods you see, and quite a few of the local tradesmen worked on the lodges when they were being built. So there's a ton of local interest, especially with the guy who died being Kirsty Bonnar's brother-in-law.'*

'Yes, I can well imagine that. Anyway, you'll be interested to know that it's been taken up now by our old friend Yash Patel, and he's commissioned Bainbridge Associates to help him with the case. A case, I should say, that we've been given just two weeks to solve, worst luck.' Succinctly, she gave him the briefest of background, reasoning that Lori could cover it in more depth when she met up with him. 'So,' she continued, 'it would be great if you get over to the lodge as soon as you can and do a detailed examination of the murder scene to see what you make of it. I'll arrange for Agnes Napier to meet you there, and Lori will travel up too.'

'Fine,' he said. *'I don't see me and Stew getting up on Ben Macdhui with my group anytime soon, not with this weather, so I could do it tomorrow if you wanted. Assuming the Lecht road stays open of course,'* he added cautiously.

'That would be dead brilliant,' Lori said. 'I'll check the train timetable as soon as we're done, and tomorrow, I'll give you as much background as we've got. There was a cast of thousands at that place, and it really made my head spin when Agnes Napier was telling us all about it. But luckily, Maggie made loads of notes, and I've memorised and swallowed them.'

'And I'll tell Agnes that you two will have more questions about everything that was going on up there at that terrible time,' Maggie said. 'She told us the atmosphere was poisonous, so we'll want her to expand on that in particular.' She paused for a moment and smiled. 'Both happy with that?' Her two colleagues instantly nodded their assent, Lori beaming a smile that betrayed how much she was looking forward to spending a whole day with Jimmy.

'Great. And whilst you're away, I'll load up with caffeine and chocolate and try to work out how the *hell* we can get to talk to the main players in this murder mystery.'

***

Thankfully the Cockbridge to Tomintoul road over the Lecht was clear on what was a crisp winter morning, although patches of packed and frozen snow made it decidedly treacherous in places. Accordingly, it had taken Jimmy nearly two hours of careful driving to traverse the forty-five miles to Nethy Bridge, where he'd arranged to meet Lori Logan in the elegant baronial hotel located right in the centre of the village, she having travelled up from Aviemore station by taxi. She was already there when he arrived, sitting in the reception area, conspicuous in a dazzling yellow quilted jacket and matching woolly hat.

'I love the gear,' Jimmy said, laughing. 'I've got a big adventure trip up the Lairig Ghru pass in a few days' time and you look as if you're ready for it yourself. Or maybe we could even tackle Everest instead.'

'Do you like it?' she grinned. 'I just got it a few days ago in anticipation of coming up here.' She held up a leg for inspection. 'And I got these wicked boots too. Real leather and a hundred percent waterproof. I tried them out in a big pile of slush at the station, and they worked, no bother.'

He gave a thumbs-up. 'Looks like you're all ready to hit the mountains then right enough.' He glanced at his watch. 'By my calculation, we've got about half an hour before we meet Agnes Napier, and the lodge is only five or ten minutes away. So can you fill me in on the background before we go?'

Lori nodded enthusiastically. 'Aye sure Jimmy. So, basically three sisters and their families had been renting the place over Christmas for a few years, until obviously that all stopped after Alasdair Macbeth was found hanged. The three are Eilish Macbeth, who's the dead man's wife and the woman who wrote that big-selling book, her big sister Kirsty Bonnar, who everybody knows, and their wee sister Isla. Her mother, who's called Nan, was also there. Then there were their other halves and the kids. Kirsty's married to a guy called Tom Harper and they live in London. Isla's got a partner, a guy called Drew, and they live in Glasgow as do the Macbeth family and the old mother. There are four kids in total. Eilish and Isla have two each, Tom and Kirsty don't have any as far as we know.'

Jimmy nodded. 'I've seen Eilish Macbeth's daughter on the television a couple of times, she looks about sixteen or seventeen, something like that?'

'That's Christabelle, and aye, she'll be seventeen on her birthday and she's the oldest one. She's Alasdair's step-daughter by the way, not his real daughter. The other kids are all much younger, between four and eight or something like that. The other thing you need to know is that Alasdair Macbeth's father had died a few months earlier and left a pile of debt when, according to Agnes, the family had been expecting to inherit a big pile of cash. So apparently relations in the Macbeth family were a bit strained because he was going to get nothing. In fact, Agnes said the atmosphere in the lodge was poisonous. Distinctly lacking in Christmas spirit.'

'Sounds interesting. And the reason this Agnes came to us was that Alasdair didn't leave a suicide note, and she thought that was out of character. Is that the gist of it?'

Lori shrugged. 'Aye, basically that's it. But she obviously felt strongly enough about the fact to get us involved. And she told that wee newspaper too, don't forget.'

Jimmy looked at his watch again. 'Well, we'd better get moving and take a look at this murder scene. Should be interesting, and I'm looking forward to talking to this Agnes woman too.'

Ten minutes later they were pulling into a parking space directly outside the door of Christmas Lodge. Built in an Alpine style and impressive in size, its roof was covered in a thick blanket of glistening snow, for all the world looking like an illustration from an upmarket ski brochure. The adjacent space was occupied by a mid-sized SUV bearing a current-year registration that Jimmy assumed must belong to Agnes Napier. Mentally, he took a note of the number, something he had found himself doing automatically since becoming a private detective, albeit a part-time one. As they got out of their own car, she opened the front door and waved.

'Welcome, welcome to Christmas Lodge,' Napier said, ushering them into an impressive galleried entrance hall. 'It's cold out there but it's lovely and warm in here. We've got underfloor heating and radiators too, and it's brilliant.'

'What a lovely place,' Jimmy said as he surveyed the room. 'I'm Jimmy by the way, Jimmy Stewart, and this is Lori of course, whom you met when you were in Glasgow. I've worked with Maggie right from the very start, but now I'm a sort of part-time consultant. But she probably told you all of that.'

'Aye, she did.' She paused. 'And she says you'll want to ask me some more questions whilst you're here. If it's alright, we'll do it in the wee study. You see, I don't like going into the big living room any more, not after what happened to poor Alasdair in there.'

He gave her a sympathetic smile. 'I can understand that of course, it must have been horrible for you.' He hesitated for a moment then said, 'but we will need you in there for just a minute or two, so you can point out exactly where it happened, and we might need to ask you a couple of questions about it too whilst we're there. Would that be alright?'

Napier sighed. 'Aye, I suppose so. Maybe we can do that now, so we can get it over with? If you don't mind?'

'No, that's fine,' Jimmy said. 'Lead on, please.'

She pushed open a door at the far end of the hall and led them into the lounge. It was huge, with a polished wooden floor dotted with colourful rugs, and comfortably furnished with squashy leather sofas. Along one wall, floor-to-ceiling windows afforded a magnificent view out to the forest, with a backdrop of snow-capped mountains beyond. On the adjacent wall was a large stone fireplace enticingly filled with logs but currently unlit. In the corner stood a beautiful pine Christmas tree, at least ten foot in height and expertly decorated for the season.

'This is absolutely gorgeous,' Lori said, as she swept her eyes around the room. 'I'd love to spend the festive season here, so I would. But I'm guessing you must have guests in over Christmas. But not the three sisters and their families this year? At least I presume not?' she added.

Napier shook her head. 'No, I don't see them ever coming back here. But aye, the lodge is fully booked for the next three weeks, right up until the New Year. The first lot are coming tomorrow in fact.'

'Gosh, you're going to be busy then Agnes,' Lori said. 'When do you get to have your own Christmas? In July or something?'

Napier laughed. 'No actually, I get a week off in December every year, and I usually go down to see my sister Maisie in Glasgow. I'm going next week in fact. Neither of us is married you see, so it's nice to spend the time together, and we exchange presents and have a big Christmas dinner with all the trimmings. The folks who rent the lodge over that period understand they have to cater for themselves during their stay. But the family who've got it this year are bringing their kids' nanny too, so they'll be alright. They're from London you see,' she added, her tone mildly disapproving.

Looking straight up, Jimmy surveyed a vaulted roof, the apex of which he estimated must be at least thirty feet above where they stood. Running across the room at a height of about twelve to fifteen feet above the floor and parallel to the fireplace wall was a series of timber beams, each in a perfect position from which to suspend a hangman's noose. He pointed at one of them and then said to Agnes Napier, 'So I guess Alasdair was found hanging from one of them, is that right?'

She nodded. 'Actually, it was the one that you're pointing at.'

He hesitated for a moment. 'Now I know this might be difficult, but I need to ask you one or two questions about it. The first one is, how high were his feet off the ground when you saw him hanging there, would you say? A foot, two feet, more?'

She looked perplexed. 'I... I don't rightly know if I can answer that accurately. He was *quite* high I suppose, now that I think of it. I don't know, three feet maybe, maybe a bit more. But I couldn't be certain.'

Jimmy smiled. 'No that's alright Agnes, I wouldn't have expected you to remember that. My second question is, was there a chair lying near the body, or something else that might have been kicked over? Or did the authorities say what he had been standing on before he...well, before he did what he did?'

'There was a chair,' she said firmly. 'Aye, definitely. One of the high-backed ones from the dining room. It was lying on its side, I remember that. I wasn't thinking straight of course, but I remember feeling a bit annoyed about that and wanting to put it back in its proper place. I know that sounds terrible, but your head's all over the place when something like that happens.'

'No, I totally understand that,' he said. 'And what did he use to hang himself? Was it a rope, or something else?'

'It was bedsheets,' she said. 'That's what he used. Like they do in prisons.'

'Bedsheets?' Jimmy said. 'That's interesting.' He looked up at the beam and thought for a moment. 'That would have taken what, four or five sheets to make a decent rope? Maybe even six. So where would he have got them from Agnes? Not from his bed, we have to assume.'

'We've got a big linen cupboard,' Napier explained, 'where we keep all the sheets and spare pillows and such like. I looked afterwards. That's where they were taken from.'

'And anybody's got access to the cupboard I presume?' he asked.

'Well, yes and no. We keep it locked.' She paused for a moment. 'We have a better class of clientele of course, but that doesn't mean we don't sometimes lose items, let's put it that way.'

'And who's got the key? You, I assume?'

'There's not a key,' she said. 'There's one of these keypads on it, and you push in four buttons to open it.'

'And who knows the number?' he asked.

'Me and the cleaners. And the laird's rental office of course. They come out once a month to change the combination and they let us know what it is.'

'But you didn't give any of the party the combination?' Lori asked.

The woman shrugged. 'No-one asked for it. So no, I didn't. But it's not always locked. Sometimes the cleaners forget and leave it on the snib, so I suppose that's what must have happened.'

He looked at her, brow furrowed. He couldn't quite put his finger on it, but there was just something in her tone that made him doubt her veracity.

'Well, that's okay for now,' he said, pausing once again to gather his thoughts. Then he said, 'Sorry Agnes, but there's just one more question I want to ask you and then we'll disappear off to the study. My question is, what sort of a guy was Alasdair? I mean physically – was he tall, short, well-built, skinny, what was he?'

'He was a big man,' Napier said. 'Over six foot and well-built too. He was from farming stock, remember.'

Jimmy nodded. 'Aye of course.' He shot her an appreciative smile. 'If it's okay, I'm just going to take a couple of photographs of the scene and then we can head for the study. And maybe you could make us all a nice cup of tea?'

***

They sat in silence whilst they waited for Agnes Napier to return with the tea, Jimmy assuming that Lori, like himself, was processing what they had just discovered and working up possible scenarios to explain what might have happened. It would have taken some organising whether it had been murder or suicide, that was what was uppermost in his thoughts. Pleating five or six bedsheets such that they formed a strong rope would surely have been at least two hours' work in itself, and with the family gathered together in close proximity, how would Alasdair Macbeth have made the time to do this? Then he would have had to secure the improvised rope over a beam that was twelve feet off the ground, then move a heavy chair from the dining room into the living room and place it in position. Logistically it would have been a complex operation, and quite difficult to see how it could have been done without detection. His thoughts were interrupted by the return of the housekeeper, carrying a tray on which was a china teapot, a jug of milk, three cups and saucers, and, pleasingly, a plate of chocolate biscuits.

'Ah lovely,' he said as she poured them all a cup. 'Thank goodness that's over, eh? So now maybe we can talk about what was happening in the days leading up to finding his body. Lori's explained to me about Alasdair's father's death and the tensions that had caused in their family. What about the others? Was there anything else going on that with the benefit of hindsight might have been significant?'

'There was always *something* going on in that family,' Napier said, shooting them a look. 'I worked it out last night, it was the fifth time they'd come here for Christmas, so I got to know them all quite well. How could I put it, there was always an *atmosphere*. It was all driven by bitterness and envy of course, all of it.'

'What was that all about then?' Lori asked.

'The two younger sisters hate the fact that Kirsty is so famous and that she and her husband Tom are so filthy rich. And of course it was particularly raw last year because Kirsty had got her Oscar nomination for that big film she did and was going on about it endlessly. Mind you, their hatred doesn't stop them sponging off their big sister of course.'

'Are they spongers then?'

'Oh *yes*,' Napier said, her disapproval evident. 'Kirsty and Tom pay for the whole Christmas break every year, the lodge, the food, the drink, everything. And I happen to know that they've had to bail out Isla and Drew on more than one occasion when one or other of their hare-brained schemes goes wrong.' She paused for a moment, then continued, mysteriously, 'Oh aye, and there was the thing about old Robert Macbeth's bank loan too. I don't think Eilish has ever forgiven them for that. Not that they did a thing wrong of course, because I wouldn't have put money into that run-down estate, especially with Alasdair being so hopeless when it came to understanding business.'

Jimmy gave her a searching look. 'Like you say, it sounds as if there was a lot going on in that family.' He paused for a moment then said, 'Would you mind elaborating on the details Agnes? Because I think it would help us a lot with our investigation.'

'I really don't think I should,' Napier said, her artful smile making it plain she was intending to do just that. 'But I suppose if it helps...'

'Aye, it would,' Lori said. 'It would help loads.'

The woman nodded. 'Very well. If I start with Isla and Drew, well what can I say? Not to put too fine a point on it, Drew Henderson is a complete waste of space.' She paused and gave a bitter laugh. 'Calls himself a property developer, but from what I can see, all he does is little building jobs, and I don't think he's much good at them either. He certainly doesn't make any money at it, given they live in a tiny little semi and drive a battered old car. But he's a charmer all right, and a great one for the ladies too.' She reduced her voice to a whisper and looked Lori up and down. 'I should have thought you would be an object of his intentions dear, should you be unfortunate enough to meet him. He likes them young you see. And poor Isla, she puts up with it without a murmur of complaint. But of course, she's away with the fairies herself. A sweet enough woman, but a bit deluded, if you want my honest opinion.'

'How do you mean?' Jimmy asked.

The woman laughed again. 'She wants to be a *writer*, would you believe? To be fair, she puts plenty of time and effort into it, but between you and me, her writing is rubbish.' She hesitated for a moment, then gave an apologetic smile. 'Perhaps I'm being cruel, but it is, it's pure rubbish. She gave me one of her books to read once, and quite frankly, I was disgusted.'

'What sort of books does she try to write?' Lori asked.

Napier harrumphed. *'She* calls it steamy romance, but it's nothing but smut, pure smut. I wouldn't have it in the house.'

'It's dead popular, that kind of book,' Lori said, causing Jimmy to raise an amused eyebrow. 'Especially the historical ones. Bodice-rippers they call them. I love them myself.'

The housekeeper gave the young detective a disparaging look. 'I'm not disputing their popularity my dear, but no-one wants to publish Isla Bonnar's terrible books, bodice-rippers or not. She's forever sending her manuscripts off to agents and publishers and getting nowhere, but it doesn't seem to stop her trying. Her partner Drew of course makes it all too clear what he thinks about the whole thing.'

'He doesn't support her writing then?' Lori asked.

Napier shook her head. 'Far from it. He tells anyone who'll listen that she's wasting her time because her books are rubbish and she'll never be a published writer. Although the language he uses is much nastier.'

'He doesn't sound a very nice guy,' Jimmy said, 'but I don't suppose it's easy to get published even if your books are quite good.' He hesitated for a moment before continuing. 'But what about that other thing you mentioned? About a bank loan or something like that?'

'Oh yes, that. It was happening at Christmas just two years ago, when they were all at the house. It seemed that the Macbeth estate was in financial difficulties again, which Robert Macbeth this time blamed on bad weather and the resultant bad harvest. Whatever the reason, the upshot was the estate needed a bank loan to continue in business, but because of old man Macbeth's poor track record, the bank wouldn't lend the money unless a guarantor was put in place with the financial means to cover the large sum involved. Alasdair and Eilish asked Kirsty and her husband Tom if they would be willing to act as guarantors for the loan, which I think was nearly three hundred thousand pounds in all.'

'That's a shed load of money,' Jimmy said, 'and I'm guessing they said no.'

'They did say no,' Napier confirmed. 'I think Kirsty might have been willing to agree to it, but her husband Tom put his foot down. I mean, I know you're not supposed to listen to private conversations, but there were a lot of raised voices and sometimes you just can't help overhearing, can you?'

Jimmy shot Lori a look which she returned with a knowing smile, as they both pictured Agnes Napier with an ear pressed against the closed door.

'So what did you hear Agnes?' Lori asked. 'I mean, when they were doing all that shouting? I bet it was dead interesting.'

Napier's superior expression suggested she was enjoying this time in the limelight. 'I heard *everything*. Tom said he appreciated the situation that Alasdair's family were in, but his father just wasn't a very good businessman and that it would just be throwing good money after bad, and it wouldn't help if Alasdair got involved because he didn't know much about business either. He told

Alasdair that he should tell his father to give up trying to play the Laird and sell up whilst there was still some value in the assets.'

'And how did Alasdair react to that?' Lori asked.

'Oh, he wasn't very happy, I could tell that, but I think in his bones he knew what Tom was saying was right. But Eilish got really angry and started saying some terrible things to Kirsty and her husband. You wouldn't believe the language she used, and in front of the wee kiddies too. But she's like that of course,' she added. 'No class.'

Lori looked at her, wide-eyed, 'God, that must have been a jolly Christmas that year right enough.'

Napier nodded. 'Aye, it wasn't a happy occasion. Especially with all the trouble Alasdair and Eilish were having with that wee madam Christabelle.'

'Oh yes?' Jimmy said, wondering if this stream of interesting revelations was ever going to end. 'What was that all about then?'

'She was going to be expelled from her school. Alasdair and Eilish were at their wits end, but Christabelle seemed to be treating it all as a great big joke.'

'What had the girl done?' Lori asked.

The woman raised an eyebrow. 'She had taken *photographs* of herself, and I'll leave it to your imagination to work out what sort of pictures we're talking about.'

Lori gave a sympathetic smile. 'I'm not saying it's right, but I bet half the kids in the school have done that at some time. That's what it's like nowadays, with all that social media pressure. I know it's awful, but they all do it.'

'These were sent to a *teacher*,' Napier said with a dramatic flourish. 'A male teacher of course, and the poor man got into terrible trouble even although he was completely innocent. It transpired he'd told her off in class for misbehaving on one occasion, and this was the little Jezebel's revenge. And she made all sorts of allegations too. I think she'd been reading too many of her aunt's trashy books if you ask me.'

'Oh dear,' Jimmy said. 'That sounds serious. So what happened in the end?'

Napier gave a bitter laugh. 'Oh, it was all smoothed over by Kirsty and Tom offering to make a big donation to the school's sports equipment fund. And then Alasdair and Eilish had to move the girl to a private school, and you can imagine who's paying the fees for *that*.'

'And is she still at that school?' Lori asked.

'She is, but I don't know why they bother making her go. She's just as much away with the fairies as her Auntie Isla. The girl wants to be a *model,* can you believe. One of these page three models if I'm any judge,' she added.

'Do the papers still run that sort of picture?' Jimmy asked, his curiosity genuine. 'I don't really read them, not that sort anyway. But aye, from what you've been telling us, I can see how relations must be seriously strained in that family. It sounds like one big giant soap-opera.' He paused for a moment as he considered his next question.

'So the big question is Agnes, if Alasdair was murdered, who do you think did it?'

She shrugged. 'Haven't a clue. That's why I came to your firm.'

'Not even a guess?' Lori asked. 'You must have some theories, surely?'

'No, none, none at all,' she said firmly. 'If it was one of the others who'd been killed, then I'd have plenty of ideas, but not with it being Alasdair.' She shrugged again, then fell silent, evidently not intending to elaborate.

Jimmy nodded. 'Well, I've got one final question for you Agnes if you don't mind. My question is, why are you doing this? Why did you decide to speak to Bainbridge Associates?'

She was silent again for a moment then said, 'It's quite simple. I want justice. Justice for lovely Alasdair Macbeth.' Her words were clear enough, but for Jimmy, the malice in her tone gave away her real motivation.

It wasn't justice that Agnes Napier wanted. Somehow, it was revenge.

Chapter 7

It had taken Frank nearly twenty-four hours of prevarication before he finally decided there was nothing for it but to let Eleanor Campbell know that he had cracked the Aquanaut Island dark web alias by doing a simple Google search. And then, right at the last minute, he had a better idea. He picked up his phone, scrolled down to his favourites, and stabbed an entry with his finger.

'DC French,' he boomed. 'How are you this fine morning? Loading up with a bit of breakfast at one of Felixstowe's finest culinary establishments I assume?'

'You're not far wrong guv,' the detective said, sounding guilty. *'But I'm just finishing up as it happens. They've got a good enough canteen at the nick, but I'm not exactly an honoured guest, so I was a bit worried they'd poison me if I ate there.'*

'Speaking of which, how's the investigation going down there? Any major breakthroughs to report?'

'Yeah, well I found the geezer who took the original call from the shipping company, a DC Lawson. He just happened to be in the office when the call came through and the call handler bunged it his way. Lawson says he wrote down all the details but told the woman who called that it was above his paygrade and that he'd get back to her as soon as he could. Then he stuck the details in an email and passed it up the chain to his DI. DI Stephanie Coombes is her name.'

'Any luck with her?'

'Yeah, as it happens guv, I managed to grab two minutes with her yesterday. She decided pretty sharpish that it was a matter for traffic or uniforms and passed it to the Inspector who looked after that squad. Inspector Barry Green is his name.'

Frank laughed. 'They obviously love a wee game of pass-the-parcel over there. So have you managed to get to the new guy then?'

'Not yet guv. But DI Coombes said the Inspector Green geezer was sympathetic to the request but that he needed to get an overtime chitty approved for the two officers that would be escorting the shipment to the distribution depot in the Midlands. So apparently that had to go to the headquarters finance team in Ipswich. That's as far as I've traced it so far,' French added apologetically. *'But I'm assuming that's where it got turned down. I'm going to put a call into there once we're done guv, to see if I can figure out what happened exactly.'*

'Great stuff,' Frank said. 'So, by my reckoning we have a DC and a DI and a uniformed Inspector and some as-yet-unnamed finance geek in HQ who got to know of this highly valuable shipment in advance. Any obvious suspects amongst that motley crew?'

'Can't be sure, but I don't think so guv, not so far,' French said. *'The DC and the DI couldn't wait to get the matter off their hands, so I don't think it was one of them. I haven't spoken to this Inspector Green yet but he's on my to-do list. And then obviously I need to find out who got to know about it at Ipswich HQ.'*

'Understood,' Frank said. 'Now Frenchie, on a related subject. You're a man with a bulging Rolodex stuffed with dodgy underworld contacts and informants, are you not?'

'*I have my sources guv, yeah,*' the detective answered guardedly. '*You know I have.*'

'And it wouldn't be beyond the bounds of possibility that one of those villains would have discovered the dodgy dark web alias for these Aquanaut Island thingies?'

'*Well yeah guv,*' French agreed, now sounding distinctly suspicious. '*I suppose.*'

'Excellent. Hold that thought and stay on the line.' He scratched his head, fiddled with his phone for a few seconds and was gratified when the screen displayed *'dialling number'* alongside the name of Eleanor Campbell. She answered promptly, he greeting her with the same *bonhomie* he had employed with French.

'Eleanor, we've had a lucky break,' he said, speaking over her terse *what do you want?* 'Your esteemed colleague DC French here found out that alias thingy we were looking for from a guy in a dodgy pub in the East End. I guess he's saved you a ton of work as a result. Isn't that great?'

'*I stayed up to like two o'clock in the morning working on it,*' she responded, evidently unamused. '*And my code worked first time. I already know what the alias is.*'

'Okay, that's fantastic,' he said, momentarily surprised but feeling relieved at the same time. 'And anyway, DC French's contact has probably got it wrong, so I'm glad you got there first.'

Instantly she asked, '*What is it Ronnie? What's your alias search phrase?*'

Mildly panicking, Frank leapt in. 'Christmas crackers, that's what your pub geezer said it was, I think? You search for Christmas crackers, and it comes up with Aquanaut Islands.' He forced a laugh. 'I mean, I ask you, how hilarious is that?'

'Yeah, that's what my geezer said it was,' French said, lying with inscrutable conviction. 'Made me laugh out loud it did.' *I owe you one Ronnie*, Frank thought. 'Is that what you got too Eleanor?' he asked her.

'Like yeah. And I've used it to search already. And I found something.'

'What?' he said, impressed. 'Already?'

'Already. I found a website selling them. At nine hundred and fifty pounds.'

'Bloody hell, that's steep,' he said. 'But that's amazing work Eleanor, well done. But how do we know that's what they're selling? The Aquanaut Islands I mean?'

'You don't. But they're described as a box of luxury crackers with an Aquanauts-themed toy in every one. So I guess you have to like trust them.'

He gave a wry smile. 'Trust them? Chances are you'll hand over your nine hundred and fifty notes and you'll never hear from them again. I don't suppose you've managed to trace their location, have you?'

'That will be super-complicated,' she said, *'because everything will be protected by an industrial-strength megabit encrypted firewall.'*

*Sh*e paused for a moment, evidently thinking. *'But there is one way we could perhaps crack their defences.'*

'And what's that?' he asked. Simultaneously, he heard French laugh. He said, *'I know what she's going to say guv. It's bleeding obvious.'*

'You could like just buy one,' Eleanor said simply. *'With a credit card.'*

Frank considered the matter for a few seconds then said, 'Are you joking? I wouldn't give my credit card details to those bandits.'

'No need, we can use a clone,' she said. *'I've got an app from MI6 that will generate a valid sixteen-digit number plus the expiry date and the security number. It's way cool. Their agents use it all the time on the dark web to entrap bad actors or pay off informants.'*

'And this is something you can do easily with this exciting spook-ware?' Frank asked, then continued before she could answer. 'And this would achieve *what* exactly?'

'They'll have to reach out to us to let us know how to pay and where we can collect the item from. I expect the contact will be by anonymous text and the toy will be left in one of these courier drop-off and collection lockers that you get at big supermarkets. We might then be able to geo-locate the mobile number they use to send the text.'

'I thought you said the text would be anonymous?' Frank said, puzzled.

'It's anonymous to like normal people,' she said mysteriously. *'But not to us. Although I expect they change the number every few hours, which is a complication.'*

He laughed. 'Okay, so I assume you have some other clever spookware that does that. So that means we can get the phone number, if only for a short window of time, if I understand what you're telling me?'

'That's right guv,' French confirmed. *'And we might get lucky with the supermarket CCTV too. We might clock the geezer doing the drop off and then we can run the old facial recognition stuff on him and see if he's got form.'*

Frank stroked his chin as he processed what his colleagues had just told him. Finally he said, 'You know, that all sounds like a very cunning plan, and so I commend it to the house. Right, off you go and do your cloning stuff and report back to me as soon as you hear anything.' He hung up then gave a deep sigh of satisfaction. Because if these dark-web scammers did in fact deliver the goods, rather than just running off with MI5's money, it would be one Frank Stewart in person who would be retrieving the nine-hundred-and-fifty-pound Aquanaut Island from that pick-up locker.

All in the line of duty, naturally.

Chapter 8

No matter what way you looked at it, Jimmy and Lori's encounter with Christmas Lodge housekeeper Agnes Napier could not have been described as anything else other than jaw-dropping. The stream of revelations, each one more astonishing than the previous one, had served to shine a penetrating spotlight on the dysfunctional Bonnar sisters and their families, at the same time throwing up a list of potential suspects for the murder of Alasdair Macbeth – assuming of course he actually *had* been killed, the view of Maggie's two associates being that the jury was still out on that one. Now she, Lori and Jimmy were gathered once again in the Bikini Barista cafe, intending to chew over what had been discovered on the trip to Nethy Bridge, and to decide the next steps in the investigation. Stevie the proprietor had been his usual efficient self and the three of them were now equipped with steaming hot chocolates, the mutual choice of beverage driven by the picture-postcard winter scene to be observed out of the cafe's window.

And now there was something else too, a piece of late-breaking news which in some ways could be judged advantageous, but on the other hand, had the potential to turn out the exact opposite. 'I'm bet you glad you drove down yesterday,' Maggie said to Jimmy as she took a cautious sip from her mug. 'I doubt you would have made it if you'd tried to come down this morning.'

He nodded. 'Yeah, me and Stew had dinner and a beer or two with a potential customer last night, so it all worked out perfectly.' He glanced out the window at the snowy vista and gave a wry smile. 'It's getting back that might be the challenge.'

'You can stay over with us if you like,' Maggie said. 'Ollie loves to have you there, and it gives him someone his own age to play with,' she added, laughing.

He grinned. 'You mean, like Frank?'

'Exactly. Anyway, it seems you two had a very productive time up there in the wilds.'

'It was a dead beautiful place,' Lori said wistfully. 'I want to go there one Christmas, so I do. But yeah, we found out a lot, definitely.'

'Including, I assume, from an inspection of the murder scene,' Maggie said. 'Any thoughts about what happened up there, having seen it?'

'Loads,' Jimmy said, nodding. 'We now know that Alasdair was hanged using a rope made from twisted bedsheets, and that they came from a linen cupboard that was usually locked but was sometimes kept on the snib and so accessible to anyone in the house. Including Alasdair himself of course. The beam that the rope was suspended from was about ten or twelve feet above the floor, so it *probably* would have needed a stepladder to be able to secure it.'

'You say probably?' Maggie said.

He nodded. 'It did occur to me and Lori that you might *just* have been able to secure it by tossing it over the beam, then having a loop that you could thread it through, then pull it to tighten it. It would take a bit of strength to throw it that high, and it might take a couple of attempts to get it over, but it could be just about done we think.'

'But we think the ladder's more likely,' Lori added. 'We didn't see one, but the lodge has a shed, and there might be one in there.'

'Interesting,' Maggie said. 'But I suppose the key question is, did you find out anything that strongly points to it being murder rather than suicide?'

Jimmy gave her an uncertain look. 'There was one thing. I asked Agnes how far Alasdair's feet were above the floor when she saw him hanging there.'

'Blooming heck, bet that was a tough one to ask,' Maggie said.

He nodded. 'It was. But what did she say Lori, can you remember exactly?'

'She said it was three feet, maybe even a bit more.'

'That's right,' he said. 'Apparently, one of the dining room chairs was found lying on its side, and it was assumed that was what he was standing on -with the noose round his neck obviously - before he jumped off.'

'But the seat of a dining room chair isn't three feet off the ground, is it?' Maggie said, puzzled. She glanced down at the seat she was sitting on, then stood up to examine it more closely. 'It's hardly even two feet by my reckoning.'

'Exactly,' Jimmy agreed. 'Agnes Napier might have got it wrong of course, but if she didn't, then it casts great doubt on the suicide theory, that's for sure.'

'So, what *did* happen, do you think?' Maggie asked

He shrugged. 'We've not worked that out yet. All we do know is that staging it to look like suicide would have been no easy task. For a start, Alasdair Macbeth was a big guy. He was over six feet tall and built like a farmer, according to Agnes, so he was probably fifteen or sixteen stone, maybe more. It wouldn't have been easy to string him up, that's for sure. But I need to think about it a bit more,' he added. 'At least me and Lori have got a picture of the scene in our heads, and we took a few photographs as well.'

'Great work, you two,' Maggie said, then gave a wry smile, before picking up her phone. 'So obviously, I was looking forward to asking you what you had found out about the family.' She held up the device and pointed the screen at her colleagues. 'Except Yash Patel got there first.'

Jimmy took the phone from her and read the first few paragraphs of the journalist's article, evidently just published that morning in the Chronicle's online edition.

'Bloody hell,' he said. 'I don't know the legalities, but isn't this stuff potentially libellous or something like that? And I'll tell you something else Maggie, the only person he could have got all of this from is Agnes Napier. Because we certainly didn't tell him.'

'Let me have a look,' Lori said, snatching the phone from him. She scanned down the article then said, 'That's exactly the stuff she told us. About Alasdair's father, about Christabelle, everything.'

'What's she playing at?' Maggie asked. 'She must know the family will be able to work out that she's the source, surely?'

'To be honest Maggie, I'm not sure I agree with that,' Jimmy said, 'because when you think about it, every single person at that lodge knew what was going on, and any one of them could have spilled the beans to Yash. And as for what Agnes is playing at, I can't answer that exactly, but whatever it is, it's driven by malice, pure malice.'

'Well, it's certainly set the cat amongst the pigeons, but maybe not in the way she was expecting.'

'What do you mean?' Jimmy asked.

Maggie gave a wry smile. 'I've got more news, something that popped into my inbox just before you arrived.' She took the phone back from Lori and clicked open a document. 'A Cease-and-Desist order from Schuster & Clark would you believe? And the Chronicle have got one too. Raised on behalf of the family, that's what it says in the letter.'

'Who are Schuster & Clark?' Jimmy asked, clearly surprised by the turn of events.

'They're a giant law firm. Their headquarters are in New York but their massive in the UK too. And Tom Harper is their Managing Partner in this country. Which, incidentally, means he's on a million a year or more.'

'No wonder him and his wife can afford to pay for Christmas then,' Lori said. 'But what's a Cease-and-Desist order when it's at home?'

'For the newspaper, it means they could be hit with an injunction if they publish any more stories in the same vein. For us, they're asking us to stop our investigation forthwith.'

'But can they do that?' Lori said. 'I thought this was supposed to be a free country with a free press.'

'They can do it,' Maggie said. 'And they *have* done it. But we don't have to comply with it, although that's a risk I don't want to take at the moment.' She smiled, 'And in actual fact, it gives us an opportunity.'

'How come?' Lori said.

'All of these orders are subject to negotiation, especially in our case, where the legal basis is shaky to say the least.' She paused and smiled again. 'But isn't it true when they say every cloud has a silver lining? Because there I was, scratching my head looking for an excuse to start talking to the family, and now I've found one.'

***

She'd spoken briefly to Yash, who'd confirmed, as she'd expected, that the Chronicle wasn't planning to take the threat of injunction lying down. The paper's editor was a passionate crusader for freedom of the press, and already they'd published a strongly-worded article condemning Tom Harper's action and threatening to fight it all the way to the High Court if necessary. The journalist had also given her the go-ahead to fly down to London – business class, on the account of her pregnancy – to meet with the lawyer at Shuster & Clark's impressive offices situated on Canary Wharf. It had been an earlier start than she would have liked, but after a four-hour journey on a busy Friday that encompassed taxi, plane, train and a final leg on the DLR, she found herself in a meeting room on the tenth floor of the office block, sipping a coffee and awaiting the arrival of Harper. Afterwards, she was having lunch with her best friend Asvina Rani, who worked nearby, a date she was greatly looking forward to.

Five minutes later than scheduled, Tom Harper swept into the room, a transparent folder under his arm. He was a very good-looking guy, but that probably wasn't so surprising given he was married to the notably attractive Kirsty Bonnar. And then a few seconds later, to Maggie's complete surprise, the actress herself joined them.

'Good morning,' the woman said, unsmiling, before pulling out a chair and sitting down opposite. The man did the same, selecting the chair alongside his wife, his face wearing a faint smile. 'I'm Tom Harper,' he said, 'and this is my wife Kirsty,' as if she needed any introduction. Without waiting for a response, he took out a letter from the folder, spun it round then said, 'I understand you want to talk about this.'

Maggie paused for a second, then nodded. 'Yes, I do. But just so we're clear, my firm won't be complying with your cease-and-desist order. As far as I can see, there's no valid legal basis to prevent us going about our lawful business, so unless the Chronicle decides to cancel our contract, carrying on with the investigation is what we intend to do.'

'Who instructed you?' Kirsty Bonnar asked, stony-faced. 'Which member of the family instructed you? Or was it that devious old bitch Agnes Napier?'

This was interesting, Maggie thought. Did they genuinely not know, or was this just a fishing expedition? But luckily, there was a ready-made answer to her question.

'None of the above in fact. Bainbridge Associates were commissioned by the Chronicle newspaper in support of the story they're currently running. It's a routine sort of matter for us,' she added pleasantly. 'We've worked a lot with the paper in the past, particularly with Yash Patel, who's the journalist heading up the story. They asked us to help, and we agreed. We're not concerned with the merits of the matter one way or another. We're simply employed to ask the questions.' It wasn't strictly the truth, but it was close enough to overcome any scruples Maggie might have had about telling an outright fib.

'It's a gross intrusion into the private grief of our family,' Harper said. 'There's no basis whatsoever for the wild allegations that paper is making, and if they or you continue down this path, there will be consequences, take it from us. Serious consequences.'

Maggie smiled. 'Forgive me for saying this Tom, but don't you think your sister-in-law Eilish has done plenty of intrusion into that private grief already? Because if she hadn't written that book and then if she and her pretty daughter weren't turning up on every available TV program to promote it, then the Chronicle wouldn't have been in the least bit interested.'

The actress gave her a sharp look. 'So it was my stupid little sister, was it? God, I wouldn't put it past her.' *Goodness, she really doesn't know who the source is, does she?* Maggie thought. *That is interesting.*

'You'd need to ask Yash Patel that,' she said, glad that she didn't have to lie this time. 'But do you really think it's something your sister would do? Would Eilish allege that her husband had been murdered just to get more publicity for her book? That seems rather hard to imagine.'

'Oh, I don't know,' Kirsty said, her tone bitter, 'she's certainly stupid enough if nothing else. But she did love Alasdair, even if he did frustrate the hell out of her. So no, maybe she wouldn't,' she added, notably softening.

'And what do *you* think Kirsty?' Maggie asked quietly. 'Do you think Alasdair *could* have been murdered?'

She tossed her head dismissively. 'Complete nonsense. My brother-in-law was in a bad place, and it all got too much for him, that's all. I'm ashamed to say I wasn't surprised when he took his own life. Although it was a great shock of course,' she added hastily, before pausing. Then she said, 'He'd had a very difficult time in the months leading up to Christmas, with his father dying and all the troubles that went with it. And it was a great disappointment to Eilish. I don't think she was very satisfied with her life, but she had clung to the belief that one day she would be lady of the manor.'

'Yes, some of that was hinted at in Patel's article,' Maggie said guardedly. 'I glanced over it on the plane on the way here.'

'Sensationalist rubbish,' Tom Harper said sharply. 'It was of course a terrible family tragedy, but he wasn't murdered. I mean, who would want to murder *Alasdair*? The very thought is ridiculous. He was a violin teacher for goodness' sake. And the gentlest man in the world.'

'You found the body Kirsty, didn't you?' Maggie said softly. 'That must have been awful for you.'

'You can't imagine how horrible,' she said, 'seeing Alasdair hanging there dead in that beautiful living room with the log fire and the huge tree, and all the kids' presents waiting to be opened. I'm just glad the children didn't see it first. That's one thing to be thankful for at least.'

'You've done very well for yourselves,' Maggie said, changing the subject. 'Both of you have.' She hesitated for a moment. 'But I suppose that can lead to family tensions. Jealousy even.'

Kirsty shrugged. 'I admit Isla and Eilish haven't had the same good fortune in life that Tom and I have enjoyed. But I'm the elder sister, and I've always felt a responsibility to look after the two younger ones. To help them out when needed. To look after them if you will.'

It seemed that the actress had, momentarily at least, forgotten the purpose of the meeting, and with it, some of her initial hostility had melted away. Even if that turned out to be only a temporary respite, Maggie meant to take advantage of it.

'Do they need looking after?' she asked gently. 'Aren't they two grown-up women?'

The actress shrugged again. 'As I said, they haven't been as fortunate in life as I have, in both the material sense, but in their choice of husbands too.' As she said it, she gave her husband a fond smile, which, Maggie noted, wasn't returned. 'Or should I say in their choice of partner in Isla's case,' she corrected herself.

'That's Drew, isn't it? Drew Henderson?'

Kirsty gave a bitter laugh. 'Yes, Drew. And what a bloody waste of space he is.'

Maggie smiled to herself, remembering that Lori and Jimmy had told her Agnes Napier had described the man using exactly the same phrase.

'He's not a nice guy then?' she asked, fishing.

'Oh, he's nice all right,' Kirsty said. '*Too* nice. What they used to call a ladies' man. And what a merry dance he's led poor Isla over the years. Mind you, she lives in a little fantasy world herself, with her stupid books and her ridiculous dream of being a writer. She wanted me to help her, by introducing her to what she calls the right people, but of course, I couldn't.' Then suddenly, she brought herself up short. 'But I don't know why I'm telling you all this,' she said sharply. 'It's none of your business, and this...this *investigation* or whatever you call it has to stop, and it has to stop now. Do I make myself clear?'

'As I said at the outset Kirsty, that's not really within my gift. We're contracted to the Chronicle, and if they decide to continue with the story, then we're duty-bound to carry on. There's nothing in law that would force us to stop as far as I can see.'

'Well, maybe we'll have to test that in court,' she said. 'And I doubt if you would have the stomach or the resources for the fight.'

'I don't think you would do that,' Maggie said. 'And in any case, our terms of engagement state that the client must indemnify us against any legal action that arises as a result of our activities on their behalf. Standard stuff as you will well understand. So if you do fancy a day in court, it'll be the Chronicle who'll be paying the bill, not us. And they've got bottomless pockets, *and* a stomach for a fight too.'

Tom Harper smiled. 'It's never very smart to go to court, we all know that. Hopefully it won't come to that.'

His wife gave him a sharp look, evidently not agreeing. She was silent for a moment then said, 'Well in any case, none of the family will talk to you, let me make that crystal clear. This is all nonsense, and we don't intend to fan the flames by speaking to journalists or private investigators either.'

'Is that what you've told them to do? To employ the *no comment* strategy, as if they were in a police interview room?'

Kirsty nodded. 'Exactly that. There's nothing to see here anyway. You and your journalist friend are wasting their time and their money. No one will speak to you or any of your associates,' she repeated. 'No one.'

Maggie nodded then smiled. 'Very well Kirsty, and at least I know where you're coming from. And Tom, it was nice to meet you too.' She stood up, picked up her handbag then turned towards the door. 'I think we've probably concluded our business, don't you? At least for now.'

***

She had an hour to kill before her lunch date with her friend Asvina Rani, which she spent relaxing in Addison Redburn's spacious reception atrium, enjoying the excellent complimentary coffee whilst pondering the case. The fact was, they were really no worse off than they had been before, injunction or no injunction. It was always going to have been tough to get any of the family to talk, even the publicity-hungry Eilish and Christabelle Macbeth, and nothing that had happened in the last half hour had changed that. But she wasn't despondent, not in the least. They had examined the crime scene and knew what had been used to hang him, and they had a list of suspects, one of which must have carried out the killing. Okay, they were rather light on motive at the moment, but that, she felt, would surely emerge after a bit of industrial-strength brainstorming. If it was indeed murder, as they now were reasonably sure it was, then staging Alasdair Macbeth's death to look like suicide must have taken sophisticated planning and execution. The exact method of how that was accomplished was still to be worked out, but she was confident that Jimmy and Lori would come up with a solution in due course. Any remaining gaps in their knowledge could probably be filled in by Agnes Napier, and they could always re-visit the scene in the event they had overlooked something vital to the case.

Then out of the blue, she remembered an old murder mystery she had enjoyed some years ago, in which the famous fictional detective had been confined to bed with a bad dose of flu or cold, she couldn't quite remember which. She seemed to recall that this novel was set at Christmas too, although she couldn't be sure of that either. Whatever the details, the sleuth was able to solve the particularly thorny case without once having to leave his bed, using the services of his faithful companion as a surrogate should the scene need to be visited, or a witness or suspect interrogated. Perhaps this would be how this investigation would pan out. They already had quite a lot of background information, and they knew too it could only have been someone in that house who was responsible for the killing. Ruling out the kids, that just left the five family members plus Agnes Napier to pick from. So what if they wouldn't talk? - a barrage of *no comments* wouldn't stop her and her team getting to the bottom of what had happened that Christmas.

But then suddenly she realised that she was looking at this all the wrong way. Because the unarguable fact was, if this *was* a murder case, then someone who had been staying at Christmas Lodge was a killer, and that person would have spent the last twelve months safe in the knowledge that Alasdair Macbeth's death had been officially recorded as a suicide, a done deal. But now, with Yash Patel's sensational campaign in full flight, that feeling of security would be rapidly evaporating. Not only that, perhaps another member of the family had had their suspicions at the time but had either suppressed or dismissed them. Now, maybe they were ready to talk, irrespective of what Kirsty Bonnar and her husband had advised. *And today was Friday.*

She grabbed her phone and called Lori, who answered promptly as usual.

'Hi Lori, two things,' Maggie said. 'Number one, can you get onto Agnes Napier and see if she can give you Isla and Drew Henderson's address? And number two, are you doing anything in particular this evening?'

'I was going down the town to get battered with my wee friend Rosie and her big pal Shania,' she said. *'That's not her real name by the way, but that's what everybody calls her because she's a karaoke fanatic and always sings Shania Twain songs. But I'm up for a better offer if you've got one, because that pair are seriously*

dangerous on a night out.' She paused for a moment. *'Have you got a better offer then? 'Cos I'm listening.'*

'Absolutely I have,' her boss replied, struggling not to laugh. 'If I can persuade Frank to babysit, you and I are off to do a bit of old-fashioned foot-in-the-door detective work. And don't worry, I'll be buying the drinks afterwards.'

Chapter 10

Much to Frank's surprise, the business of ordering one of the stolen Aquanaut Islands using MI6's dodgy credit card had gone without a hitch. According to the villains' glossy website, what you were actually buying was a collection of two dozen Aquanaut-themed Christmas cards, which, at nine-hundred and fifty quid a box, worked out at an eye-watering forty pounds a card, and that was before you added the mandatory shipping charge of fifty quid, bringing the grand total to a round one thousand pounds. It was an outrageous sum, no doubt about that, but there were plenty of parents willing and able to stump up the cash to make sure their little Johnny or Joanna got the Christmas they were dreaming of. He was reminded that that stolen cache comprised twenty thousand units, and it wasn't exactly rocket science to do the maths. Twenty thousand multiplied by a grand a piece equalled two million smackers, a nice wee business right enough. And what were their costs? A few hundred quid to pay off a bent copper in the Suffolk Constabulary, a tankful of diesel for their stolen getaway van, and a month's rent for a scruffy lock-up on an anonymous West Midlands industrial estate. Add on a wee bag of low-grade cocaine for the spotty IT geek who'd knocked up the website, and you were looking at no more than five grand in expenses, tops. There were probably no more than half a dozen hoods involved in the scam, each who could look forward to clearing a cool three hundred and fifty thousand. Who said entrepreneurship was dead in modern Britain, he thought ruefully.

As Eleanor had predicted, collection of the goods was to be from a pick-up locker. You weren't given much choice of location, which was why Frank was camped up in his BMW in the carpark of a large supermarket near the post-war housing scheme of Castlemilk, an area of the city he was not familiar with. The heater was blasting, a takeaway americano steamed in the cupholder and a chocolate bar sat on the passenger seat, untouched but radiating temptation. This being the run up to Christmas, the facility was doing a roaring trade in both collections and deposits, and whilst the frenetic coming-and-goings had the potential of making today's task more difficult than he would have liked, he had a good view, and he was also pretty sure what he was looking for. The confirmation email from the hoods said that his Christmas cards – yes, that description still made him smile – would be available for pick-up from 2pm, which at least had narrowed down the time window during which he would have to hang around in the freezing cold. But now it was three-thirty, and the winter sunlight, such that it was, had long since dropped to the misty horizon, and in ten minutes would have disappeared entirely. No doubt that was the plan, to await the cover of darkness before making the drop, but there was a potential flaw in that plan which Frank hoped to exploit to his advantage.

It was nearly twenty minutes later before he saw what he was looking for. A youth of about fourteen or fifteen leapt out of the passenger seat of a lowered hatchback, made his way to the rear of the vehicle, opened the tailgate and took out a bulky cube-shaped package. As Frank had expected, and as seemed to be the prevailing fashion amongst these wee housing-scheme neds, he was dressed from top to toe in white, the soft cotton tracksuit complimented by a pair of dazzling trainers. No chance of losing him in the crowd then, he thought, congratulating himself on his foresight. *Right, here we go.* He jumped out of the BMW and crossed the carpark at a fair lick, arriving at the bank of storage lockers just behind his quarry, who had now placed the package on the snow and was studying his mobile phone, no doubt to retrieve the instructions for the drop.

Frank tapped him on the shoulder and said, 'How's it going pal? Are they my Christmas cards you've got there? I'll just take them off your hands right now, save you all that bother of opening and shutting the big locker.'

Startled, the boy spun round, gave him a questioning look, then said, 'Naw, ah cannae dae that. I've got to do the drop proper then send a picture otherwise...'

With a stealthy movement, Frank shot out an arm and grabbed the phone from him, taking the boy by surprise. 'Hey, whit are you doing?' he said indignantly as he tried without success to retrieve the device. Thwarted by Frank's steely grip, he nodded towards the car he had come in. 'See my mates over there? I just need to give them a shout and they'll come and sort you out good and proper.'

Frank gave a wry smile. 'I can't be arsed to get out my warrant card, but just so you know, you're talking to DCI Frank Stewart of New Gorbals nick. Still want to get your mates over pal? Please, bring it on. Because I get a nice wee cash bonus every time I make a multiple collar.'

'Shit,' the boy said, his face turning pale to match his attire. 'Look, I've no' done anything here, I'm just dropping this off for a guy.'

'What guy?'

The boy shrugged. 'I don't know him. He was just cruising round the scheme in a van, and we got talking, and he gave me and my mates thirty quid to do this.' That was almost certainly the truth,

Frank thought, and there was no point in asking if he got the registration number, because that van would almost certainly have been driving round on false plates.

'But he gave you a phone number too, didn't he?' Frank asked. 'So that you could send that picture of the drop, to prove you done it.' He paused, waved the phone in the air then shot the youth a menacing look. 'So what's that phone number pal? Come on, cough it up.'

'I cannae do that,' he said. 'I'll get killed.'

Frank smiled again. 'Listen son, what's your name?'

The boy returned a defiant look. 'Ah don't need to tell you that. Ah know my rights, so I do.'

'And I don't need to handcuff you and take you down the station where they'll rough you up in your cell, then take your fingerprints and a DNA swab, after which every cop in Glasgow will know who you are. So come on, don't play silly buggers with me. What's your name?'

'It's Shug,' the boy said, his resistance melting.

'Shug what?'

There was no answer.

'Shug what?' Frank repeated. 'Or do I have to beat it out of you?' he added in an amused tone. 'Because that's what I do when wee scumbags like you mess me around.'

'Shug Wilson,' the boy said finally. 'It's Shug Wilson.'

'You're facing a wee dilemma then Shug, aren't you?' Frank said. 'That's assuming you know what the word means, which I doubt. You see, if you don't give me that number, I'm going to confiscate your phone and you won't be able to send that picture, and so the bad guys will think you're a little toe-rag who's ran off with their Aquanaut Island so that you can flog it yourself. And when I say bad guys, I mean *really* bad guys, not the pound-shop types that swan around your scheme. I guarantee they'll come looking for you, and when they find you, they'll probably cut off your hands first so that you can't do any more thieving. Then they'll cut off your balls and stuff them in your mouth so that you've got a souvenir of their visit. And then they'll probably kill you to make sure you don't blab to the police. But of course, you know all that already. Whereas I will let you take your picture, and I'll let you send it too, and then I'll give you back your phone and you and your pretendy-gangster mates will be free to go.' He paused for a second. 'So how about it? What's it to be? Your choice.'

'You've already got the number in your hand,' the boy said. 'I stored it in my phone.'

Frank grinned. 'That's brilliant. Now you just go ahead and put the box in the locker as arranged, and you can take your photograph, and then I'll stick the number in my own phone, and we'll be good to go. And whilst we're at it, I'll video the whole thing for posterity.'

With a truculent air, the youth did as he was told, afterwards shooting a defiant one-finger salute in Frank's direction as he ran back to his mates' car. But Frank wasn't bothered. He'd got that precious phone number, and although it might only remain in service for a few more hours, that might be long enough for Eleanor Campbell to work her cyber magic and trace its owner. But better than that, he had an email with a four-digit code that would spring open the locker he was currently standing in front of. And inside that locker was a gaudily printed cardboard box containing one brand-new, never-played-with, ready-for-Christmas Aquanaut Island. He simply had to punch in four numbers and it could be his.

Now *that* was what you would call a dilemma.

Chapter 11

For Maggie, it had been a bloody long day, starting with the taxi arriving at the Milngavie bungalow just after five to take her to the airport for her flight to Heathrow and the meeting with Tom Harper and Kirsty Bonnar. On the positive side, the lunch with her best friend Asvina had been lovely but the rich food and plenty of it had caused her to sleep all the way through her flight back to Glasgow. The plane had landed at six-thirty, precisely on schedule, and she would dearly have loved to have jumped straight into another cab and headed straight home to where Frank and Ollie would be waiting for her. But no, work had to come first, even in her current pregnant state, and since this was Friday, it had to be done now if at all. So instead, the taxi had taken her to a new-built housing estate on the north-western edge of the city, where she had arranged to meet with her young colleague. The Henderson's house was a modest mid-terraced property, located in a row of what the planners liked to call affordable housing, this an island in an ocean of four-bedroomed executive homes. But what grabbed Maggie's attention most of all was the 'for sale' sign mounted on a wooden pole and attached to a gatepost. Characteristically, Lori was already waiting for her when she pulled up at the kerbside, wearing the yellow quilted jacket and matching woolly hat that was fast becoming her winter trademark. Conscious that this might turn out to be the shortest meeting in the history of Bainbridge Associates, Maggie asked the driver to hang on for five minutes before he drove off.

'Thanks so much for giving up your big night out,' she said as she stepped out of the cab. 'And nice to see you're dressed for the weather. Because it's bloody freezing, isn't it?'

Her colleague grinned. 'I love this jacket, so I do. And I'm not bothered about giving up my Friday night because if this goes the way I think it might, I'll still have plenty of time to get down to the town and meet my pals.'

Maggie gave a wry smile. 'Yes, you're right, we might not get past the doorstep. But we can give it a try at least.'

'Why did it have to be a Friday?' Lori asked. 'Not that I mind.'

'Remember, Agnes Napier told us this is the night Isla's other half usually goes out on the town with his mates. I'm hoping she'll be in on her own with the kids and might take the opportunity to vent about him if we turn up unexpectedly.'

'Or she might think we're Jehovah's Witnesses and slam the door in our faces.'

'Yeah, very possibly.' Maggie nodded towards the doorbell. 'But let's find out, shall we?'

Lori stuck out a finger and jabbed the button, being rewarded by a loud but obviously synthesised *ding-dong*. Through the frosted glass panels of the door, they saw a light being switched on, and a few seconds later a woman opened it, remaining half-hidden behind it and keeping a cautious hand on the handle.

'Yes?' she said, studying them with a suspicious expression.

'Isla?' Maggie said, smiling. 'I'm Maggie Bainbridge, and this is my colleague, Lori Logan. We're working for the Chronicle newspaper, and we wondered if we could grab five minutes of your time?'

'I know who you are,' she said. 'Kirsty says I've not to talk to you.'

Maggie smiled again. 'Yes, I know, she told me that when I met with her and Tom in London today.' She paused for a moment before continuing. 'And if that's what you want, Lori and I will leave right now.' She glanced over her shoulder. 'Look, I even asked my taxi to wait for me. It'll be no problem if you want us to go. We're not here to harass you, believe me. We just want to ask you a couple of questions.'

The woman gave them an uncertain look and for a moment it seemed she might be about to invite them in. But then she said, 'No, Kirsty told me I mustn't talk to you or that Patel guy.'

'I totally understand that,' Maggie said, 'but the thing is, your sister Eilish and her daughter Christabelle are hot property at the moment, and I don't think the media are going to leave them alone for one minute, irrespective of what Kirsty says. Obviously, we don't have a clue whether your brother-in-law Alasdair was murdered or not, because we weren't there, but someone who *was* there has been talking to that newspaper, and the sad fact is, those allegations aren't going to go away anytime soon.' She paused again. 'And when allegations start flying, sometimes it's the innocents that get caught in the crossfire. This might be your chance to put your side of the story, if there's anything that's been bothering you all this time. That might help you if the police get involved.'

The woman looked suddenly alarmed. 'But poor Alasdair killed himself. Why would the police want to get involved after all this time?'

'Someone thinks he was murdered,' Maggie said. 'If that turns out to be the case, the police are definitely going to be asking questions. It won't be just us and the Chronicle.'

Isla hesitated. 'I don't know anything. But I suppose it won't do any harm for you to come in for ten minutes.'

Maggie smiled. 'I'm sure that's all we'll need. Just hang on a second and I'll ask my taxi man to wait for me.' She returned to the cab, opened the passenger door and spoke a few words to the driver, relieved that it would be the Chronicle who would be settling the rapidly- growing fare.

'Right, ten minutes, that's all we'll need,' she repeated, as she returned to the doorstep. 'I promise.'

The woman led them through to a small lounge, tidy but cheaply furnished with flat-pack furniture. A bottle of white wine and a glass sat on a small coffee table, the bottle half-empty, the glass completely so. 'It's Friday, end of the working week,' the woman said, catching their glance. 'We all like to unwind, don't we? Anyway, would you like to join me in a glass? There's enough left for all of us I think.'

'Not for me, thank you,' Maggie said. 'I'm off it for the duration, worst luck,' she added, patting her tummy.

'Not me either,' Lori said. 'I'm hitting the town later. But don't let us stop you.'

Isla Bonnar reached across and began to unscrew the top of the bottle. 'Maybe I will have another glass, just a little one,' she said as she started to pour a generous measure.

'What is your job anyway?' Lori asked.

The woman smiled. 'I'm an author. I write, full time.'

'That's brilliant,' Lori said. 'Do you write detective books or something like that? There magic, aren't they?'

'Not exactly,' she said. 'Romance is more my line.'

'My granny reads hundreds of them, so she does. The girl always gets the guy, doesn't she? Not like in real life,' she added, with a mild wistfulness.

'Okay Isla,' Maggie said, 'we don't want to interrupt your evening unduly, so quickly, I was just wondering what you made of the allegations that have appeared in the paper. Can I ask you straight out, do you think Alasdair could have been murdered?'

The woman shrugged. 'I don't see how. I mean, everybody was in the house the whole time so someone would have seen or heard something, surely.'

'No-one saw him preparing to kill himself either though, did they?' Maggie mused. 'I mean, if that's what happened, like the official version says. It would have been quite an elaborate operation.'

Lori gave Isla a puzzled look. 'You said everyone was in the house for the whole time you were up there. But what were you all doing? Because if it was *my* family stuck together in a house for all that time, there'd be an international incident within ten minutes. Didn't you get really bored?'

'We just relaxed,' she said. 'I did a bit of writing, and I played with the kids. Tom was working the whole time as per usual and Kirsty was trying to learn the lines for a film she's going to be in. Christabelle was glued to her phone or watching re-runs of Love Island on the telly.' She paused for a moment. 'And my mother just sat around complaining about everything and everyone as usual.' There was no hiding the bitterness in her tone. 'And what about Alasdair and Eilish?' Maggie asked.

Isla shrugged. 'Eilish was being horrible to him, but that was nothing new. She thought she was going to be rich, and then suddenly she wasn't.'

'But that wasn't her husband's fault, surely? And he must have still been very upset about the death of his father.'

'He was. Of course he was. But that didn't stop her going on and on, did it?' she said.

'But she's rich now I suppose?' Lori said. 'With her book doing so amazingly well.'

The woman nodded. 'Yes, two authors and a famous actress in the family now. Isn't that lovely?' It sounded less than sincere, and no wonder, Maggie thought, with one sister an effortless million-seller and the other still unpublished despite years of yearning.

'And what about your husband?' Maggie asked. 'And by the way, is he in tonight? Because we wouldn't mind asking him a couple of questions too.'

She laughed. 'No, it's Friday and that's Drew's night out with his pals. It's sacrosanct.' Outwardly at least, it didn't seem to be concerning her. 'And he's not my husband,' she added. 'He's my partner.'

'Where does he go?' Lori asked.

'Their favourite is a pub called the Burns Tavern,' she said. 'It's just off George Square. He's taken me there a few times, but it's not really my scene.'

'That's where me and my pals go too,' Lori said. 'There's a dead good atmosphere and they've got a mega sound system and a wee dance floor with an old-school disco ball. It's cool.' And probably packed with young women your age, Maggie thought, and a bunch of older guys chancing their luck.

'And what was *he* doing when he was at the lodge?' she asked.

'Sitting about. Drinking. Watching football and old movies. That's Drew for you.'

'Was he close to Alasdair?' Maggie asked. 'I mean, would he have talked to Drew about how he was feeling?'

She laughed again. 'With Drew? No, you must be joking. He doesn't do feelings. But Alasdair was talking to Tom. A *lot*,' she added, emphasising the point.

'What about?' Lori asked.

Isla shrugged. 'How should I know? I don't go around eavesdropping on other people's conversations.'

'I thought that was what writers *did* do?' Lori said. 'I thought that's how they got their inspiration.'

'Well I *don't*,' the woman said. 'But I think that perhaps Tom and Alasdair were trying to make up after the big fall-out the previous year.'

Maggie ostentatiously raised her arm and peered at her watch. 'I know we said we wouldn't out-stay our welcome, but I'd love to know what that was all about, if you don't mind sharing it with us. Just a couple of more minutes.'

Isla nodded her assent. 'Alasdair and Eilish asked Tom and Kirsty for a loan to help his father keep the estate going. But Tom wouldn't agree. He said it was just throwing good money after bad and that they should sell up whilst the assets might still have some value. I think words were said, and that caused a lot of bad blood, but what did they expect? They're more than generous with their money already, but some people always expect more, don't they?'

Maggie hesitated, wondering exactly where to go next with this conversation. At least, like her sister, Isla Bonnar had seemed to have forgotten that she was not meant to be answering any of their questions. The problem was, everything she'd heard so far, right from the start of the investigation. suggested that Alasdair Macbeth was the last person on earth that anyone would want to murder. And no one seem to have a motive either, except perhaps his wife Eilish, bitter that her prosperous future had been taken away from her by the incompetence of her late father-in-law. But was that bitterness enough to drive her to murder her own husband? It seemed a bit of a stretch, to say the least.

Struggling to find anything more to ask, she said simply, 'So what do you think Isla? Do you think Eilish could have killed her husband?'

'*No*,' she shot back. 'I mean Eilish can get a bit emotional at times, but I don't think she could ever *murder* someone. No, definitely not. Alasdair killed himself and everybody just has to accept that.'

Maggie let the answer hang in the air for a moment then motioned towards her colleague, indicating that it was time to go. Getting to her feet she said, 'I really appreciate your time Isla, thank you. And we won't be bothering you again.'

'But the paper will still be writing these stories, won't they?' she said. 'Vile slander, all of it.'

'Yash Patel will run out of new things to say soon enough,' Maggie said. 'It'll be old news before you know it.'

Isla gave a half-smile. 'I hope so. Anyway, let me see you to the door.' She led them down the short hallway and opened the door for them. As they stepped onto the path Maggie said, 'I see you're moving. Where are you going if you don't mind me asking?'

The woman smiled again. 'I've not really decided yet. But my writing's finally paying off, and it seems like a good time to go. I might get a flat down by the river, they're really nice.'

'I wish you the best of luck then,' Maggie said. 'And thanks again.'

***

The taxi driver beamed a smile into the mirror which indicated he couldn't believe his luck, with a drop-off up the town and then a lucrative trip all the way out to Milngavie, delivering a stonking three-figure fare for a couple of hours work.

'Good evening again, ladies,' he said, giving them a wave. 'You just relax in the back there and I'll have you delivered in no time, snow or no snow. But we'll have to take it easy because the roads are a wee bit slithery.' He fiddled about with his meter for a moment and then just as he was about to pull away from the kerb, he heard the parp of a horn followed by a flash of headlights. 'Hang on a minute,' he said, peering out the windscreen. 'Here's one of my taxi mates trying to do a drop off. Same company as mine.' He peered through the windscreen again. 'Oh aye, it's big Ally. He's a right character, so he is.' He gave a thumbs up to the other vehicle to indicate he was just vacating the parking space. 'Nae bother, off we go,' he said when, a minute or so later, the manoeuvre was complete.

'So Miss Logan, what do you think to that?' Maggie asked her colleague. 'Because we didn't really find out anything we didn't already know as far as I'm concerned.'

Lori nodded. 'Aye, I know, it's a bit hopeless, isn't it? But I suppose there is one thing. A couple of people have said Drew Henderson's a waste of space, but his partner doesn't seem to share that view. She doesn't seem bothered that he goes out shagging on a Friday night with his mates, does she?'

Maggie laughed. 'Do you think that's what he does? Goes out shagging, as you so colourfully put it?'

'Why else would they go to the Burns Tavern?' her colleague said.

'Is that what happens there? And Miss Logan, is that why you go?'

'Not me, no way. I just go for the dancing. But Shania doesn't think she's had a proper weekend unless she gets a nice wee shag on a Friday night.'

'Goodness, what a sheltered life I've led,' Maggie laughed. 'And aren't I glad of that. But you're right, there doesn't seem to be any obvious issues with the Henderson relationship, does there?'

'And they had absolutely no motive to kill Alasdair. Nobody had, that's the problem.' The girl paused for a moment. 'You don't think old Agnes did it, do you?'

Maggie gave her a sceptical look. 'No, why would I think that? And what motive could she possibly have anyway?'

'She's a nutcase serial killer who gets pleasure from watching someone die in agony?' Lori said, breaking into a giggle which she then struggled to control.

'Yes, exactly. But the fact is, Alasdair Macbeth was found with his feet dangling three feet above the floor of that living room. And as we've said a million times...'

'Not the old Sherlock Holmes chestnut again?' Lori said.

'The same. Once you've eliminated the impossible, then what remains must be the truth, no matter how improbable. Or words to that effect. He was murdered, we know that. Definitely. We just don't know how, why or by whom.' She paused for a moment. 'But you know, today's not been a bad day all-in-all. We've talked to half the suspects already and having had these initial conversations, there's always an excuse to go back if we think of more questions. So that's good in my book.'

Lori grinned again. 'And maybe I can add a fourth suspect to that tonight? Because believe you me, there aren't many men who can resist when Shania comes onto them. She's a proper temptress, so she is.'

'You mean with Drew? No, you can't do that,' Maggie protested. 'That would be like entrapment. We're not allowed to do that.'

'She'll only be chatting him up,' Lori said dismissively. 'She does that with all the older guys when she fancies a few free drinks. And I'll be chaperoning her to make sure there's no funny business. She'll ask if he's married, and he'll say no, but he won't mention he's got a partner and kids. And he'll be a bit pissed by them and hopefully he'll start talking, which is what we want, isn't it? And I promise, if he tries anything, I'll take him out with a single blow.'

Maggie laughed. 'All right then, but like you say, no funny business, okay?'

But of course, they had no way of knowing in advance that Lori and her promiscuous friend Shania would be the last people to see Drew Henderson alive. Apart, that was, for his killer.

Chapter 12

The news that an as-yet-unidentified body had been found in a back alley just behind the Central Station had caused a frisson of excitement around New Gorbals police station. Contrary to its historic reputation, violent deaths were rare in the fine city of Glasgow and if you were fortunate– or unfortunate, depending on how you looked at it – you could spend quite a few years as a murder squad detective without actually working on a murder case. The city did spawn a goodly dose of late-night violence of course, ninety-nine percent of which was alcohol-fuelled, but no more than any other major city in the country. The only problem with this particular crime was it was coming up to Christmas, and a fair proportion of the New Gorbals serious crime squad had bagged much-coveted leave to spend time with their families, and they wouldn't be too thrilled if it was taken away from them. With a vague sense of foreboding, Frank could imagine the phone call from one of the brass, asking him what he had on at the moment.

Still, he would worry about that if and when it happened. Right now, there had been serious developments on the Aquanaut Island case which called for an urgent team meeting. The venue, naturally, was the basement canteen at New Gorbals, the sustenance, naturally, was a strong americano and a roll and sausage with brown sauce.

'Right Lexy, let's get them on the line,' he said to the DC, who was also mid-way through the sustaining breakfast. 'I'm particularly interested to hear what Ronnie's got to say for himself.'

'Okay sir,' McDonald replied, punching a few keys of her opened laptop. 'Right... here they are now.' The features of DC Ronnie

French and Senior Forensic Officer Eleanor Campbell popped up in separate windows on the laptop's screen.

'Morning all,' he boomed. 'You still in Felixstowe, Frenchie?' he added, not sure if he recognised the office his DC was camped in.

'Nah guv, scooted up to Ipswich this morning to have a word with them finance geezers,' he explained. *'I'm in their HQ right now.'*

Frank nodded. 'Okay, got it. So this has all got a whole lot more serious with the news that the poor lorry driver has died from his injuries. What exactly happened Ronnie, do you know?'

'Brain haemorrhage guv, undetected. The poor guy just dropped dead at home last night, in front of his wife and kids too, bloody awful. Definitely caused by him being coshed, so it's a murder case now, no question. The Northamptonshire boys are running with it as we speak.'

'Well maybe we can give them a helping hand with that,' he said. 'Eleanor, how did you get on with tracing that mobile number I sent you?'

She shrugged. *'Good and bad, I suppose. I traced the signal as it travelled from Glasgow to a place called Gretna.'*

'Aye, that's at the border, so I guess they were heading back to the Midlands after doing some drops in Scotland. And what happened at Gretna?'

'The van stopped for fuel in the services, and we got a capture on CCTV.'

'That's brilliant,' Frank said, feeling his excitement rise.

'Like not brilliant,' Eleanor said, and he felt it drop again. *'Look.'* She punched some instructions into her keyboard and immediately their screen filled with a hazy video image. It was a fuel station forecourt, the detail difficult to make out through the flurries of snow that danced around the CCTV camera. But even if the images had been crystal clear, it wouldn't have helped. The driver who was filling the van with diesel wore a large shapeless anorak, the hood pulled down over his forehead. He had a scarf around his chin and mouth and to complete the disguise, he wore a pair of sunglasses, incongruous on a dark December evening, but effective.

Lexy sighed. 'I don't think we should have expected anything else sir. They're professionals and they're not going to get caught out by that schoolboy error.'

'And they drove off without paying too,' Eleanor said.

'Of course they did,' Frank said in a resigned tone. 'Somehow, I didn't expect them to leave their credit card details. So what happened after that Eleanor?'

'We lost it just before a place called Penrith,' she said.

'They'd have chucked the SIM card out of the window,' French said, *'then stuck in a new one. That's what they do so they can't be traced.'*

'Bugger,' Frank said. 'But like you say Lexy, no more than we should have expected.' He hesitated for a moment, then scratched his head. 'So where do we go now, that's the big question?'

He glanced at his young DC colleague, whose ruffled forehead signalled furious thought, always a promising sign in his experience.

'I detect the old brain's shifted into a higher gear,' he said, grinning, 'which suggests a brilliant idea is about to give birth. Come on wee Lexy, out with it.'

'It is an idea sir, but I'm not sure it's brilliant and I'm not sure you'll like it either,' she said, giving him an uncertain look.

'I'll be the judge of that. Come on, let's hear it.'

She nodded. 'Okay. So yesterday you sent me that video you took of the wee Castlemilk ned putting the package in the locker, and I sent it on to Eleanor this morning.'

'I got it,' Eleanor said. *'Want me to show it?'*

'Yes please.'

After a few clicks, the video appeared on the screen. She pressed play and they watched its few seconds of footage, and then Lexy said, 'Great. Now can you play it backwards Eleanor?'

'Yeah, 'course,' the forensic officer said, *'but like why?'*

Lexy laughed. 'Let's just look at it and you'll soon work that out.'

Eleanor did as instructed, the team watching the footage with growing amusement. It was Ronnie French who spoke first. *'That's hilarious. It looks like the urchin's making off with it, don't it?'*

'It bloody well does,' Frank said, laughing. 'And now I think I can see where you're going with this Lexy.'

She nodded. 'It's a very cunning plan, even if I say so myself. Firstly, you send an email to the hoods complaining that you handed over the cash but when you went to collect it, the locker was empty.'

He laughed. 'Aye, I expect they've got a whole customer service department all geared up to handle complaints.'

'That's just so they get to know of the issue,' she said. 'But the next bit's the genius bit. And again, I say that in all modesty.' She paused for a moment. 'We speak to our friend Yash Patel, and we get him to run a story in his paper. *Beware the Aquanaut Scammers*, or something like that. The story warns you that you'll send your thousand pounds, but you won't get anything. But here's the real genius bit. We then get Yash to post our wee backwards video in their online edition, and he writes a supporting story saying that rival criminal gangs have hacked the scammers' website and are stealing the goods as soon as they are delivered to the pick-up lockers. And as corroborating evidence, here's a video of a bandit called Shug Wilson in live action.'

'Bloody hell Lexy, that *is* genius,' Frank said. 'The murdering hoods see their business model crumbling before their very eyes, and just to rub salt in the wound, a wee Glasgow nobody has double-crossed them. They're not going to like that, are they?'

'No, they're not sir,' Lexy said. 'Not at all. I think Shug might be in a spot of trouble.'

He laughed. 'And it'll be us who'll have put him there, don't forget. But yeah, it's a brilliant plan, no question. So tell me, what happens next?'

'Well sir, I'm going to track him down and warn him there's every chance he's only got twenty-four hours to live. We tell him to lie low, and then we wait for the hoods to turn up and start cruising the streets looking for him. Because they will turn up, I guarantee it. For them, it'll be a matter of honour. And when they do, we nip in and nab them. Simple.'

***

Frank wasn't exactly surprised to find his tiny office occupied when he returned from his meeting with the team, nor was he surprised that the occupier was the corpulent figure currently filling his chair. The backrest had been reclined to an alarming angle to allow Detective Superintendent Charlie Maxwell to lounge back with his feet up on the desk.

'How's it going Frank?' he said in a languid tone. 'I hear you and your team of reprobates are chasing a truckload of Christmas toys around the country right now. Important work, right enough.'

Frank laughed. 'Very important sir. The happiness of the nation's wee ones depends on it. What about you? Have you got kids sir, and do they want an Aquanaut Island from Santa?'

He gave a wry smile. 'My boy's seventeen, he's expecting Santa to drop a bloody hatchback down the chimney this year. Anyway, how come your squad is working on this investigation? I thought you were strictly cold cases?'

'Cold cases and internal corruption sir,' Frank said. 'There's been allegations that someone in the Suffolk force leaked the details of the last shipment to the bad guys. And it's all got seriously serious of late, because they coshed the lorry driver, and he's just died from his injuries.'

Maxwell whistled through his teeth. 'Aye, that is seriously serious. But your squad isn't leading the murder enquiry, surely?'

He shook his head. 'No sir, the Northamptonshire boys and girls are leading on that one, because that's where the heist took place.'

'Understand. Well, it sounds like your wee toy job is just part-time, meaning you'll have plenty of headroom to take on another case I've got for you. You see, there's been a murder.'

Frank nodded. 'I heard. Near the Central Station.'

'That's right. A guy in his forties by the name of Drew Henderson. We let his family know over the weekend and obviously it's still really raw for them. He had two kids as well. What a bloody Christmas eh? We've not released the name to the papers yet because we don't want a media scrum when they're still in shock.'

'How did he die?' Frank asked.

'Stabbed. Three times and in the back, according to the initial scene-of-crime officers. The body's in the morgue now awaiting further examination. But he wasn't found until about eight on Saturday morning, and we think he must have been attacked about one o' clock or thereabouts. The poor guy bled out, that's what they're saying. Might have survived if he'd been found earlier.'

'Poor guy right enough,' Frank said. 'But can I ask what it's got to do with me?' It sounded more brusque than he'd intended, but Maxwell seemed unconcerned. He swung his feet off the desk and straightened up, letting the chairback spring into its natural position.

'Thing is Frank, and just between you and me, we're a bit short of DCI talent in this neck of the woods here right now. We've had one or two screw-ups of late and I can't afford another.' He paused again. 'I know you've got that DC McDonald seconded to you at the moment and she's a right wee bright spark. My original plan was to steal her back off you, but then I thought, why don't I nick the organ-grinder as well? A sort of two-for-one package if you will.'

'I suppose I should be flattered sir,' Frank said. 'But if you want to steal me, I'd need to check with my boss before I commit.'

Maxwell gave him a wry look. 'I checked, and you don't actually have a boss at the moment, as far as I can see. Other than some faceless civil service geek.'

He laughed. 'That's Trevor sir, and he's my admin assistant, not my boss. I think it'll actually take an act of parliament to get me moved. I'm a proper government agency you see. A one-man quango.'

'Well, I'm commandeering you, quango or no quango, and I'll sort out any paperwork crap that ensues afterwards. What other resources have you got other than DC McDonald?'

'I've got a huge squad sir. Comprising one superannuated Cockney DC and a brilliant but pain-in-the-arse forensic officer. Who, by the way, is pregnant and not far off her maternity leave.'

'That's it?' Maxwell said, surprised.

Frank nodded. 'We run lean and mean sir. Although we occasionally supplement our resources by using subcontractors. We know a wee team of private investigators, one of whom I happen to be married to. We wouldn't use them on a murder investigation though, obviously,' he added quickly.

'I know all about the Bainbridge bunch,' Maxwell said. 'We should nationalise them, if that's still a thing. Anyway, I think I can rustle you up half a dozen or so officers, some pretty good ones amongst them you'll be pleased to hear. And you'll have Room 9C downstairs as the murder room. It's not the biggest, but it's got a big whiteboard, and all the IT gear is set up and ready to go.' He stood up and stretched his shoulders. 'So Frank, you start tomorrow, alright?' Then he laughed. 'No, scratch that. You start right now.'

Chapter 13

It had taken five days for the news of Drew Henderson's death to filter through to Maggie and her team, it first emerging in a dinner-table conversation with Frank, where he shared the news that he had reluctantly accepted an assignment to lead a fresh murder investigation. When in confidence he had named the victim, her initial reaction was that it couldn't have been the same man. But the police had quickly found his address from the driving licence in his wallet, and they'd been to his house to give the terrible news to his partner Isla. Now Maggie and Lori sat in their Byres Road office awaiting the arrival of DC Lexy McDonald, who was to conduct the interview with Lori, one of the last people to see Henderson alive. Also due at the office was Lori's friend Shania, real name Ruth Thompson, who had also been present at the Burns Tavern on the previous Friday evening. The two other women arrived almost simultaneously, DC McDonald radiating her usual cool competence. Ruth Thompson aka Shania, however, was not at all like Maggie had been expecting based on Lori's description of her friend. Instead of the wild temptress of her imagination, this young woman was smartly dressed in a trouser suit and pink blouse, with her hair neatly tied up, an appearance which suggested she might hold a responsible managerial position in a respected organisation. But undoubtedly, she was very attractive, if rather more demure in appearance than Lori had described her.

'Sorry, it's a bit tight for space and we only have these plastic chairs,' Maggie said, indicating for the women to sit down, 'but I didn't think it would be a good idea to do this at the Bikini Barista.'

Lexy smiled. 'That's no problem, and I didn't want to haul you all down the station either.'

Maggie nodded. 'Is it all right if I sit in on this interview Lexy? Even although I wasn't actually at that bar on Friday night, so there's nothing I can tell you about that.'

'No, that's fine,' Lexy said. 'Frank's given me some of the background of the case you're working on, and I think I'll need you to fill in the gaps at some point.' She paused for a moment. 'So Lori and Ruth, can you tell me about Friday night at the Burns Tavern please?'

'It's a place we go quite a lot,' Lori began. 'It's always got a dead good atmosphere on a Friday, and they play brilliant music. And when me and Maggie heard from his partner Isla that Drew Henderson liked to go there too, I thought we could combine work and pleasure. With the help of my pal Shania ...sorry, Ruth here. It was just the two of us,' she added. 'Rosie stood us up for a guy she'd been chasing for ages.'

'And I assume you did see Drew Henderson?' Lexy asked. 'And by the way, how did you recognise him?'

'I'd seen a photograph. The housekeeper at Christmas Lodge showed me and Maggie a family snap. And aye, we did see him. He was there with a mate.'

'And did you manage to speak to him at all during the evening?'

Ruth said, 'That didn't go exactly to plan, but yeah, I did speak to him, briefly. Or rather, he spoke to me.'

'What do you mean?' Lexy asked.

'Him and his pal were already with a couple of girls,' Ruth said. 'A couple of wee schoolgirls actually, they didn't look more than sixteen. It's supposed to be twenty-one minimum in that place, but everyone's got fake ID,' she added, her tone scathing. 'Anyway, that was Lori's plan shot down in flames before it even started.'

'But you did speak to him, you said?'

Ruth nodded. 'Aye, I did. When the two scrubbers went off to the ladies, he went to the bar to get more drinks. So I went and plonked myself on the stool beside him and just said hi.'

'And what did he say?' Lexy asked. 'Anything?'

'Aye, he did, the cheeky bastard. He said, *I bet you'd be dead good in bed darling,* then he asked me for my phone number.'

Lexy didn't seem surprised. 'I've heard that line plenty of times before. Chancers, the lot of them. So what did you say?'

'I said, *in your dreams pal*, or something like that, and he said, *your loss*, then he went back to his table. That was it I'm afraid. Although I did see him looking at me a few times during the rest of the evening.'

'*Everybody* looks at you though,' Lori said, laughing. 'We had a couple of more drinks and chatted to a couple of guys and did a bit of dancing, but we kept an eye on him until they left.'

'Did he speak to anyone else during the night?' Lexy asked. 'Somebody he might have known, other friends, something like that?'

Lori shook her head. 'Don't think so. The girls went up for a couple of dances and left him and his mate at their table, but no, I didn't see him talk to anyone else.'

'So when did he leave?'

Lori shrugged. 'About half-eleven I suppose. The girl went with him. Mind you, I'm surprised she was able to walk given the number of drinks he'd been plying her with.'

'And where was his friend by this time?'

Lori shrugged again. 'Don't know. I suppose he went off with the other lassie somewhere. I didn't notice them leave.'

'So what do you think?' Lexy asked. 'Was Henderson and this girl going back to her place? Because he couldn't very well take her home, could he?'

'I doubt she had her *own* place,' Ruth said sceptically. 'She looked like she was still at primary school. More like they were going for a quick one up against a wall somewhere.' The matter-of-fact way she said this hinted at knowledge of the practice, Maggie thought, struggling not to laugh out loud.

'Would either of you recognise this girl if you saw her again?' Lexy asked. 'Because she might be a witness, and if she saw the attack, she'll be scared out of her wits I would imagine.'

'I would recognise her,' Ruth said. 'Definitely.'

Lori nodded. 'Me too, nae bother. As long as she's not in her school uniform, that is.'

'That's good,' Lexy said. 'We'll obviously be looking at the pub's CCTV so we should get a shot of this girl from that. We'll ask if anyone there knows who she is, otherwise we might put out an appeal on local media. I'm sure we'll track her down fairly quickly.'

'But wouldn't she have come forward if she'd seen anything?' Maggie asked, then answered her own question. 'No, I suppose if she's under-age and had lied to her folks about where she was going that night, that would be the last thing she'd want to do.'

Lexy nodded. 'Yeah, I fear so. But we'll find her.' The detective constable paused for a moment, gathering her thoughts, then said, 'I think that's probably all I need from you Ruth, and thanks for making the time to talk to me.'

'Nae problem,' the girl said. 'I'll get back to the office now then. I'll be just in time for my lunch break.'

'Where do you work?' Maggie asked out of interest.

'Up the town, West Nile Street. I'm a claims handler with a big insurance company.' She sighed. 'I just hope his poor partner had a good policy on his life. But unfortunately, that's one of the big problems with the unmarrieds. In the eyes of the law, the woman who's left behind is a nobody.'

***

Maggie of course had told Frank everything they knew about the Alasdair Macbeth case, sketchy though her knowledge undoubtedly was. Now they'd arranged a big get-together with all the team, this time at the Bikini Barista cafe, to chew over the implications of what they had found out, and to decide the next steps in what looked like becoming two closely-interlocked investigations. Present were Maggie, Lori, Frank and Lexy, with Jimmy on video call from Braemar. Refreshments were in place, courtesy of Stevie the proprietor, the atmosphere serious. It was Maggie who spoke first.

'I can't believe Drew Henderson was murdered so soon after we talked to his wife,' she said. 'And we had him as one of the suspects in the Alasdair Macbeth matter too. I know it seems a stretch, but do we really think there could be a connection? Or was he just the victim of some random act of violence on a Friday night?'

Frank shook his head. 'Obviously I don't know if there's a connection or not, but what I'm reasonably certain of already is that this was a targeted murder. If there'd been a drunken punch-up or an argument with a stranger, then the stab wounds would likely have been to his front, whereas Henderson was stabbed three times in the back. And there would have been signs of a struggle, and yet the post-mortem didn't show up any indications that he had been in a fight. None of that points to a random act of violence.'

'You mean someone must have been waiting for him then?' Lori asked. 'That it was premeditated?'

He nodded. 'Very probably. Maybe the killer hung about outside the pub waiting for him to leave, then followed him down that wee lane before doing the evil deed.'

'But remember, he left with the girl sir,' Lexy said. 'She must have seen something, surely?'

'Aye, that's why we need to find her,' he said. 'And fast. But let's hold back on the media appeals for now, just in case it makes her go to ground.'

'Understand sir,' Lexy said.

'There's something I need to toss into the proceedings,' Jimmy interrupted, sounding apologetic. 'Because I've been thinking a lot about Alasdair Macbeth's death after my visit to the lodge, obviously.' He paused for a moment. 'And to be honest, I'm now struggling to see how it could have been murder.'

'What?' Maggie said, surprised. 'But I thought you ruled out suicide because of how high his body was suspended? You thought he couldn't possibly have jumped off the chair that they found in the room?'

He gave her a despondent look. 'That's what I thought, but I must have missed something, I *must* have. Because the logistics for it being a murder just don't add up right now. The thing is, Macbeth was six-foot-two and sixteen stone, and if he was murdered by hanging, he presumably wouldn't have gone quietly, and he wouldn't have been an easy guy to restrain. And it was Christmas Eve, so the three wee kids would have been hyper with excitement and wide awake, so you couldn't have done it without causing a huge commotion. No, I can't explain why his feet were suspended three feet off the ground, but I can't come up with a credible scenario for murder either. I'm sorry, but I can't.' He hesitated for a moment. 'But don't worry, I'm not giving up. I'm going to have to go back to Christmas Lodge and look at everything again. I'm going to attempt a full reconstruction in fact. Because I think that's the only way I'll find the missing piece that I'm looking for. If it exists at all of course,' he added.

'I don't know how you'll be able to do that,' Maggie said. 'Because the lodge will be booked solid right through Christmas, won't it? I don't think the guests would much like a murder being recreated whilst they relax in front of the log fire.'

'I've thought of that,' he said. 'I talked to the Glengarry agency that handles the rentals and there's a five-hour window on a Saturday when they do the changeovers and they've got the cleaners in. I can drive over then and take another look. I need to do this Maggie, because it's doing my head in.'

Frank sighed. 'It sounds like we've got a bit of work to do before we can say our two cases are related then, haven't we?'

Suddenly Maggie had a worrying thought. 'When were you planning to release Henderson's name to the media Frank? Because once that's in the public domain our friend Yash Patel will be on it like a rabid dog. Even if we don't think there's a connection, that won't stop him spinning a lurid tale. You know, *Shock Murder of Kirsty and Eilish Brother-in-law Prompts More Questions*, that kind of thing.'

He laughed. 'Aye, I hadn't thought of our boy Yash as a rabid dog, but that's a good description. But to be honest, we've no pressing need to name him. To be honest I want to leave it as long as possible to protect his wife and kids from the hordes of doorstepping reporters, especially with it being so close to Christmas. We'll probably hold off on releasing his name for a week or two. That'll stop Patel feasting on the two cases and dreaming up wild connections.'

'But this one's *definitely* connected to our case,' Lori protested. 'I don't know how you can't see that. The Henderson guy was knifed in the back by someone who was waiting for him, and that someone must be the person who killed Alasdair Macbeth. Who else could it be?'

Maggie nodded. 'I do see your point Lori. But aren't we ignoring the most obvious suspect?'

'Yes, that's just occurred to me too,' Lexy said. 'The *girl*.'

Lori gave a snort. 'You didn't see her. She was a skinnymalink with legs up to her armpits and weighing six stone in her underwear. But nah, she couldn't slice an apple, never mind kill somebody with a knife. No way.'

Frank shrugged. 'Aye well, we need to find her before we decide on that. But Maggie, I don't think it would do any harm for you lot to carry on with your investigation, for the time being at least. But remember if anything pops out of the woodwork that you think might have a bearing on the Drew Henderson murder, you tell us right away, okay? Meanwhile Lexy, we need to head back to New Gorbals and meet our new team. Because the Chief Super says he's assembled a crack squad for us. But I'll believe that when I see it.'

As he spoke, a text message pinged through on Maggie's phone. 'Sorry, I forgot to put it on silent,' she said, raising a hand apologetically. But of course, such is the addictive nature of these infernal notifications, she was unable to resist looking to see who it was from. *Yash Patel.*

'Sorry, better just read this quickly,' she said. 'Won't be a sec.' She scanned the message, then gasped as it stopped her dead in her tracks.

'*What*? Bloody hell. *Bloody* hell.'

'What is it Maggie?' Lori said, stretching across the table in an attempt to read the text over her boss's shoulder.

'You are not going to believe this, but Yash has set up an *interview* with Eilish and Christabelle Macbeth,' she said incredulously. 'And not just that. They're doing a bloody *fashion* shoot for the paper's style editor. It's tomorrow at Edinburgh Castle and it's going to be in next weekend's magazine.'

'I can't believe this,' Lori said. 'So much for them not talking to the press. This is completely nuts.'

'Exactly,' Maggie said. 'It sounds like Eilish and her daughter are drunk on fame and have given the proverbial two fingers to her big sister Kirsty. Like you say, completely nuts.'

'But her brother-in-law has just been murdered,' Jimmy said. 'What sort of woman is she, for goodness' sake?'

Maggie smiled. 'That's what we're going to find out. Because Lori and I are going to gatecrash that ridiculous fashion shoot.'

Chapter 14

Following receipt of the astonishing text message from Yash Patel, Maggie was desperately keen to speak to the man himself. Accordingly, five minutes after the fruitful Bikini Barista meeting had ended, she found herself dialling his number. He answered on the first ring, with a bubbly, *'What do you think to that then Maggie? Am I a bloody genius, or am I a bloody genius?'*

'Bloody hell Yash,' she said, laughing, 'you're a bloody genius all right. And by the way, that's the fourth time I've said *bloody* in the last ten minutes. Five times actually, if you count that last one. I'm glad I've not got a swear box, otherwise I'd be bankrupt in a day. But what's going on? Because I don't understand it.'

He laughed. '*We're being played, Maggie dear, totally played. But I don't care, it's absolutely wondrous for me and the paper.*'

'What do you mean, played?'

'*I've witnessed this scenario a thousand times before,*' he said. '*It's what celebrities do, day-in, day-out. Media management they call it.*'

'Are Eilish and Christabelle celebrities?' she asked, sounding sceptical. 'And what do you mean, media management? Is that a thing?'

'The Macbeth women are one of the biggest stories in town right now, and as to what celebrities do, well I detect the hidden hand of a very clever public relations campaign behind all of this.'

'What, a PR agency is orchestrating this?'

'Not necessarily an agency, but this has all been very carefully plotted out, right from the start. I can smell it,' Yash said. *'Trust me, I can spot these things a mile off. It's all about keeping the celebs constantly in the public eye.'* He paused for a moment. *'Just think about it. Eilish and Christabelle have had a good few months in the spotlight since the publication of the book, and they've done amazingly well, but inevitably interest starts to fade. Whoever is behind this will have known this was going to happen, so they'll have had another event up their sleeves, an event that will get the subject back to the top of the public's agenda.'*

Maggie could feel a sinking feeling in her stomach. 'You don't mean the murder allegation, do you? Come on, you've got to be kidding. Tell me you're kidding.'

'No, I'm not kidding. I strongly believe this murder accusation was fabricated to get the Macbeths shooting back onto the front pages again. And it worked, didn't it? And this interview is the follow-up, when Eilish gets to tell the world how much she loved her husband and how every day is pure torture for her and why she can't understand why someone would make these vile accusations.'

'So did they approach you?' she asked. 'I suppose they must have.'

'Yes, they did, surprise-surprise. As I said, Eilish wants to have the chance to deny the allegations in the strongest possible terms, and to tell the truth about her marriage to the wonderful Alasdair. Her words, not mine.'

'So you're not a genius then?' she said affectionately. 'It just sort of fell into your lap without you doing anything.'

'That's a fair cop,' he said. *'But you know me, Maggie. Always happy to take the glory.'*

'And now they're doing a fashion shoot for the paper too. And whose idea was that, might I ask?'

He laughed. *'Take a guess. But our style editor was bouncing up and down with excitement at the prospect. The Macbeths are very photogenic women, mother and daughter alike.'*

Suddenly Maggie had a thought. 'But does this mean that the housekeeper at Christmas Lodge must be in on it too? Don't forget, it was Agnes Napier who approached us with the story. That's where it all started.'

'Yes, I spoke to her a couple of days ago,' he said, sounding mildly apologetic. 'I meant to mention it to you, but well, you know, I've been crazily busy. She told me a few things about the family, about half of which I believed. But I printed them all anyway,' he added, laughing. 'But afterwards, I wondered if that was why she didn't go to the police with her murder allegation. If in actual fact she had made the whole thing up.'

'Why would she do it though?' Maggie asked, then before he could respond, she answered her own question. 'For money, obviously.' She could feel her heart sinking as she recognised the irrefutable logic in what Yash was telling her. 'But if you suspected this all along, why are you still running with it?'

He laughed again. *'I'm afraid you don't understand newspapers Maggie. It doesn't have to be true for it to be a great story. And there'll be more revelations along the way, I guarantee it. Just you wait and see. I know it's a cliché, but this is a story that's going to run and run.'*

'And these cease-and-desist orders?' she asked. 'Are they part of it too?'

'It wouldn't surprise me if they were part of the same campaign. Just look at it. My editor has been running leaders for the last few days ranting on about unwarranted attacks on the freedom of the press. It's never been out of the headlines. And that means more publicity for the Macbeths, and that sells more books.'

She shook her head. 'No, that just seems a step too far to me. Because that would mean that Tom and Kirsty Bonnar were in on the affair too, and he's a very successful lawyer. He wouldn't risk his career for a scam like this.'

'Yeah, but don't forget his wife is a famous actress, and she'll be no stranger to the dark arts of public relations,' he said pointedly.

'No *way*,' she said, her tone disbelieving. 'That's a conspiracy theory too far, even for you.'

'Just saying. It's not impossible, is it?'

But now, potentially throwing a huge spoke into the wheel, was the murder of Drew Henderson. That brutal act, if it was connected, suggested there was much more to the Christmas Lodge affair than a cleverly orchestrated PR campaign. She was about to voice that thought when, just in time, she remembered that his name was not yet in the public domain, catching herself before it slipped out to the journalist.

'Anyway,' she continued, 'the main reason for my call was to cadge an invitation to that photoshoot. I want to see it and I want to talk to them too.'

'No problem,' he said. *'You can sit in on my interview and ask as many questions as you like.'*

***

The photoshoot had been arranged to take place on the iconic esplanade of Edinburgh Castle, famous as the venue for the spectacular annual military tattoo. That event took place in August, when even in the notably chilly East of Scotland, you could expect the occasional warm evening. This morning though it was absolutely freezing, with a further overnight dusting of snow adding to the picture postcard scene but lowering the temperature a couple of degrees or so. Two hired campervans and a catering van were parked up against a rampart, the former doubtlessly serving as dressing rooms for the models and a warm base for the Chronicle's team, who had flown up from London the previous evening. Maggie and Lori had taken a taxi from the station and were enjoying a takeaway coffee with Yash Patel as they awaited the next shoot to begin. Alongside them was an expensive-looking camera equipped with a giant lens, mounted on a tripod in preparation for its next action.

'The collection has been put together by a fashion brand called House of Kinross,' he said, grinning. 'That's what Emma Harding tells me, she's our style editor. They don't do men's clothes apparently, so I can't say I've heard of them myself, but Emma says they're very upmarket and very expensive.' As he spoke, a woman in a bright-red puffer jacket, black bandana and designer sunglasses emerged from one of the motorhomes and headed towards them.

'Speak of the devil,' Yash said. 'Maggie and Lori, this is Emma. Maggie and Lori are private investigators. They're working with me on the Macbeth story,' he explained to his colleague.

'Hoping to solve the big murder mystery I suppose?' she said with a wry look. 'Anyway, nice to meet you both but if you'll excuse me, I need to have an urgent word with Yash.' She placed a hand on the reporter's elbow and took him to one side before beginning what looked like an intense conversation.

'Her jacket's even brighter than yours,' Maggie said once the woman was out of earshot.

Lori laughed. 'I'm not sure about that but hers is dead nice. It must be a great job to be style editor on a big paper like the Chronicle.'

Maggie gave her assistant a rueful look. 'Yes, but I fear you have to look and sound like Miss Harding for that. And in my case, be ten years younger too.'

'Aye, she did sound dead posh. But look,' Lori said, pointing towards one of the motorhomes. 'Here's the two of them now. And these coats are absolutely gorgeous.'

'Yes, I love Kinross's dark navy woollen coats,' Maggie said. 'Classical and timeless. And about fifteen hundred pounds each if I'm not mistaken.'

'You know this brand, do you?' Lori asked.

Maggie grinned. 'Yes, but only from the magazines.'

Emma Harding had finished her chat with Patel and now was in discussions with the photographer who answered to the name of Henry. He gave Harding a thumbs up, then directed Eilish and Christabelle over to the nearest rampart, this evidently chosen to be the location of the shoot. After some words of explanation, he arranged the pose so that they were standing arm-in-arm, each pointing slightly inwards, then with a demonstrative sweep of his hands, got them to look in opposite directions to each other, heads tilted upwards to the sky.

'Right, that's perfect,' he shouted, running back towards his camera and examining a remote viewfinder which had been mounted on a separate stand. 'Now just hold it there please. One more...perfect.' He paused for a moment then said, 'Okay, so let's try it with the coats open so we can see the tartan skirt and sweater. And the boots too of course, we want to see the boots. Same pose, and just the hint of a smile this time please if you will. Excellent.'

The shoot continued for a further ten minutes or so, with occasional consultations between Henry and Emma, the latter clearly delighted with how it was all proceeding if her broad smile was any guide. Finally, it seemed it was over, Henry and Emma ostentatiously applauding the Macbeth women like football managers saluting their star players at the end of a match. 'Right then, let's get you out of the cold,' Harding said, pointing towards one of the motorhomes, 'and then we can take a look at some of Henry's excellent work.'

Yash wandered over to Maggie and Lori, grinning. 'They look like professionals, don't they? They're obviously loving this, the pair of them.'

'What was your conversation with Emma about?' Maggie said. 'If you don't mind me asking? Because it looked quite serious from where I was standing.'

He laughed. 'The Macbeths wanted to know how much they were going to get paid for all of this. And before you say anything, the answer is a big fat zero. But you can't help but admire their cheek. Anyway, let's grab something from the catering van whilst we wait for them. They should be ready in ten minutes.'

***

The interview venue was the larger of the two campervans, taking place around the cramped dining table at the front of the vehicle. Eilish and Christabelle Macbeth sat on one side, still dressed in their House of Kinross cashmere sweaters and woollen skirts, and Maggie had to admit, both looking effortlessly stunning. She wondered if they would get to keep the items for their personal wardrobes. Certainly, given that they seemed to be angling to be paid for agreeing to the interview and photoshoot, it wouldn't have surprised her if they asked to do so. She and Yash sat on the other side of the table, he with his tablet computer resting in front of him, she with her little notebook and chewed ballpoint. There was no room for Lori around the table, so she stood on the steps that led down to the closed entrance door. As had been previously agreed, it was the journalist who was to lead the interview.

'That was a brilliant photo-shoot, wasn't it?' he started with. 'Did you enjoy it? I guess Henry has shown you some of his pictures. I saw a couple of them, and I thought they looked amazing.'

'Very nice,' Eilish said. 'Yes, we're very pleased with them, aren't we Christabelle?'

'Yeah, like *cool*,' her daughter said, with just a hint of a smile. Maggie had learned that the two women had spent almost an hour with a make-up girl prior to the shoot, but despite this, or perhaps because of it, Christabelle had amplified her signature goth-cum-punk-rock look, picked out by thick black eyeliner and glossy lipstick of a matching shade. The effect was dramatic without detracting from her natural attractiveness. Lori had told her the girl now had over a hundred thousand social media followers and that her look was now being widely copied in schools the length and breadth of the land. For the Macbeths, this had become big business.

'Okay then,' Yash continued. 'First of all, thank you for agreeing to this interview, which I'll be leading. Maggie and Lori here have been helping me with researching the story, and they may have some supplementary questions to ask, but this is mainly an interview for the Chronicle, and I'll be writing the final piece. Does all of that make sense?'

Eilish nodded. 'And do we get to see the piece before it's published? And do we get to make changes if we don't like something you've written?'

Yash smiled. 'No, I'm afraid not, that's not how it works. But I promise that I'll report what you say fairly and accurately. So, in that respect, it's you two who dictate what appears in the paper.' Maggie laughed inwardly at that. Yes, that was true from a literal standpoint – Yash would report their words accurately - but it was what he made of those words that would carry most weight in the piece, and she knew from experience that his analysis could be brutal. As he was fond of telling her, he had been born with a highly-tuned bullshit detector, and if he detected even a hint of the stuff, he wouldn't hold back.

'So Eilish, I think it was you and your daughter who have asked for this interview,' he said. 'I think you want the chance to comment on the rumours that have begun to circulate about the tragic death of your husband. Is that right?' Maggie smiled again to herself, sitting as she was alongside the man personally responsible for spreading these rumours.

'I loved my husband,' she said emphatically. 'I would never have killed him. Poor Alasdair was in a bad place, and he was overcome by it all, despite the support of his loving family. That's why I wrote my book, so that no other family has to go through what we've gone through. Why would anyone think I could kill him? I don't understand that.'

'As far as I can make out, no specific accusations have been made,' Maggie said. 'There's speculation he might have been murdered, but no-one has been accused.'

She gave them a disbelieving look. 'Sure, but it's *always* the wife, isn't it? That's what everyone will be thinking.'

'But you don't think *anyone* killed him, that's what I understand,' Yash said.

'No, I don't,' she said, spitting out the words. 'The suggestion is ridiculous. Completely ridiculous. Who would want to kill Alasdair?' she repeated.

Maggie left the question unanswered and asked instead, 'Forgive me if this question is rather intrusive, but do you remember him getting up during the night? I mean, around the time it's believed he took his own life?'

The woman hesitated, evidently considering how she should answer. Then in a quiet voice she said, 'Alasdair and I weren't sharing a room. I was sleeping with the three young children. They had bunk beds, and I had a single.'

'And was that just for Christmas Eve?' Lori asked. 'Because the wee ones were so excited? You were looking after them?'

She bowed her head, then shook it slowly. 'Alasdair and I hadn't been sharing a room for a while. We thought it would be good to give each other space whilst we tried to work things through. As I said, he'd been going through a lot and his head wasn't in a good place. But it was all going to be fine. We would have got through it, I know we would have. Because we loved each other.'

'There were some issues with money though, in the family I mean,' Yash said. 'We heard from a source that your sister Kirsty and her husband had been asked to bail out Alasdair's family estate, but they wouldn't. And that they were in the habit of paying for the family Christmas getaway each year. I wondered how they felt about that and if it caused tensions in the family. And if it contributed to Alasdair's death in any way.'

'Kirsty and her money and her fame,' Eilish said, bitterness creeping into her tone. 'She's always thought that she is better than us, with her fancy career and her fancy husband.' The statement gave an interesting insight into the emotions that clearly bubbled below the surface of the family, and how it would go down with all of them when Yash Patel played it back in the pages of the Chronicle could only be imagined.

'And Christabelle, how were you getting on with your dad during this difficult time?' he asked.

'He's my stepdad,' she said, unsmiling, 'but like, okay I suppose.' It wasn't a ringing endorsement of the relationship, but then again, she was a teenager, so it was about par for the course.

'And do *you* think your stepdad could have been murdered Christabelle?' Maggie asked.

The girl shrugged. 'I suppose. But I don't think so. Everybody thought he had killed himself and why should I have thought any differently?'

'You must miss him awfully though,' Lori said. 'I don't know what I'd do if anything happened to my dad.'

Christabelle paused for a second before answering. 'Like yeah, of course I do.' She paused again. 'But it was like *really* selfish of him, wasn't it? And now we just have to get on with it, mum and me. We can't bring him back, can we?'

There was more than a hint of sadness in the girl's voice, and for the first time, Maggie felt herself feeling some sympathy towards her. But then again, the death of her stepfather, irrespective of whether it was murder or suicide, had transformed her life and that of her mother too, so maybe she shouldn't feel *too* sorry for her.

For a few seconds, no-one said anything, until finally Yash asked, 'I don't know if either of you have anything to add? Because if not, I think we can probably call this a wrap.'

Eilish gave him a look tinged with sadness, a look that, to Maggie, appeared theatrical – and like any diligent actress, it seemed she'd made the effort to learn her lines. 'I didn't kill Alasdair,' she said plaintively. 'No-one killed Alasdair. We might wish it was otherwise, but it isn't. That's why Christabelle and I are dedicating the rest of our lives to making sure no-one has to suffer the terrible pain that we've suffered.'

'But you've made a ton of money out of it, and now you're nearly as famous as your sister,' Lori said, raising an eyebrow. 'That's probably going to go a long way towards easing the pain, so it is.'

***

Afterwards, Maggie sat in silence for several minutes, trying to make sense of what she had just heard. Thinking about what Yash might write in his next article, he probably wouldn't write it as bluntly as Lori had just said it, but there was little doubt that the focus of the piece would be on the remarkable contrast between the Macbeth women's self-professed suffering and their astonishing rise to wealth and fame on the back of it. There was every likelihood that his story would also question how reliable the murder speculation was and whether it might be part of a carefully-conceived plan by their advisors to keep the pair in the public eyes. The story too would unveil the cracks in the Macbeth's marriage and the fact that husband and wife were no longer sharing a bed at the time of his death. Yash had plenty to write about, that was for sure, a fact that would doubtless please the hidden hand or hands who were masterminding Eilish and Christabelle's burgeoning media profile.

But who were these mysterious public relations Svengalis, Maggie asked herself, if indeed the existed at all? Yash had suggested that the actress sister Kirsty Bonnar might have had a hand in it, given she was familiar with the dark arts of public relations as he put it, but that was plainly ridiculous. As she thought about it some more, the answer – or at least *an* answer – popped into her head. Could it be Eilish Macbeth's publishers, or at least someone closely connected to them? A couple of days ago she'd tried to work out how much money Macbeth had already made from *My Daddy's Dead*, based on reported sales of something north of half a million copies. Internet searches suggested that authors who had managed to strike a good deal with their publishers might make as much as one pound per book in royalties, which meant Eilish might already have tucked a cool half-a-million quid or more in her back pocket. But the thing was, the publisher could expect to make half as much again in profit from a hit title, after deducting printing and promotion costs. As such, it was very much to their benefit to keep interest in a book sky-high. Yes, she would need to talk to these publishers as a matter of urgency and see what they had to say for themselves about the matter.

But the one thing that had struck her above all else was the fact that their brother-in-law's very recent brutal murder had not seemed to have affected them at all. Granted, the police would have told all members of his close family not to say anything about the terrible event to anyone, especially the media, but surely that would be easier said than done with the event so raw? But no, there was nothing in their manner to suggest it was troubling them in the slightest. Perhaps the pair were so truly self-obsessed that the enormity of it had not yet registered with them, or maybe they just didn't care.

And there was a second oddity, one that struck Maggie as equally puzzling. Because *not once* had either woman asked who it was who had brought the murder allegations to Bainbridge Associates. Surely that would be the first thing you would want to find out in a situation like this, doubly so when the spotlight of suspicion was pointed at you?

Unless, of course, you already knew.

Chapter 15

The snowploughs had been out early, evidenced by the banks of snow lining the road as Jimmy and Frida descended from the Lecht summit towards Tomintoul. But now the machines would have long returned to their Aviemore depot having done their work, meaning the pair could anticipate a clear run all the way to Nethy Bridge. It was Saturday, the sky a shimmering crystal blue, the morning sun projecting a glorious light onto the stunning winter landscape.

'It's brilliant you could come with me,' Jimmy said, glancing at his girlfriend in the passenger seat, then letting his eyes drop to her tummy. 'Actually, that both of you could come.'

She laughed. 'How do you know it's not twins or even triplets? You're always saying I'm getting enormous. Which, by the way, is not very flattering.'

'You look amazing,' he said. 'But it's your scan the week after Christmas and then we'll know for sure. That'll be exciting.'

'It will,' she agreed. 'Anyway, what was your conversation with Maggie last night all about? It seemed to go on for ages. I fell asleep before you were finished.'

'Developments,' he said. 'She and Lori had a chance to talk to Eilish and Christabelle Macbeth and some *very* interesting stuff emerged from that conversation.'

'Relevant to the case?'

He nodded. 'Very. Seems there's a suggestion that the murder allegation is all part of an elaborate public relations scam to keep the Macbeths in the papers and on the telly.'

'No way,' Frida said, astonished. 'Do you believe that?'

He shrugged. 'I don't really know to be honest. But if is true, then Agnes Napier must be in on it, which seems rather astonishing.'

'But you were doubting that it could be a murder anyway, weren't you? I mean, you couldn't see how logistically the thing could be done. So doesn't this mean that you're right? That it isn't murder, but just some scam as you put it?'

He gave his girlfriend a rueful smile. 'Aye, except for one thing. Something else that Maggie and Lori found out from the Macbeth women.' He paused for a moment before continuing. 'As you just said, it was the physical logistics of the thing that convinced me more than anything that murder was impossible. Because how could someone have dragged six-foot-two, sixteen stone Alasdair Macbeth out of his bed without waking his wife who was lying beside him?'

'They couldn't,' Frida said. 'But *she* could have done it I suppose? Although I've seen her on television, and she's very petite. *Beautiful*, but petite.'

He nodded. 'Luckily, I now know that particular scenario no longer applies. Because yesterday, Eilish revealed that she and Alasdair hadn't been sleeping together for a while. It turns out that during her stay at Christmas Lodge, she was sharing a room with the three youngest children, and he was sleeping on his own. Which, confusingly, now puts murder back on the agenda again.'

She smiled. 'Yes, I can see that.' She paused for a moment, thinking. 'But that still doesn't solve the logistical puzzle as to how it could have been done, does it? Not that I can see.'

'You're absolutely right,' he said. 'Which is exactly why I brought you along.'

***

They were nearly at Nethy Bridge before they got a half-decent mobile signal, but when Jimmy tried to get Agnes Napier on his hands-free mobile, the number rang out and gave no opportunity to leave a voicemail message.

'I was hoping she would tell me who was in which room,' he explained to Frida. 'I can kick myself for not asking that the last time I was here. But no matter, we can probably work it out.'

'Why do we need to know that?' Frida asked.

'I shouldn't have thought you could move a big bloke like Alasdair Macbeth around the place in the middle of the night without someone hearing something. I want you to be my ears, to tell me what can and can't be heard in the various rooms of the lodge.'

Ten minutes later they arrived at Christmas Lodge, where the cleaners were already at work, as evidenced by the small van parked at the front door bearing the logo *Highland Maids*. They found the front door was closed but not latched, pushing it open and stepping into the hallway.

'Hello?' Jimmy shouted. 'All right if we come in? It's Jimmy Stewart from Bainbridge Associates. The agent said it would be okay if we came and looked around.' A woman of about thirty marched into the hall, her hair tied up and wearing an apron over a navy sweatshirt and faded blue jeans. 'Hello, I'm Jana,' she said, frowning. 'Sure, you can look around. But I can't make coffee or tea. We have very tight schedule, and I don't want to clean kitchen twice.' The accent suggested eastern European, Polish or Czech perhaps, not that it was of any significance, other than it reminded him of a former girlfriend who he had been very much in love with, or so he thought. But looking back, he realised that had been nothing in comparison with the feelings he now had for Frida.

He smiled. 'No, that's no problem Jana, we're here to work too. And by the way, this is Frida, my detective colleague.'

His girlfriend shot him an amused look. 'Hi Jana,' she said. 'It's nice to meet you.'

'Okay Jana,' Jimmy continued, 'we won't take up too much of your time, but there's a couple of quick things we need you to help us with before we get started. Firstly, do you know if there's a shed or something where a stepladder might be kept? And secondly, could you point me in the direction of the linen cupboard and let me have the key if it's locked, which I understand it normally is.'

The woman nodded. 'Shed is on left side of house, but I don't think there is ladder in there, just some old skis and garden tools. Key is hanging there,' she added, pointing to a row of hooks next to the door. 'I take you upstairs to linen cupboard. It is locked but there is no key.'

'No key?' he said, feigning surprise, because he already knew it was secured by a combination lock.

'There is keypad,' she explained. 'Two-one-five-two is number at moment.'

'Ah right,' he said. 'And who knows the number, do you know?'

'Me and colleagues in Highland Maids, letting agent, housekeeper. It is changed every month, and we all get email. We don't tell residents unless they ask, because sometimes things go missing.'

'Okay, we'll follow you upstairs Jana, because that's where we want to start. Lead on.'

The cleaner skipped up the wide staircase and pointed out the linen cupboard, located next to the stairs and alongside another cupboard housing the oil-fired central heating boiler and hot water tank. A quick visual survey revealed that the bedrooms were arranged along each side of a wide hallway, a count confirming that the property had seven of them, as he had expected. The lodge had been architected as two distinct wings, joined at an angle of about one hundred and twenty degrees, and an earlier glance at the website had showcased the wing featuring a luxurious master suite comprising a large bedroom with an outdoor balcony and an elaborately equipped his-and-hers en-suite bathroom. But now it was time to see them for themselves.

'It's absolutely lovely, isn't it?' Frida said, as she pushed open the door of a bedroom. 'They're beautifully decorated, and the bedlinen looks *so* luxurious. I feel like jumping right onto that bed and snuggling down in the duvet.'

He laughed. 'Best not to in your current condition, and I think the cleaner would have a fit if you did. But aye, it is lovely. Anyway, let's see if we can work out what the sleeping arrangements were. We'll start at the fancy end, that's this way,' he said, pointing along the corridor. The largest bedroom was exactly as he'd remembered it from the website, airy and spacious and super-comfortable. The en-suite bathroom was equally impressive, a quick mental calculation suggesting that in floor area, it was about the same size as his old London flat.

'Nice,' Frida said, grinning. *'Very* nice. Can we stay for the week? *Please?'*

He laughed again. 'I wish. Anyway, I bet this would have been Tom and Kirsty Bonnar's room. Because if I was paying for this place, I'd make bloody sure that I at least got the best one.'

'Agreed,' she said. 'And it looks like there's another two bedrooms on this wing, next door and one opposite.'

He nodded. 'Yep, I noticed that on the website. Let's have a wee look.'

They walked over to the first door and pushed it open. 'Tiny but perfectly formed,' Jimmy said, sticking his head through the door. 'I think this would have been the old granny's one. Apparently she was complaining she got the worst room and had to shuffle along the landing to get to the bathroom in the middle of the night.'

'Which is just here,' Frida said, pushing open the door opposite. 'About three or four steps from her door.'

'Okay, that's good,' he said. 'Let's take a quick look at the one opposite.'

He stuck his head through the door and looked around. 'Tiny, this one. Just wide enough for a single bed and there's a wee cabinet with a couple of drawers and a lamp on top. This'll be the housekeeper's I expect. She only stays over occasionally I think, because she lives close by in the village.'

'Was she there that night?' Frida asked.

'Aye, I think she was, although I'll need to check with Maggie and Lori. Anyway, let's head for the other wing now and see what we can deduce.'

The first room they came to was another single, but much bigger than the previous one, large enough to have a dressing table and chair as well as the single bed, which in fact was more like a small double in size. On the wall was mounted a large flat-screen television, the stickers on its perimeter frame revealing it to be equipped with subscriptions to the major on-demand channels. This would have been Christabelle's, Jimmy decided. Next door was a much larger room, furnished with two sets of bunk beds and a single. This was no doubt designated the nursery, a room obviously designed to accommodate the nanny or au-pair who would have typically been part of the entourage of the rich families who could afford to rent the lodge. This is where Eilish Macbeth and the three under-tens had slept.

'So far so good,' he said to Frida. 'By my calculation, that leaves Isla and Drew, and then just Alasdair himself. That should be easy enough to figure out.'

The single room that the victim had occupied was next door to the nursery, and next to that was the final double room of Isla and Drew, this one also endowed with an en-suite, of more modest size than that of the master suite but still luxuriously equipped.

'So that was good work, and quite easy too,' he said with a satisfied smile, 'and we now know where everybody slept on the night when Alasdair Macbeth died.'

'Or at least where they started out,' Frida corrected.

'Aye, you're right about that. But now, we can maybe start thinking about some scenarios.' He paused for a moment. 'What is interesting is that Alasdair's room is right opposite the top of the stairs. That means if he was taken downstairs against his will, at least his abductor wouldn't have had to drag him along a hallway.'

She shook her head. 'Yes, that's true, but we have to dismiss that as a theory, surely? He was a big guy, even bigger than you. One, I doubt if anyone or even a *bunch* of people could have got him downstairs against his will, and two, even if they did, he'd have been kicking and screaming and woken up the whole house. Whilst on the other hand, if he had planned to kill himself, he could easily have got up and crept down the stairs without disturbing anyone.'

He nodded. 'Aye, I get that. But let's for a moment assume that he *was* murdered. How could that have been accomplished, that's what we need to work out.'

'The postmortem definitely concluded he was hanged?' she asked. 'Because that's another thing that so difficult to get your head around. How can you hang someone against their will, without them shouting the house down?'

'You can't,' he conceded. And then, out of the blue, it came to him. 'But you *could* strangle someone with a noose as they lay in bed, if say, you managed to gag them and restrain them at the same time.'

'It would take more than one person though,' Frida said. 'And I thought hanging broke the neck? That's different from strangling, isn't it?'

'Aye, but I'm sure the neck would still get broken even if the victim was already dead,' he said, although he felt far from certain about it. 'Once you'd strung them up, I mean. At least I think so.'

'Or maybe he was incapacitated in some way, whilst he lay in his bed?' his girlfriend suggested. 'Drugged perhaps? Or knocked unconscious? And then it was the hanging that killed him.'

Jimmy gave her a doubtful look. 'If he'd been bashed on the head then I guess that would have come out in the post-mortem, and I'm pretty sure it didn't. And can you still get chloroform? That's what used to happen in the old movies. A cotton wool pad infused with the stuff and held over the mouth and nose.'

'I don't know, but I doubt if it's easy to get a hold of nowadays,' she said. 'I suppose there might be a modern equivalent. But I really don't know. But he could have been smothered with a pillow,' she added

He nodded. 'Yes, I guess that's a possibility.' He hesitated, unsure where to go next. Finally he said, 'Okay, well let's park the *how* for the moment, and also the *who*. Let's assume Alasdair was either killed or incapacitated by person or persons unknown, then taken downstairs to the lounge to where the hanging was staged.'

'Is the lounge under one of the bedrooms?' she asked.

He pondered the question for a moment. 'Actually, it isn't, now that I think about it. We'll go down there in a second, but no, it's a huge full-height room with a vaulted ceiling.' He paused again, thinking. 'Yeah, it's at the end of the wing where the master suite is. As I said, full height, right up to the roof. Next to it on the ground floor level is the dining room, and at the higher level it must share a wall with Tom and Kirsty's fancy en-suite bathroom.'

'So quite a distance from the bedrooms, even Tom and Kirsty's,' Frida mused.

He nodded. 'Aye. I think it's reasonably unlikely that anyone would have heard anything, whilst they were faking the suicide I mean. But to be fair, I'm not exactly sure about that. That's what we need to test out.'

'And you think it's definitely a *they*?'

'Got to be. It would take two people to move a guy that size, let alone string him up on a beam. Anyway, let's wander down and take a look.'

He wasn't sure if he would learn anything from a second visit to the room, but this time he was planning to carry out the first of two experiments. He said, 'Hang on a minute, I'm going to fetch a chair from the dining room.' A few seconds later he returned with the object, then said to Frida, 'It's pretty echoey and noisy in here with this wooden floor, isn't it?' He lifted the chair slightly then laid it down firmly to demonstrate, dragging it a few inches as he did so, generating first a thump and then a grating screech. 'See, quite hard to be quiet in here.'

'Would you mind going upstairs and trying every room?' he asked Frida. 'Whilst I bang about down here with this chair. See if you can hear anything in any of them. Or we can swap jobs, if you're getting tired.'

She gave him a mock scolding look. 'I've never felt fitter in all my life. I'll be back in a minute.'

For the next ninety seconds or so, he lifted and laid the chair, alternatively treating it roughly to emulate the sound it would have made if it had been kicked over by a dying man, then moving it as gently as he could, as if seeking to avoid detection.

'Interesting,' she said on her return. 'The only room I could hear you bashing about was in the master en-suite It wasn't *very* loud, but you could still hear it. Even when I guessed you were trying to be quiet.'

He nodded. 'That makes sense given it shares a wall with this room. And that was the only room in which you could hear anything?'

'The only *room*, yes. But I could hear you a bit in the hallway. I guess the sound travels up the stairs. Anyone who'd gone to the bathroom during the night would certainly have heard something.'

'Anybody without an en-suite then, not counting Tom and Kirsty,' he said, thinking out loud. 'Although I'm not sure exactly how that helps us, to be honest.' He paused for a moment. 'Anyway, next on our agenda is a wee bit of art and crafts. We're going to discover how long it takes to turn a sheet into a rope. Four or five sheets to be exact, and it's probably best if we don't mention this to Jana. You know, the old forgiveness rather than permission thing.'

Unfortunately, the tactic fell at the first hurdle when they found the cleaner polishing the wooden floor in front of the linen cupboard. Apologetically, they explained what they were planning. She didn't sound exactly thrilled but nor did she expressly forbid it, especially when Jimmy, with some reluctance, promised to iron the sheets once they were done with them.

'Let's grab four to start with,' he said to Frida. 'We just need to make the rope long enough so we can see how easy it is to chuck it over the beam, then see if we can thread it through a loop to pull it tight. There doesn't seem to be a stepladder in the place, so that's how it must have got up there.'

'It would be good if somehow there was a weight tied into one end,' Frida said. 'That would make it much easier to throw it over.' She paused for a second, wrinkling her nose. 'Wait a minute, did you see these two big planters alongside the front door, the ones with the conifers with the Christmas lights on? Because I'm sure they had a bed of big pebbles covering the soil. I noticed them because I thought something like that would look great at the front door of my tearoom.' She leaned over and kissed him on the cheek. 'Don't go away, I'll go and grab one.'

Sitting on the floor, it took three-quarters of an hour of laughter and frustration before they managed to fashion a serviceable rope from the twisted bedsheets. 'What do you reckon?' Jimmy asked her. 'We've got about four or four and a half metres, something like that? That should be plenty long enough for our experiment.'

And so it proved. His first three throws failed to clear the beam, and failed by a considerable margin, much to Frida's amusement. She nailed it with her first attempt, prompting her to jog a lap of honour around the room in mock celebration, arms thrust above her head. She then ran to him and wrapped him in her arms, squeezing him tight before kissing him full on the lips. 'Did you know you had such a *clever* girlfriend?' she laughed, stroking his hair. 'Clever, and *very* much in love with my wonderful Jimmy.'

'And I love you crazily too, and yes, you're bloody clever, no question,' he grinned. 'But anyway, now we know how the rope could have been put in place. Pretty easy really, as long as you're not a rubbish thrower like me. And to be fair, I would definitely have got it the next time if you hadn't taken it off me.'

She laughed. 'You really think so? I think you would have been here all day. But seriously, that's how they got the rope up, but how would they have got *him* up there? That doesn't look easy at all.'

He frowned. 'It would have taken two people minimum. You would have to set up a couple of these dining room chairs, one either side of him, with one person standing on each of them. You'd then have to hoist him up by the armpits, then stick his head through the noose then drop him and bang, his neck's broken. Then you push over one of the chairs to make it look as if that was what he'd been standing on when he killed himself, move the other one back into the dining room, and the job's done. Then you just have to quietly creep up the stairs and go back to your bed, waiting for him to be discovered in the morning. Not that you'd get much sleep I'd imagine, after you'd murdered someone.'

'That's how it was done then?' she asked. 'You're sure of that?'

He shook his head. 'I'm far from sure about it. It's a theory, that's all, and the only half-plausible one I can come up with at the moment. And remember, we still have no idea what happened up in his bedroom, before all of this. My money is on him having been strangled by the noose that was then used to hang him, but that's just a supposition.'

She hesitated for a moment then said, 'But *surely* one of the men would have to have been involved? Because you said that the three sisters are all slightly-built women. It seems a stretch to think that one or more of them could have had the strength to have done it on their own.'

He nodded. 'I suppose if the three of them were involved in some crazy pact they might just about have had the strength to manage it between them, but that really does stretch credibility to breaking point.'

And as he said it, he realised how far away they remained from solving this thorniest of murder mysteries. Means, motive and opportunity were the three wise men of crime-solving, to which he always added *evidence of prior intent*. On the credit side of the ledger, they had developed a half-arsed explanation of the method, and as to opportunity, well at a stretch, maybe each of the adults in the household could have had the chance to throttle him, drag him downstairs and stage the hanging. As for means, any one of them might have gained access to the linen cupboard to fashion the rope that was an essential part of the crime, but as Frida had pointed out, it would have taken great strength to both move him and string him up. Did that mean that one of the male members of the household had been involved? *Possibly, but not definitely*.

But the thing that was missing from all of this was perhaps the most important of the three pillars of crime-solving, and that was the motive. Aside from perhaps his wife Eilish, who could possibly have had the desire to kill this gentle giant? Sure, his wife was disappointed that he wasn't to inherit a great fortune, but was that a reason to kill him? He thought not. And as far as the rest of the family was concerned, there didn't seem to be any animosity towards the victim, in fact, on the contrary, he seemed to have been well-liked by everyone, other than by the old mother, who was bitter that he hadn't attained the financial success of his brother-in-law Tom Harper. But then again, she was apparently bitter about everything, so that didn't mean anything.

Luckily though, this was something that Maggie was brilliant at. She could look at a situation and by examining the dynamics between the players, she could tease out the underlying jealousies, betrayals or passions that might drive someone to commit the ultimate crime of taking someone's life. As soon as they left Christmas Lodge, he would get her on the phone and tell her everything he had found out, and he was sure that, although it might take some time, her agile brain would soon work out the motive, and *that* would lead to the solution of this crime.

'Right then darling Frida,' he said, nodding sagely, 'I think we've done all we can here, unless you can think of something we've missed? We've got ourselves a plausible theory, which is progress to say the least. Yep, we're done here, I think. Let's get going before it starts snowing again. We'll just nip downstairs again and say cheerio to the cleaner and then we'll get off.'

They found the woman in the kitchen, a cleaning spray in one hand and a wire scrubbing pad in the other, looking at the grease-laden cooker hob with an air of repugnance. 'Guests would never do this in own homes,' she said acerbically. 'It is disgusting.'

Jimmy gave her what he hoped was a sympathetic smile. 'Aye you're right Jana, it is disgusting. Anyway, that's us away now. It's been nice to meet you and thanks very much for your help.'

'I remember something,' the cleaner said unexpectedly. 'About that day when families arrived. Something I had forgotten.'

'What was that,' he asked, his instincts telling him that this was going to be important.

'Poor man wanted combination to linen cupboard,' she said. 'He wanted extra pillow for teenage daughter.'

Bloody hell, he was about to say but managed to restrain himself. Instead he said, 'And by poor man, I guess you mean Alasdair Macbeth? The man who died?'

Jana nodded. 'Yes.'

'You were still here when the Macbeth's arrived then?' Frida said, 'I thought guests weren't allowed in until three o'clock?'

'They arrive at two, but it was cold,' Jana said. 'We don't leave guests to freeze in car park.'

Frida smiled. 'No, of course you don't.'

'And you're quite sure?' Jimmy said. 'You gave Mr Macbeth the combination?'

'No, I did not *give* combination, I said he *asked* for combination. It is not my job to give extra pillows or sheets. That is job of housekeeper. Instead, I left note for Agnes.'

'Agnes Napier knew that he had asked for the combination then?' he said.

The woman shrugged. 'Only if she read note. But I left it here,' she said, nodding towards the large island unit. 'And I write in big letters.'

'Okay,' he said, his mind racing. 'Look, this has thrown a bloody big spanner in the works, and we need to get our brains working on what it means as soon as we can. So we'll be off now.'

She looked at him, uncomprehending, then said, 'You forget. You forget something.'

He gave her a puzzled look. 'Sorry, don't think I'm with you Jana.'

The woman smiled before replying. 'You said you would iron sheets. Come, I show you where ironing board is located.'

Chapter 16

Frank realised it had been a while since he'd been involved in a proper murder investigation, almost five years in fact, when he'd been on the case that became known as the Regents Canal murders. That killer had preyed on young women taking an early morning jog along the towpath, feigning an ankle injury to make them stop, then dragging them into the undergrowth before raping and murdering them. He'd claimed four victims before he was eventually caught, the Met using a brave young PC as bait. Frank had only been a DI back then and so he wasn't in charge, that dubious honour going to the idiot DCI Colin Barker. The punch that he had administered to Barker during the course of that investigation hadn't been his finest hour he had to admit, leading to him being exiled to Atlee House and Department 12B, but it had been highly satisfying nonetheless. And now here he was, five years on, improbably in charge of his own murder case after a long road featuring many twists and turns along the way. Detective Superintendent Charlie Maxwell had promised to rustle him up a half-dozen or so officers for his team, but in the event - and not unexpectedly- he had ended up being allocated just three, a conscientious but unimaginative Detective Sergeant called Andy McColl and two DCs. Still, with DC Lexy McDonald now available pretty much full time, other than the few hours a week she would be spending on the Aquanaut Island case, and his ability to call on Ronnie French and Eleanor Campbell as required, he reckoned he had just about enough to get by.

They were in the investigation room and DS McColl was standing in front of the white board, marker pen in hand, summarising where they had got to in the five or six days the investigation had been up and running.

'Okay, so we've been busy as you know, ticking off the obvious lines of enquiry. Probably the first thing to say is we've had no joy yet in tracking down the murder weapon. We can't say for certain, but the forensic guys think it was probably an ordinary kitchen knife. There are millions of them around, obviously.'

Frank shrugged. 'We'll probably never find it, so don't worry about it too much.'

'No, I guess not sir,' McColl agreed. 'As far as identifying and eliminating suspects is concerned, we of course started with the immediate family. DC Lawrence went with the family liaison officer to speak to the victim's partner, that's Isla Bonnar. Naturally, we checked where she was on the night her partner was murdered, and she told us she was at home looking after the kids. She'd had a visit earlier that evening from a Maggie Bainbridge and her associate - who I subsequently found out is your wife sir – and then she'd gone to bed.'

'Aye, that's right Andy,' Frank confirmed. 'Maggie's firm's working for the Chronicle newspaper, investigating an earlier possible suspicious death connected to the same family.'

'Strictly speaking, Isla doesn't have an alibi for the *exact* time of the murder,' the DS continued, 'but I think it's reasonable to assume she wouldn't have left her young children alone in the home. She's not ruled out, but I think she's probably low down the list.'

'We've got a list already then Andy?' Frank said, amused. 'That's good.'

McColl shook his head. 'Not as yet sir. Some possibilities maybe, but nothing concrete.' He paused for a moment, glancing at his notebook. 'Oh yeah, the victim's sister-in-law and brother-in-law. They live in London...'

'That's the fancy lawyer and the actress,' Frank interjected.

'That's right sir. DC French spoke to them and confirmed they were both in London at the time of the murder. They'd gone out to dinner apparently, and DC French has confirmed their alibis with the restaurant. That definitely rules them out.'

Frank nodded. 'Aye, seems to. And then we've got the author sister Eilish, and her daughter Christie-something.'

'Christabelle,' McColl supplied. 'Eilish Macbeth had her mother Nan Bonnar staying with her for the weekend, and they were both at home with her youngest child on the evening in question. Christabelle was at a sleepover with a school friend. I checked that one out myself and the mother of the friend confirmed that Christabelle had gone to their house directly after school, and that they had tea together as a family before the girls disappeared upstairs to her daughter's bedroom for the rest of the night.'

'Okay, so that sounds like the immediate family is pretty much ruled out,' Frank said. 'Then I asked you to chase up on the mate Henderson was with at the pub, and to check out any other pals or work colleagues. And of course there's the girl he got off with that night. How's that all going?'

'His mate's called Shug Campbell,' Lexy said. 'I managed to speak to him yesterday.'

'What, another Shug and another Campbell?' Frank laughed. 'That sounds suspicious. What did he have to say for himself?'

'Well sir, given what he and his mate Drew had been up to that night, he was anxious that I didn't come to his house, so he popped into the station. He's married, you see.'

'Very considerate of you Lexy. And what was his story?'

'He said these two girls got chatting to them and that they seemed really up for it. His words, not mine sir,' she added. 'He left before his mate Drew, at about a quarter past eleven, and told the girl he knew somewhere quiet where they wouldn't be disturbed.'

'A true romantic, and in the middle of bloody December too,' Frank said. 'God, he must have been desperate right enough.'

'Perhaps sir. But in the end, nothing happened. He said the girl suddenly changed her mind and said she wanted to go home. According to him, he just said fair enough then waited until her Uber turned up. And then he called another taxi and went home.'

Frank hesitated for a moment. 'I think you said that the two girls got chatting to them. So that was how it was, not the other way round?'

'Definitely that way round sir,' Lexy said. 'I picked him up on that when he said it, and yes, the girls came on to them.'

'Interesting. Now then Andy, how are we getting on with identifying the pair of them?'

'Ongoing sir,' McColl said. 'DC Black and I went to the pub and looked at their CCTV. It caught them going in, it caught them talking to the two men during the evening, and it caught them when they left. We also talked to a couple of the bar staff who were on that night to see if anybody knew them, but we drew a blank. One guy said he was pretty sure they'd never been there before.'

'How could he be so sure?' Frank asked.

'He described them as very fanciable, although he put it a bit more crudely. He said he would have definitely noticed them if they'd been in before.'

'And what about their age? Because one of Maggie's team was there that night and she said they looked very young. That they might even have been underage.'

'You can have a look at the footage yourself sir,' McColl said, 'but yeah, I wouldn't be surprised if they were only sixteen or seventeen. We got pretty good face shots for both of them, and so we were able to run a visual search against the criminal records system, but that drew a blank. Then we ran an image search on Google, but that drew a blank too.'

'That probably means they're *under* sixteen,' Lexy said. 'The social media giants have a voluntary policy to protect the privacy of minors. They switch off facial search when they think the image might be that of an under-age person.'

'Is there anything we can do about that?' Frank asked her. 'Isn't there something in the settings menu you can click on to turn it back on?'

Lexy laughed. 'No, I don't think so sir. But maybe this is a job for Eleanor. I'm sure she could tweak it with just a couple of lines of code.'

He sighed. 'Aye, that's what she always says, but do I really want to have that conversation?' He paused. 'Let's hold that for a moment. We'll go old-school to start with, with some posters up on the wall of the pub.'

'Already done that sir,' McColl said. 'Hopefully someone will know them.'

'Have we considered an appeal in the media sir?' Lexy asked.

Frank nodded. 'Aye, I've thought about that. Maybe we'll get the lassies' mugshots on the local six o'clock news, see if anybody recognises them.'

'Someone's bound to sir, if we do that,' she said, then smiled. 'Would you like *me* to have a word with Eleanor? Because she might already have a search app that ignores the age restriction. I would imagine it's something the security services would have developed. And I think that would be the quickest way to identify them.'

He laughed. 'Very nice of you to offer to take one for the team Lexy, but I couldn't let you do that. I'll give her a wee call when we're done, I'm sure she'll be delighted to hear from me.' He paused for a moment then said, 'Finally then Andy, what about the victim's working life? Anything of interest emerged from that direction?'

He shrugged. 'Nothing specific sir. At the time of his murder, he was working as joinery sub-contractor on a new-build housing project down in Port Glasgow, for McCallum Homes. DC Black had a word with the site manager and got a bit of a lukewarm response as far as Mr. Henderson was concerned. Apparently, he was a bit unreliable, and the quality of his work was no better than okay. He seemed to get on fine with his workmates. No reports of arguments or anything like that.'

'Doesn't sound as if that line of enquiry is going anywhere,' Frank said. 'So exactly as we said before, finding that wee temptress must be our top priority. I'll talk to the press office about getting it on the news, and I'll seek out our tame forensic genius too.' He paused for a second, thinking, then said, 'I believe that's about it, and thanks for your good work, all of you. Off you go detecting and we'll have another catch-up tomorrow.' He nodded at Lexy. 'And DC McDonald, if we can just have five minutes or so on that other matter of ours?'

***

They headed down to the canteen to grab a quick coffee, the beverage inevitably accompanied by an iced gingerbread square. After ordering at the counter, they commandeered a corner table in preparation for their call with Ronnie French.

'What do you make of our new DS?' he asked, taking a sip from his drink. 'Nice guy, but I don't think he's got a career as a stand-up comic if this job doesn't work out.'

'I like him,' Lexy said. 'And I like the fact that he's serious. There're too many idiots around here who think they're comedians.

Present company excepted sir,' she added hastily. 'You're funny, but you're not horrible and sexist like some of them.'

He felt himself reddening up from his young colleague's unexpected compliment. 'Well, that's nice of you to say so Lexy. And I agree, there's still too much of that stuff that goes on around here. Dinosaurs, the lot of them.' Then he smiled. 'But you'll be the boss of them all one day, you mark my words. Chief Constable Alexa McDonald. It's got a nice ring to it. And talking of rings, let's see if we can get Ronnie on the line.'

'Morning guv,' French answered, sounding bright as usual. *'How's tricks?'*

'All good here Frenchie. I've got Lexy with me and we're just going to have a quick update on the Aquanaut case. Are you still in deepest Suffolk by the way?'

'Nah guv, back in the Smoke now. I'm sitting at my desk in Atlee.'

Frank smiled. 'I take it that must mean you have good news for us. Am I right, or am I right?'

'I reckon so guv,' the detective said. *'To cut a long story short, I'm pretty sure it's a woman in the finance section who did the leaking. Name of Alison Stewart. No relation, I hope.'*

'No, I bloody hope not too,' Frank grinned. 'Anyway, tell us more.'

'Well, you might remember it was the Inspector Green geezer who put in the request for permission to escort that shipment, and to do that he had to get a chit filled in by the finance section in Ipswich, to make sure it got allocated to the right budget and cost centre and all that bollocks. And it was this Alison Stewart who got the job of

doing it. They all work in this big open plan office with the boss lady in the biggest desk in the corner. So I went to see her and announced at the top of my voice the reason I was there. Ten minutes later this Stewart bird announces she's got a headache and needs to go home right away, and I thinks 'hello hello, what's going on here?' To cut a long story short, I swiftly organised for a couple of the local lads to rush round to her place with a warrant and confiscate her phone and laptop, and did a bit of a search too, where they uncovered another pay-as-you-go mobile. We've asked the phone company for the records and I'm expecting it in my inbox within the hour.'

'Nice work Frenchie,' Frank said. 'Feels like we're closing in on a result, a kind of pincer movement from all directions. Talking of which Lexy, what's happening in the wild south-east of our fair city?'

She smiled. 'All planned out sir. Yash Patel is putting the video on the Chronicle's website this evening and his story will run in the paper tomorrow. Also looks as if it will get featured on the TV news tonight.'

'And the message is going to be *don't buy from these scam artists because you'll get ripped off?*'

'Exactly that sir. I'm hoping that'll spur the bad guys into action and they'll turn up in Castlemilk tomorrow looking for our Shug Wilson.'

'And have you warned wee Shug that these guys will be after him?'

She gave a guilty smile. 'Eh, not exactly sir. He's well-known to the local cops as a hooligan and small-time drug dealer. And they say he doesn't normally surface until midday, when he walks to the wee row of shops in the scheme to buy cigarettes. Then he hangs about with his mates for a while, trying to look menacing. So I decided that rather than warn him, we'd just head down there tomorrow and keep him under close observation.'

'The bad guys might come mob-handed,' Frank said. 'You need to make sure there's back-up on hand. And remember, they might be armed. I don't want any heroics, because this is only about a bloody toy at the end of the day.'

'Understand sir. I've talked to the sergeant here and he says he'll notify the response team management that they might have to scramble some armed officers if the worst comes to the worst. And there's two detectives coming up from Northamptonshire too, so we'll be fine. But I'll be careful, I promise.'

He nodded. 'Make sure you are. But this is all good news, isn't it? There's every chance that soon we'll be revered across the nation as the cops who saved Christmas. But before I get carried away with myself,' he added gloomily, 'I'd better go and phone Eleanor.'

Chapter 17

Jimmy's second visit to Christmas Lodge had, in Maggie's opinion, been quite the success, although whether it left her more confused or less confused about the case was a moot point. Because the question remained: had there really been a murder, or, as Yash Patel maintained, was the allegation simply part of a cleverly-orchestrated PR campaign designed to keep Eilish Macbeth's book at the top of the best-sellers list? Jimmy's careful investigations, with the help of his lovely girlfriend Frida, seemed at first to confirm that murder was at least possible, only to have that theory thrown into doubt with the revelation that the cleaner had told them that Alasdair Macbeth had asked for the combination which unlocked the linen cupboard. At least it was now established beyond doubt that if it *was* murder, then it couldn't have been carried out single-handedly. Adding to that, Frida was of the belief that because of the brute strength required to lift the limp body of sixteen-stone Alasdair Macbeth off the ground, then a man would have had to have been involved. Did that mean then that either Drew Henderson, now dead, or the lawyer Tom Harper had conspired with another member of the household to carry out the crime? Or, she suddenly reflected, could they *both* have been involved, either just the two of them or with another party? That other party could only have been one of the three sisters, or at a push, Eilish's teenage daughter Christabelle. As she had reflected earlier, this was a classic country house murder mystery, with a strictly limited number of possible perpetrators, which in theory should make it easier to work out who did it. If you included Agnes Napier – and she would be giving that woman more attention in a little while – then there were seven adults present in the house that evening, not including the victim. The problem was though, if you were speculating which pair might have done it, then the mathematics presented you with twenty or more possible combinations, which wasn't helpful at all. But what was making this case one of the most baffling they had ever tackled was the annoying fact that no-one seemed to have had a motive to murder Alasdair Macbeth, a frustration that she knew Jimmy shared. If it had been murder, then two of the seven adults present at the beautiful lodge must have done it. But the question remained. *Why?* Until they worked that out, she knew the solution to the crime would continue to elude them. Still, she was experienced enough to know that the motive would eventually present itself, as it had always done in the past. It was just that they didn't have enough facts at this stage in the investigation to be able to figure it out. Luckily, there was plenty for them to work on to change that.

Lori was sitting opposite her in the Bikini Barista cafe, aware that her boss was in deep thought and unwilling to interrupt that process. But eventually she could contain her curiosity no longer. 'How's it going Maggie?' she asked tentatively. 'Have you managed to work it all out yet? Because your brain seemed to be going ten to the dozen. I could see wee red lights flashing and steam coming out of your ears.'

She laughed. 'Not quite Lori, but at least I've worked out what we need to do next. Two things in fact. We need to chase up Eilish's publishers to see if they are indeed running some cunning publicity stunt, and we need to talk to Agnes Napier to find out why she's been telling lies, or perhaps to be more accurate, lying by omission.'

'She's been telling fibs then?' Lori asked. 'Mind you, I've met her twice and both times I thought there was something that didn't quite add up about her.'

'Well, she didn't tell us that Alasdair had asked for the combination to the linen cupboard, did she?' Maggie said. 'And you would have thought that was a pretty vital piece of information to have passed on to us.'

'You're right,' Lori said, looking thoughtful. 'But that wouldn't support her new story, would it? That Alasdair killed himself. Because if he had access to the cupboard, it was very likely that it was him who took the sheets and turned them into the hanging rope.' She hesitated for a moment. 'And bloody hell, there's something else too. Something that's just occurred to me in fact.'

'What's that?'

'She had a brand-new car, a nice silver four-wheel drive. It was parked outside the lodge when me and Jimmy went there. I don't know much about cars, but I know new ones cost a lot of money.'

Maggie nodded. 'True, but not many people properly buy them these days. They sort of rent or lease them for a monthly payment, then give them back after three years or something like that.'

Lori nodded. 'Even still, I bet the monthly payments are really high, and I bet Agnes doesn't earn that much. I just found it a bit odd.'

'Interesting,' her boss said, her mind whirring furiously. 'So are we now thinking that the car is part of a pay-off for her keeping her mouth shut about the identity of the murderer? Are we saying that

Agnes Napier is a *blackmailer*? That seems unbelievable, quite frankly.'

'I don't think it's *so* unbelievable,' Lori said. 'What if the killer or killers were paying her off, but she got greedy and decided to ask for more? And what if they refused, so she decided to come to us with her allegations of murder, to get her revenge? You've got to admit, that's more than half-plausible. More plausible than her being part of some ridiculous PR stunt if you ask me.'

Maggie was silent again, her mind focussing on a detail that now seemed to be growing in significance. 'Remember, it was Agnes that told you and Jimmy that when she saw Alasdair hanging, his feet were dangling three feet or more above the floor. It was that fact more than anything that persuaded us that murder couldn't be ruled out. In fact, the opposite. It made suicide look problematic.'

'But we now know she's less than truthful,' Lori said, giving Maggie a knowing look. 'So that might have been a lie too. She might have just made that up to support her story.'

'That's the problem, we don't know whether it's a lie or not,' Maggie said ruefully. 'But thankfully, it doesn't really alter what I think we should do.'

'Which is?'

'We pursue both theories in parallel until one of them falls away. One, we talk to Eilish Macbeth's publishers to see if they really are pulling the strings, as Yash suspects, and two, we chase up Agnes Napier and confront her with her untruthfulness, to see how she reacts.'

Lori grinned. 'You're dead brilliant Maggie, you really are. But there's a couple of other things I've just thought of which might help us too. First, we could ask Kirsty Bonnar if she remembers how far off the ground his feet were dangling. Because she was the person that discovered him hanging there, and I don't think it's a sight you would forget in a hurry. Second, we could do with finding out whose idea it was to cut him down. I mean, if I'd discovered a dead body hanging like that, I'd have probably called the emergency services right away and wouldn't have touched him, but that's not what happened, is it? Someone took the decision to cut him down, and if you were the murderer, and you noticed that by mistake you'd left him hanging too high for it to be suicide, you wouldn't want to leave him there for the police and paramedics to see, would you?'

Not for the first time, Maggie marvelled at the perception of her young colleague. Shooting her an admiring look, she said, 'And you, young Lori, are dead brilliant too.'

***

It wasn't hard for Maggie to find out the name of Eilish Macbeth's publishers, it being printed prominently on the back cover of her book, but it was a lot more difficult to get anyone in the firm to talk to her. It had finally taken a strongly worded email from Yash Patel to the company's Managing Director, threatening to name the firm in the Chronicle as the party behind the Alasdair Macbeth murder allegation, before The Clarkstone Press would take her call. But eventually a name, an email address and a mobile number were forthcoming, that of one Kate Strong, who laboured under the title of *Executive Vice-President, Non-Fiction*. After an exchange of email correspondence, Miss Strong was finally persuaded to set a date and time for a telephone conversation.

The publisher picked up on the first ring with a brisk *'Kate Strong.'*

'Hi Miss Strong' Maggie said brightly. 'It's Maggie Bainbridge from Bainbridge Associates. I hope you're expecting my call?'

'Sure, you want to talk about My Daddy's Dead, is that right? And it's Kate, please.'

'Thank you Kate,' Maggie answered, 'and yes, my call is about the book and about Eilish Macbeth too if you don't mind. And I'll try not to take up much of your time because I know you must be terribly busy.'

'Aren't I just?' the woman said, her tone audibly softening. *'There're just not enough hours in the day in this crazy business. Anyway, how can I help you?'*

'I'll get straight to the point if you don't mind,' Maggie said. 'You'll have no doubt heard of the murder allegation related to Eilish's husband Alasdair. It's been suggested to me that the allegation was invented as part of a super-clever marketing campaign that you guys are running, and I wondered what you made of that suggestion?'

She heard the woman laugh. *'What do I make of it? It's a ridiculous conspiracy theory, that's what I make of it. Let me make it clear that neither I nor the Clarkstone Press would ever pull a stunt like that. It's simply beyond preposterous.'*

'But you can't deny it's been effective in keeping the book in the public eye, and very useful for sales too? It was still top of the non-fiction chart the last time I looked.'

Strong laughed again. *'Yes, it is, and I don't deny that all the publicity the book has been attracting has been incredibly useful. But if you'll forgive me, it's clear you don't understand the first thing about the publishing business.'*

'You're right about that without a doubt,' Maggie agreed, taking no offence. 'But is there anything specific that leads you to say that?'

'You obviously think publishers like us have a giant promotion budget we use to power a book into the charts, but it's not like that at all. Quite the opposite in fact. True, we'll commit a modest launch budget in the few weeks leading up to a book's publication, and we might keep the spend going for four or five weeks once it hits the shelves, but after that, a book and its author must stand on its own two feet.' She paused. *'The thing is, publishing is essentially a gambling business. You might not know that Maggie, but it is. Every year we take a punt on a few hundred books in the knowledge that only a handful will make significant sales. The few that are successful pay for the rest, but the problem is we never know in advance which is which.'*

'No, I didn't appreciate that,' Maggie said truthfully.

'Not many people do. The fact is, a book either takes off through word of mouth, or it dies a slow death. Unless of course the author is prepared to put their own resources behind it, either time or money or both.'

Maggie hesitated for a moment. 'And is that what's happening with this book? Is Eilish Macbeth putting lots of resources behind it?'

'The book has done amazingly well through word of mouth of course, and that's because one, it's bloody good and two, it has resonated with the public. But Eilish and her daughter have supported it with their media appearances too. It's been a very effective campaign on their part.'

Maggie hesitated for a moment. 'And tell me Kate, has she planned all this herself do you think, or has she had professional help? From a PR agency for example?'

'I can't say. But obviously her older sister is an actress used to being in the public eye, and she would have ready access to these kinds of people I would expect. Or perhaps her other sister has been helping her.'

The last remark was puzzling. 'I'm sorry Kate,' Maggie said, 'but I'm not sure I understand that. Are you saying you think Isla could have been involved? But how could that be?'

'Isla is with a literary agency, and it tends to be these firms who provide writers with career guidance. Which might extend to advice on what genre to write in and how to promote both a title and its author.'

'She's got an *agent*?' Maggie said, surprised. 'Forgive me for saying this, but I thought Isla Bonnar's literary career had been a bit of a damp squib.'

'Celebrity sells books,' Strong said, sounding faintly apologetic. *'Even if it is only celebrity by association.'*

'You're referring to her sister Kirsty I assume?'

'Exactly. A link like that gives us publishers something to hang our marketing on. "Read the explosive debut novel of Isla Bonnar, younger sister of award-winning actress Kirsty". That kind of thing.'

'But she hasn't actually had any books published as far as I'm aware. So why is the agency sticking with her? And who is this agency, by the way?'

'The firm is called The Barbour Agency, founded and run by a lady called Claudette Barbour,' Strong explained. *'And as to why they're sticking with Isla, then you would need to ask Claudette that question yourself. But if you want my opinion, it's no more than another punt. It doesn't particularly cost anything for an agency to have an aspiring author on its books. I guess Claudette is sticking with her in the faint hope that Isla might eventually write something half-decent. And then of course she can finally leverage the celebrity of her sister to promote it. Or should I say sisters, now that Eilish has also achieved a certain fame,'* the publisher added.

Maggie laughed. 'You were right when you said there's a lot about the publishing business I don't understand. Were any of Isla's books offered to you, by the way?'

'I only deal with non-fiction, but yes, my fiction colleagues have looked at a couple of them.' She paused. *'Romance is a very competitive genre, and there are a lot of very accomplished authors in the field. It's very difficult for a new author to break through unless they offer something special, especially if they write in one of the sub-genres.'*

'I understand she writes what you publishers call steamy romance? Is that a sub-genre?'

'Yes, it is, and a rather popular one too, especially with the younger demographic,' Strong said, laughing. *'It's like Mills & Boon but with a little dash of sex thrown in. The heroine always wins the hero in the end, but she enjoys a bit of bedroom action on the journey, usually courtesy of the rogue. Which she then of course bitterly regrets.'*

Maggie laughed. 'I've read a couple. They're embarrassing. But why were Isla's efforts rejected do you know?'

'They just weren't very good,' she said simply. *'She's quite a nice writer, but her plots were cliched even by the standard of the genre, and she wasn't very good at writing sex either. The secret is that the bedroom scenes can't be in any way graphic, yet they must convey the sense of forbidden pleasure. It's a lot more difficult than it looks, believe me. And as I said, there are plenty of authors who already do it better.'*

As Strong was speaking, a question popped into Maggie's head. 'Does Claudette Barbour's firm represent Eilish too? Because I was just wondering how her book came to you guys.'

'It wasn't at all typical, because you're right, it's normal for us to only pick up on titles that have been pitched to us through literary agents. But this one came to us directly from Eilish and we thought it would do well, so we took a chance on it. So no, The Barbour Agency doesn't represent Eilish.'

'And how did she know about you? Was that through her sister? Isla, I mean? Because it's not exactly easy to get your contact details, as I found out,' she added, laughing.

'Yes, I apologise for that,' she said, *'but if we made them public, we'd get even more unsolicited manuscripts than we get now, and we're already swamped. But yes, I assume it was Isla that shared my details with her sister. One day out of the blue, I received an email from Eilish that described the premise of the book with a few sample chapters attached. I had half an hour to spare so I gave them a quick skim and decided it might be a success. And by the way, she did mention right at the start of the email that she was Kirsty Bonnar's sister. I must confess that encouraged me to read on.'*

'Okay, I understand,' Maggie said, 'and you've been really helpful Kate, thank you.' She paused before continuing. 'Just finally, would you be willing to give me a contact number for Claudette Barbour? It would be great to ask her a few questions, but obviously if that's something you'd rather not do, I would completely understand.'

'She spends most of her time in New York or LA,' Strong said, *'so you'll struggle to catch her on the phone I would think. But I can give you her email and you could try that. And I don't mind if you mention my name when you contact her. It might help.'*

'That's amazing Kate,' Maggie said, genuinely grateful that Strong had been so unexpectedly helpful. 'And thank you again.'

***

Reflecting afterwards, it did seem that Yash Patel's murder-as-PR-stunt theory if not completely sunk, was seriously holed below the waterline. The Clarkstone Press had firmly ruled themselves out of any involvement, and since Eilish did not have a literary agent, the PR campaign, if it existed at all, was not being masterminded from that source either. But had Isla been given some general marketing advice from her own literary representatives The Barbour Agency, advice that she was now using to steer the promotion of her sister's book? It seemed unlikely, but if Claudette Barbour responded to the email Maggie intended to compose, then that would be swiftly ruled in or out. But what did all this mean for the case? Perhaps before her conversation with Kate Strong it had been fifty-fifty whether Alasdair Macbeth's death had been murder or suicide, but now the scales were firmly tipping in favour of murder. But as Lori had said, the one fact unarguably pointing to foul play was a fact supplied by the unreliable Agnes Napier, the fact that Macbeth's feet were suspended too high above the floor for him to have jumped off the dining room chair. That fact needed urgent corroboration, and it seemed that Oscar-nominated Kirsty Bonnar was the person best-placed to do so.

That would be Maggie's next call, following which it would be time to tackle the lying housekeeper.

Chapter 18

It had always been Frank's view that any conversation with Eleanor Campbell should be approached with a certain trepidation - a trepidation which had been well-earned through bitter experience - and this one had been no different. But, in a stunning and unexpected tearing up of the form book, she had answered his call on the first ring with a *Hi Frank* that was almost bubbly in tone, then had immediately hung up, saying she would ring him back, this time via video call. Nonplussed, he awaited the call-back with growing bewilderment, until a minute or so later his phone sprang into life and the familiar features of the young technical guru popped onto his screen. *And she was nearly smiling.*

'I know it's coming up to Christmas,' he said, eyebrow arched, 'but you seem full of the joys of spring.' He'd almost interjected an *unexpectedly* but thankfully had checked himself just in time. 'Mind you, I'm feeling pretty bouncy myself. Ding-dong merrily on high and all that.'

'Can I show you something?' she said. *'It's like super-awesome.'* The image wobbled wildly as she moved her phone, before it settled on a shot of her bulging tummy. *'Lulu seems to have grown like crazy in just the last two weeks,'* she said, her head out of shot. *'Can you see? And she like kicks all the time. I can feel her little feet. It's amazing.'*

'That's absolutely lovely,' he said, genuinely touched that she wanted to share her excitement with him. 'She's going to be quite a girl, I can see that already.'

'Yes, she is. Lloyd says she's definitely going to be a footballer with a kick like that. But I'm guessing you didn't call just so I could show you my tummy?'

He laughed. 'No, I didn't, but I'm really glad I saw it. What it is, we need some help with facial recognition technology on this new murder investigation we're working on. A man called Drew Henderson is the victim. Stabbed three times in the back in a Glasgow back alley.'

'I heard about it,' she said. *'Lexy told me.'*

'Aye, of course,' he said. 'I forgot you two were best pals. Anyway, on the night the Henderson guy was murdered, he picked up a young lassie in a pub and they left together. An hour later, he was dead, and she's not been seen since. So as you can imagine, we're rather anxious to find out who she is. But we're drawing a blank when we do an image search on the internet, and Lexy thinks it's because she's under-age and the social media giants don't let you search for kids. We've got a good CCTV capture of her and also the mate she was with on the night, and we're hoping having two images will increase the chances of us identifying our mystery girl.' He paused for a moment. 'To get to my point, Lexy thinks you might have some spook-ware that can turn off that age restriction. Is that right?'

To his dismay, he saw she was shaking her head. *'No, it's wrong.'*

'But Lexy was pretty sure it was something us law enforcers had access to,' he said.

'She's wrong,' Eleanor said, her trademark curmudgeonly manner making an inevitable return.

'Aye well, she's not got your great expertise,' he said soothingly. 'She probably just Googled something.'

'There's a CIA app, that's maybe what she meant. But we can only use it if we ask permission. And then we need to apply for a login and password, and we have to set up three-factor authentication. It's complicated and we need an executive sign-off.'

'Well can we ask for one of them?' he asked with a tinge of impatience. 'Because this is important.'

She was silent for a moment, evidently considering his request, then she said, *'We don't need to. I think we can use grandmothers.'*

'Grandmothers?' he said, puzzled. 'What do you mean, grandmothers?'

She returned the puzzled look. *'Grandmas. Grannies. Nans. Your mum's mum. Your dad's mum. That kind of thing.'*

He laughed. 'Aye, I know what a grannie *is*. But I haven't a bloody clue what the hell they've got to do with finding that girl.'

'Grandmas always post pictures of their grandchildren on their Facebook pages, don't they? In fact, half of them use a picture of their grandchildren as their profile picture. It's super-cute but it's like super-dumb too. My grandma used to do it with old pictures of me until I told her not to. Now she just posts pictures of her cat. But millions of grandmas still do it.'

'You know, you're right,' he said, cottoning on. 'In fact, Maggie's mum's got a picture of Ollie as her profile picture. Wearing an England football shirt,' he added wryly, 'but we'll soon put that right. But that still doesn't explain what you're proposing I'm afraid,' he added.

'I can do an image search of social media databases with a demographic age filter set to over fifty so that it only accesses like old peoples' pages,' she said.

'I'm coming up to forty-five myself, but I'll let the insult pass,' he said. 'Go on, please.'

'Because I'm restricting the search to older demographics, the age blocker won't kick in. If your girl has a grandma, we might find her page through that. Her grandma's page I mean.'

He laughed. 'The laws of nature say she'll definitely have a grannie. Two grannies, in fact. And I think what we're saying is if either one of these grandmas has a social media page and has posted a photo of their beloved granddaughter, which is highly likely, then we're in business. Is that right?'

She nodded. *'Like yeah.'*

'Great. We track down the grannie and the grannie leads us to the granddaughter.' He nodded his head in approval. 'That's brilliant Eleanor, it really is. And is this standard stuff,' he added, 'or do you need to write some fancy code or whatever it is you do technically?'

'I need to interface the application programming interface, then code a formatted search string, then build a data uploader,' she said, her wrinkled brow suggesting she was already composing the digital hieroglyphics in her head.

'And how long will that take?' he asked cautiously.

'It's complicated. I'll let you know when I'm finished,' she said, the transformation back to old Eleanor evidently now complete. *'So if we're done, I'll get started. Bye.'* Abruptly, she ended the call, Frank consoling himself that he'd at least got a *bye*, which was more than he was normally honoured with. With that matter satisfactorily dealt with, he could now turn his attention to something that had been quietly ticking away in the background, something he hadn't yet focussed his murder team on. And for that, he needed to speak to Maggie, not that he needed much excuse to do that.

'Hello darling,' she said, answering on the first ring. *'This is as unexpected as it is lovely. Considering it's only two hours since we met over breakfast.'*

He laughed. 'As you well know, my brain can only focus on one thing at a time, and at breakfast all I was thinking about was my bloody call with wee Eleanor.'

'How did it go?'

'Weirdly well. She showed me her bump and I even saw her smile twice. It just wasn't like her at all. For a minute I thought I'd dialled a wrong number.'

'It's the hormones. Their levels go through the roof during pregnancy. Lots of women say they've never felt better, including me. Even though I'm so terribly old.'

'Old? No way, you're younger than a spring chicken, and you look even younger than that,' he said. 'But the reason for my call is to talk about your Macbeth investigation. I'd sort of parked it for the time being whilst we got our case up and running, but now I'm thinking us cops need to focus on whether it really was murder or not.'

'Are you now thinking the two cases might be connected?' she asked.

'There's no hard evidence to support that right now but it's difficult to believe they're not, let's put it that way. Two of the three guys who were at that family gathering are dead. That's unusual, to put it mildly.' He paused. 'But anyway, and just to prove I was listening to you this morning, I think you said you were planning to talk to Kirsty Bonnar to see if she remembers how high off the ground the victim was hanging when she walked into that room.'

'That's right,' Maggie confirmed. *'We've only got the say-so of Agnes Napier the housekeeper that he was dangling too high to have stepped off the dining room chair, and she's already proved herself to be an unreliable witness. I was going to try and catch up with Kirsty today and ask her the same question. And there was another thing too. They cut down the body you see, and I thought it would be good to know who instigated that.'*

'Good point. But do you think she'll talk to you? Because it was her and her husband who were behind that cease-and-desist order, wasn't it?'

'I don't know. I was going to send her a text explaining in advance what I wanted to talk about. To give her time to think about it. And also to point out that her answer might put an end to the murder speculation once and for all.'

He hesitated for a moment. 'Maybe that might not be a good idea. Texting her, yes, that's fine, but I wouldn't give her advance warning about the subject.'

'Oh God, you're right,' she interjected. *'Because if she's involved in the murder, she might not have realised the significance of how high his body was dangling. If I tell her the question in advance, it'll give her the chance to think about how she should answer it.'*

'Aye, it would be better to spring it on her in my opinion. More chance of getting a truthful response.'

'But she might still lie,' she said, sounding a little deflated. *'I hadn't thought of that either. You see, that's why you're such a clever professional detective and I'm still a well-meaning amateur.'*

He laughed. 'It's true I get paid to do it, but I wouldn't say I'm clever. But the thing is, I'm beginning to see a win-win situation emerging here.'

'How do you mean?'

'If Kirsty Bonnar corroborates the housekeeper's story, then that gives good cause to open a formal police investigation, because it means that two separate witnesses are providing evidence that he couldn't have committed suicide. If she *doesn't* corroborate it, then we have two conflicting accounts, and *that* gives us a reason to ask some questions too. Maybe we won't be able to open a full-on murder enquiry, not at first anyway, but I can still send in my DS Andy McColl to ask some awkward questions. We'll ask them all to come down the station one at a time so they can understand how seriously we're taking it.'

'That would be brilliant,' she said. *'And just so you know, if it was murder, then we think two people must have been involved, because of the logistics involved in moving Alasdair's body. And the maths says there are more than twenty separate possible combinations.'*

'Sounds complicated right enough,' he said, 'but I guess we only need one of them to crack under questioning and then we're in. I've not worked with DS McColl before, but I get the feeling he'll be really good at that. Anyway, I'll be really interested to find out how you get on with Miss Bonnar. Let me know as soon as you find out anything. Cheerio and see you later.'

As he hung up, he felt that old familiar feeling in his gut, the one that told him the chase was on. Irrespective of what Kirsty Bonnar would tell Maggie, he just *knew* that the actress's brother-in-law Alasdair Macbeth had been murdered and that it had to be connected to the death of Drew Henderson in some way. How and why, he didn't know yet, but eventually it would all fall into place as it always did, and it wouldn't surprise him if, as usual, it was the wonderful Maggie Bainbridge who worked it all out.

Now, with the satisfaction that everything was moving nicely forward, he could take a leisurely drive over to Castlemilk, meet up with DC Lexy McDonald, and renew his acquaintance with the criminal mastermind that was wee Shug Wilson.

Chapter 19

Maggie's conversation with Frank had been sobering, bringing her up short as she realised how close her rashness had come to blowing the whole investigation out of the water. But she had quickly recovered, deciding that it might be more effective if the text approach to Kirsty Bonnar came from Yash Patel and the Chronicle rather than her. Accordingly, Patel had composed a message, the gist of which was that the paper's investigations had thus far failed to find any concrete evidence to support the assertions of the anonymous whistleblower, and if nothing emerged in the next day or two, they would spike any future articles and print an apology. But before that, they just needed the answer to a couple of little questions. Okay, it wasn't quite the truth, but it wasn't exactly a lie either, and Maggie had long ago learned that the printed media employed a very loose definition of what constituted either. Whatever the moral merits of the approach, it had done the job, the actress instantly responding that she would accept a call the following morning. And so, precisely on schedule, Maggie rang her.

'I'm glad this stupid thing is finally coming to an end,' Kirsty said immediately the opening pleasantries were over. *'It's been terribly stressful for the whole family, especially since it's all such utter nonsense. And now on top of everything we have Drew's awful murder to deal with.'* As she said it, Maggie heard a gasp. 'Shit, I wasn't supposed to say that.'

'Don't worry, I know about Drew,' Maggie said, 'My husband has been asked to lead the murder enquiry. He's a detective chief inspector, I can't remember if I mention that.' She paused for a moment. 'I can understand how hard it must be for all of you. Especially for Isla and her family.'

'She's gone to pieces as you can imagine,' the actress said, *'and the kids are distraught, naturally. Of course he was out doing his womanising,'* she added bitterly, *'but he must have picked the wrong target this time and her husband or lover took his revenge.'* She paused for a moment. *'Or more likely it was a father, given how much Drew liked them young.'*

'Do you think that's what happened?' Maggie asked, surprised. 'That it was the work of a jealous lover or a vengeful father?'

'What else could it be?' she shot back. *'I always suspected this was how he would meet his end, and so it's proved.'*

It seemed an astonishing thing to say, making Maggie wonder if there was some history that provoked it. But on the other hand, Kirsty Bonnar was an actress and perhaps over-dramatisation came naturally to her.

'Well, I assume the police will be investigating that line of enquiry along with all the others,' she said non-committally. 'But there are just two questions I want to ask you before we bring this thing to a close. The first one might bring back some unpleasant memories, so I apologise in advance for any distress it might cause.'

'Okay,' she said, sounding wary. *'Fire away.'*

'The first question relates to when you discovered Alasdair that terrible Christmas morning.' She paused. 'Can you remember, I wonder, how far his feet were off the ground? Was it two feet, three feet, perhaps more?'

The line went silent for a moment, then Kirsty said. '*What an extraordinary question that is. You'll forgive me when I say that it never entered my mind to consider that. I was just stunned by the scene as you can imagine. My only thought in fact was that the young children shouldn't see it, and I was so so glad they were all still in bed and hadn't come down to open their presents.*'

'I know it must be terribly difficult for you,' Maggie said softly, 'but perhaps you can try to picture the scene again and see if there's anything that might bring it back to you. I know it must be painful to go back to that morning,' she added, 'so don't worry of it's too distressing for you.'

There was silence again, much longer this time, and for a moment Maggie wondered if the actress had ended the call. But then she said, '*I remember looking up at his face. I looked up at his face.*' Maggie heard a gentle sob, before she said for the third time. '*I looked up. I stood right next to him, and I had to push my head right back to see it, almost as far as it would go. I didn't want to look, but I had to see if he was still alive. In fact, I prayed he was.*'

Unknown to Kirsty, Maggie had experimented by pushing her own head as far back as she could, until it began to hurt. *And what it revealed was, if you were looking at his face at that angle, Alasdair Macbeth's feet must have been at least three feet off the ground.*

'It must have been very distressing for you,' she said, feeling her excitement growing. 'You were very brave.' She paused for a moment then said, 'But at some stage, it must have been decided to cut him down, rather than wait for the emergency services to arrive. How did that come about, can you remember?'

'*That was Tom,*' she answered instantly. '*Everyone else was in a state, but he was quite calm. Alasdair's eyes were open you see, so Tom thought there was a chance he was still alive and he should be given CPR as soon as possible. And I think at the same time he was worried that the wee kids would come down and see him hanging there. So someone went off to fetch a kitchen knife to cut the rope then Drew and Tom lowered him to the ground as gently as they could. But it was too late of course, he was already dead. But at least we tried,*' she added sadly.

'It's so tragic, I really feel for you,' Maggie said. 'And yes, if Tom thought there was a chance to save Alasdair, well he did the right thing in cutting him down.'

'*He wasn't sure if it was the right thing,*' Kirsty said. '*Afterwards I mean. But no-one knows what the right thing is in a situation like that, do they?*'

'No, I guess not,' Maggie said, then she paused for a moment, seeking to bring the call to a natural close. 'But look, I won't take any more of your time, because the less time we spend thinking about that terrible event the better. Thank you so much for taking my call, it's been very helpful. Goodbye Kirsty and thank you again.'

And it had been very helpful, *extraordinarily* helpful in fact. Now, any element of doubt about the cause of Alasdair Macbeth's death had been firmly squashed. If Kirsty Bonnar had been involved in the murder, she could and would have lied to support the suicide theory. *But she didn't.* No, Bonnar had been telling the truth, of that there could be little doubt. But what was to be made of the fact that it had been her husband Tom Harper who had instigated the cutting down of Macbeth's body? Was her explanation of his reasoning plausible, or was this the hallmark of a murderer anxious to conceal his crime? Perhaps that was something that would emerge under the questioning of the steely DS McColl. With a smile of satisfaction, she composed a two-word text and sent it to Frank, copy Lori and Jimmy.

Game on.

Chapter 20

Despite several phone calls and an equal number of WhatsApp messages, Maggie had been unable to make contact with Agnes Napier, which was now beginning to concern her rather a lot. If she'd remembered correctly, this was the week when the housekeeper should have been staying in Glasgow with her sister Maisie, celebrating an early Christmas, but of course, these arrangements could easily have changed. Perhaps the Glengarry estate had asked her if she could postpone her break and stay on at Christmas Lodge, where perhaps she was too busy to respond to Maggie's messages. But that was all speculation. The fact remained that Napier was critical to the case, and they would be unable to move forward until they had talked to her. She picked up her phone and swiped down to Jimmy's number.

'Hi Jimmy, how are you?' she said brightly. 'And more importantly, how's Frida and her little bump?'

'Aye, all good, and it's not so little now,' he said. *'I'm stuck in the office catching up on some admin. It's too wild to take anyone up on the mountains right now.'*

'And what about getting across to Nethy Bridge? Would that be possible today?'

'Yep, the pass is open as far as I know. Why, do you want me to pop over there?'

She laughed. 'I know it's more than an hour's drive, but yes, it would be great if you could. Our housekeeper Agnes Napier's gone missing you see. Or at least she's not responding to any of my calls or messages.'

'She's a sleekit wee woman,' he said. *'I wouldn't trust her as far as I could throw her, which isn't very far. But I guess you want me to check out her house and Christmas Lodge too, to see if she's there? And I could speak to the Glengarry estate letting agent in case she can shed any light on her whereabouts. Because sometimes they ask her to cover other properties, and the phone signal can be a bit iffy in some of these places.'*

'That would be brilliant Jimmy. And I'll see if I can track down the sister. I seem to remember she doesn't live far from my office in fact. Anyway, let me know if you discover anything, and we'll touch base later. Over and out.'

'Roger that,' he said. *'Speak soon.'*

Sleekit. Yes, the peculiarly Scottish word described Agnes Napier to a tee. There was just *something* about her, something vaguely untrustworthy that made you question anything she said, and now that impression she radiated had been validated by the business of the linen cupboard lock. However you described her, she wasn't a very nice woman or a very clever one either. And now Maggie believed that her foolishness may have put her life in deadly danger. Yesterday, Kirsty Bonnar's evidence had proved beyond doubt that Alasdair Macbeth had been murdered. *But Agnes Napier had known that already.* She must have seen or heard something during the Bonnar family's stay at Christmas Lodge, which she had decided to use for her personal pecuniary advantage. As they had already postulated, perhaps the blackmailer's victim had decided they'd had enough of the arrangement and had abruptly stopped the payments. Vengefully – and stupidly – Napier had decided to spill the beans but thought she would be clever by going to a private detective agency rather than the police and, in parallel, dripping some heavy hints to a local newspaper. She must have thought it was all going swimmingly, until suddenly Drew Henderson is found stabbed to death in a Glasgow alleyway and it stops being such an amusing game.

Lori had been sitting at her desk, engaged in writing up notes on the case to hand over to Frank's team. Looking up, Maggie saw she was chewing on a pencil, evidently deep in thought.

'Sorry to interrupt,' she said. 'You look as if your brain is seriously whirring away.'

Her assistant laughed. 'Yeah, I'm just picturing the layout of Christmas Lodge in my head after my visit and then trying to add in what Jimmy told me about the upstairs. I want to include a wee diagram of who was sleeping where in my notes and how that relates to the big living room where Macbeth was found.'

'That's a good idea. But can I just ask you a quick question? What I want to know is, can you still get directory enquiries? I mean, if you want to look up someone's phone number and where they live? Because you don't get these big thick books through your door any more.'

'Everything's on the internet now,' Lori said. 'Just tell me who you're searching for, and I'll have a look for you. There are one or two sites that do it.'

'It's Agnes Napier's sister. She's called Maisie, and she lives in Partick or Dowanhill. She's not married either according to her sister so her surname will be Napier too of course. Maisie Napier.'

Lori smiled. 'Easy-peasy that. But I'll tell you what, I'll just search *Maisie Napier Partick* first and see what pops up. We might get lucky, you never know. Hang on.' She punched a few instructions into her laptop, and pressed *enter*. Five seconds later she was peering at the screen, open-mouthed. 'Wow, we *did* get lucky. Would you believe I've found a Maisie Napier who's secretary of the West Glasgow Bowling Club? It must be her, surely?'

'You're joking,' Maggie said, amazed. 'You found her in five seconds? That's crazy.'

Lori shrugged. 'Nobody's got a private life any more. And look, I've even got a picture. And yeah, it's her alright.'

Maggie stepped over and glanced over her colleague's shoulder. 'Yes, that must be her as you say. A bit older, but the likeness is unmistakable.'

'Defo,' Lori said. 'And it even gives her address. Look, 24 Caird Drive.'

'That's near here, isn't it?'

Lori nodded. 'Out the door, turn right at Highburgh Road, left at Hyndland Street and then it's third on the right. Ten minutes' walk even if you're dawdling.'

Maggie gave a wide smile. 'Well, this is all just amazing. So how about we go and pay her a visit right now?'

***

A light overnight dusting of snow followed by a hard frost had made the pavements somewhat treacherous underfoot, so the trek to

Caird Drive had taken nearly twice as long as Lori's over-optimistic estimate. It was an elegant street, lined with the red sandstone tenements which were such a signature of this part of the city, and which shouted prosperity. The entrance to the communal area – the *close* in Glasgow parlance – was guarded by a glass-panelled door adjacent to which was a keypad and a row of intercom buttons labelled with the flat number and the name of the resident.

'Look, there she is,' Maggie said, pointing to one of the buttons. 'M. Napier, Flat 2B. That must be on the second floor I'd guess.' Giving Lori a hopeful look, she pushed the button. After a few seconds there had been no response, so she tried again. *Nothing.*

'Looks like she's not in,' Lori said, disappointed. 'But maybe she's just popped out to the shops or something. We could wait ten minutes I suppose, see if she comes back.'

'Or we could try 2A,' Maggie suggested, pointing to the adjacent button. 'D. Prentice according to the label.' She extended a finger and pressed the button, holding it for several seconds.

Lori laughed. 'They'll definitely have heard that okay. If they're in of course.'

A moment later, the intercom crackled into life. *'Hello?'* a man's voice said.

'Mr Prentice? I'm Maggie Bainbridge and I'm a private investigator. I'm really sorry to disturb you, but I'm very anxious to get in touch with your neighbour Maisie Napier on a matter of critical importance, and I wondered if you had seen her today? And I also wondered if you knew whether her sister was staying with her or not?'

'*She's not here,*' he said in a sharp tone. '*They went away a couple of days ago, and she asked me if I would feed her bloody cat. Vicious wee bugger, so it is. I'll tell you what, if he scratches me again, he can bloody starve, Christmas or no Christmas.*'

'Oh dear, he does sound a little tearaway,' Maggie said. 'But did they tell you where they were going? And how long they were going to be away for? I assume they told you that at least?'

'*They were going to a hotel somewhere, right through to the New Year. They never said where, but I wasn't interested anyway. I only do it for her so she'll return the favour when me and my wife are away. And by the way, our wee cat's not mental like hers is.*'

Maggie laughed. 'And was this something that had been planned for a while?'

'*No, it wasn't,*' the man said, sounding cross. '*She sprung it on me at the last minute, and I had a mind to tell her where to get off. But we've got our daughter and our two wee grandsons coming to stay with us at Christmas, and the boys like the wee furry bugger. So I said, okay, I'll do it. But he's not getting any bloody turkey, believe you me.*'

Maggie laughed again. 'Yes, best to keep it out of his reach I would think. And how were they travelling do you know? I mean were they driving, or did they perhaps get a taxi to take them to the station or the airport?'

'*I didn't see them leave. But old Maisie doesn't keep the best of health, and she needs her wee mobility scooter to go any distance, so I doubt if they were going abroad, because she wouldn't get travel insurance for a start. Anyway, are we about finished? I can't stand here all day answering your questions.'*

'No that's fine Mr Prentice,' she said. 'And thank you for your time, you've been really helpful. And have a lovely Christmas with your family.'

For what seemed like an age, all Maggie and Lori could do was stare at each other, open-mouthed.

'She's done a runner hasn't she?' Lori finally said. 'Gone into hiding. A fugitive.'

Maggie nodded. 'Looks like it. She must be scared out of her wits to go to those lengths.'

'Do you think they've checked into a hotel under an alias, like Agatha Christie did that time she ran away from her husband?'

'Probably. But she is very stupid. They can't run away for ever, not if they're paying a hundred pounds a night and more for a hotel room.'

'They must be hoping the police catch the murderer before they run out of money,' Lori said. 'But what I don't understand is why she doesn't go to the police now, if she's so frightened?'

Maggie shrugged. 'Because she's stupid and greedy in equal measure, that would be my guess. I think she asked the murderer or murderers for a whopping increase in her keep-silent money, and she's still hoping they might pay up.'

'That's stupid,' Lori said. 'They've murdered before. And they always say once you've done it once, the second one is easier.'

'And remember, her killing might be the third one,' Maggie said. 'That is, if we believe the murderers of Alasdair Macbeth also killed Drew Henderson. Which I firmly believe they did.'

'But the killers won't find it easy to find Napier and her sister, will they?' Lori said. 'So they'll be safe for a wee while at least.'

'They'll be safe from the killers, but not from us. Because we've got Frank, and Frank's got Eleanor Campbell, and they've got neither.' She smiled. 'And before I forget, I better call Jimmy and give him our news. He's probably just arrived in Nethy Bridge. *Oops.*'

Chapter 21

It had surprised Frank that Yash Patel had decided to fly up to Glasgow to meet with him and Maggie in person, given that their business could just as easily have been transacted in a video call. But when he thought about it some more, the developments of the last twenty-four hours had been highly significant, perhaps even verging on momentous, events which were going to drop a blockbuster story right into the lap of the award-winning journalist, so perhaps it wasn't so surprising that he wanted to hear of them straight from the horse's mouth. By habit, Patel liked to schmooze his contacts through generous deployment of the generous expense account provided by his employer, and accordingly he'd offered to buy them brunch at a city-centre restaurant of their choosing. However, Frank wasn't going to fall for that old trick, where the provision of even some modest hospitality resulted in an obligation it was difficult to wriggle out of. Instead, they had colonised a corner table in the canteen of New Gorbals police station, and he would be picking up the tab.

'Let's get you a wee coffee Yash, and welcome to our Michelin-starred establishment,' he said, grinning. 'And I'm having a roll and sausage too. What about you two? They're dead nice, especially with the brown sauce.'

'I'll have one please,' Maggie said. 'Of course.'

'I'll pass thanks,' Patel said, 'I had breakfast on the plane.'

'Do they still do that?' Frank asked. 'I thought you just got given a packet of cheesy snacks from the trolley nowadays. But I forgot, you probably flew business class.'

He laughed. 'Naturally. Anyway, you said you had something big for me Frank, and I'm excited to hear what it is.'

'It's pure gold, Yash my boy. I'd be clearing your diary for the next awards ceremony if I was you.'

The journalist gave a wry smile. 'I'll judge that when I hear what you've got to say.'

'Okay. Well first, we've got that murder that happened about ten days ago, the guy who was stabbed in a wee back alley after a night on the town. We're now able to name him as Drew Henderson, a forty-two-year-old male from the north-west of the city. He's the partner of Isla Bonnar, youngest sister of the actress Kirsty Bonnar and the writer Eilish Macbeth.'

'Bloody hell,' Patel exclaimed. 'You're not joking, right?'

'We're not joking,' Maggie said.

'So Yash,' Frank said, 'you're allowed now to name the victim and give a bit of background, and you can even speculate on motive if you like, because I know I couldn't stop you doing that even if I wanted to. But there is one matter that we want you to hold your fire on for a day or two.'

'Depends on what it is,' the journalist said sourly.

Frank sighed. 'This is important Yash. Henderson was seen leaving the pub in the company of a young woman, and obviously we're anxious to trace her. But we're not doing a wide media appeal right now, not until we've exhausted all other channels, because we don't want her to find out that we're making a big effort to locate her. So far, all we've done is stuck up a few posters in the pub, low-key stuff like that.'

'Because you're worried she might go to ground if she gets spooked?' Patel said.

'Exactly. We're deploying some hi-tech facial search technology behind the scenes and we're quietly confident that will come up trumps. But if it doesn't, we'll resort to a general media appeal, and you'll obviously be first to know about that.'

'That's fair,' Patel said. 'And what about suspects? Have you got any?'

'Let's just say we're pursuing a number of lines of enquiry.'

'So that's a *no* then?'

Frank gave him a sharp look. 'You heard what I said, and that's what I expect you to report.'

Patel shrugged. 'Fair enough. So what about the other story?'

'There's been progress on the Alasdair Macbeth matter,' Maggie said. 'We're now sure that his death was murder, and as a result, the police will be opening a formal enquiry in the next day or two. Meanwhile, Bainbridge Associates will continue to pursue the investigation on behalf of your paper until the police are in a position to take over.'

'Bloody hell,' he said again, 'So that old bat Napier was right then, was she? And the same question. Any suspects to report?'

'As you've hinted in your previous articles, the killer or killers had to be someone who was staying at Christmas Lodge, which narrows it down to seven, one of whom is now dead.' She gave Frank an enquiring look. 'Is Yash allowed to say more than that in anything he writes?'

'There's not much more to say at the moment,' he said. 'We'll be bringing each of them into the station for formal questioning and we'll see where it goes from there. You can write that if you want.'

'Where will you be questioning Kirsty Bonnar?' Patel asked. 'Because my photographers would climb over their grannies to snap her walking into a police station.'

'She lives in London, so we would ask her to attend her local station,' Frank said wryly. 'But just so you know, you'll be the last person we'll be telling about it, and no offence. We appreciate the media's help, but we don't want a media scrum either. The last thing we need is her buggering off to her Mallorca villa in the middle of the enquiry.'

'We can send a snapper out there no problem,' Patel said. 'That might be an even better picture.'

'Don't even go there,' Frank said, 'and I mean that both figuratively and literally, if that's the correct expression. You can write your stories and I'm sure there'll be no limit to your imagination on that score but go easy on the doorstepping. Is that clear?'

'Perfectly,' Patel said, with dubious sincerity. 'And thanks for this you two, because there's enough material here to keep me on the front page for a month.'

'I'm sure,' Frank said, laughing. 'Now there's one other matter I need to bring to your attention, and it's a matter I need you to take really seriously.' He paused for a moment. 'It's come to our attention that the whistleblower or whatever you want to call her has gone to ground.'

Patel frowned. 'Agnes Napier?'

'Exactly. She's not the brightest sandwich in the picnic so her actions are unpredictable to say the least, but given her history, we think there's a chance that she might just possibly try to contact you or the Chronicle. It's our belief that she knows the identity of at least one of the murderers, and that makes her extremely valuable to us, but at the same time it puts her in great danger. So should she try to make contact, then you need to tell us right away.'

'What, do you believe *she* might get murdered too?' Patel said, surprised.

'Yes, we're worried that she might,' Maggie said. 'It seems highly likely that Drew Henderson's murder was connected to the earlier killing in some way, possibly to stop him revealing something he knew. And if the killers have struck a second time, then it gives an indication of how ruthless they are.'

Patel hesitated. 'I should tell you guys that I was intending to head up to Nethy Bridge later today. I wanted to see Christmas Lodge for myself so I could describe it properly to my readers. And I was going to try and talk to Napier whilst I was up there. In fact, I was going to do a feature on her. *Is this woman the key to the Christmas Lodge mystery*, something like that.' He gave a wry smile. 'Maybe I'll park *that* one for a while. But I'm still going to go and see the lodge and take a few photographs. It's what I like to do. It gives me a better feel for the story if I've been at the scene myself.'

Frank nodded. 'Well as it happens, I've got a proposal for an alternative wee trip for you this afternoon, and it's all thanks to yourself and that video you posted for us, the one starring the handsome if vertically challenged Shug Wilson.'

'Has that had the result you expected then?' Patel asked.

'Apparently so, at least according to the latest update I've had from DC McDonald. But anyway, you'll be able to come along and see it all unfolding in glorious technicolour. The location's not quite as picturesque as the beautiful Cairngorms, but it'll be another cracking story for you. It's a place called Castlemilk, one of our fair city's most attractive suburbs.'

***

But before he headed a couple of miles south-east to assist Lexy in what he hoped would be the finale of the Aquanaut affair, there was the urgent matter of Agnes Napier's disappearance to be dealt with. Bainbridge Associates were a highly capable little firm, but they obviously didn't have access to the powerful information and communications cyber-technology that was the exclusive preserve of the law enforcement agencies. Having said that, much if not all of the stuff that he had used on past cases wasn't readily available to the regular police either, much of it being dubious spook-ware cooked up by a shady army of IT geeks in the employ of the security services. Through a network of equally dubious first-name only contacts, Eleanor Campbell seemed to have access to this mountain of tech, on the premise that she was able to provide real-life scenarios to test its efficaciousness under battle conditions. Now he needed her urgent services again, whilst being only too aware that she was already working on the pressing matter of finding Drew Henderson's under-age pick-up. Not for the first time, he was glad he had Maggie by his side for what might prove to be a difficult call. But then, in an admission of cowardice, he decided that it would be better if his wife made the call herself, especially since, technically speaking, it was still her investigation.

The forensic officer had evidently looked at the screen of her phone to see who was calling, answering with a bright *Hi Maggie,* although she quickly added that she was busy on another important job, and asked if it was a quick one. There was then a slight but perceptible frosting of the atmosphere when Maggie announced that her husband was alongside her and she was switching to speakerphone. Despite claiming to be pressed for time, Eleanor was able to spare considerable amounts of the stuff whilst they compared notes on the progression of their pregnancies. But eventually, Maggie was able to bring up the matter in hand.

'It's another missing person affair,' she explained, 'but this time we know quite a lot about the person who's disappeared, which I assume will help us. We know her name and we know her address for a start.'

'And we know the registration of her car too,' Frank added, remembering that Maggie had mentioned that Jimmy had recorded it the first time he'd visited Christmas Lodge. 'And we know where she works, so it should be straightforward to get her bank details from their payroll department if you think that would help.'

'Oh yes, and she travelled with her sister, and we have the sister's name and address too,' Maggie said.

'Sure, all of that's good,' Eleanor confirmed. *'And is this case more important or less important than the one I'm already working on?'*

Maggie shot him a look that said *you answer that*. He thought about it for a moment then said, 'I think you know what I'm going to say, that they're equally important. But I appreciate you can't do both at once, so finish the first one before you move on to this new one.'

'And I appreciate you'll need to think about it,' Maggie said, 'but do you have any idea how you would approach this?'

'Do you know how they travelled and where they might be going?' Eleanor asked. *'Car, train, boat, plane, taxi?'*

'How they travelled, we don't know,' Maggie admitted. 'As to where they were going, a neighbour told us the sister didn't keep the best of health so we assume they would stay in the UK. But we don't know that for sure.'

Eleanor was silent for a moment, then said. *'A lot of this stuff is like super-easy. I can show Maggie how to do most of it, if that's like allowed. She's smart,'* she added, evidently in support of her proposal.

'She certainly is,' Frank said, 'and I'm sure it's allowed, especially if I don't tell anybody about it. But seriously, that would be great if you could,' he added, feeling his spirits rise. 'But exactly what sort of stuff are you referring to?'

She reeled off the list. *'Automatic number plate recognition, that's easy. Check credit card and debit card spending history, that's easy. Geolocate a person using mobile cell triangulation, that's easy.'*

'Are you sure you can teach me how to use all these apps, if that's what they are?' Maggie said dubiously. 'I know I'm a little more IT-savvy than Frank...'

'Who isn't?' he interrupted, grinning.

'...but they sound complicated.'

'Ordinary policemen use them every day, and you're smarter than ordinary policemen,' Eleanor said.

'Fair point,' he said. 'So how does this work Eleanor? What does Maggie need?'

'She just needs a laptop and then I can train her in like ten minutes.'

Frank nodded enthusiastically. 'She's got a laptop, and she's got ten minutes. Sounds like we're good to go.'

'And I won't be doing anything illegal?' Maggie asked him, evidently concerned.

'We've got a ton of civilian staff working in our nicks who do this stuff routinely,' he said. 'And often, they're temporary contract staff. So no, you wouldn't be doing anything illegal.'

She nodded. 'That sounds okay then. But what stuff *is* hard Eleanor? What would only you be able to do?'

The forensic officer thought about the question for a moment then said, *'Do you know where the sister works?'*

Maggie shook her head. 'We don't even know *if* she works. Although she looks old enough to be retired, I would say. But we don't know that for sure.'

'In which case it'll be like impossible for an ordinary person to find out her bank account details, if she hasn't got a job with a payroll department you can ask. But I can hack the council tax database using her name and address and get it from there.'

Frank laughed. 'You're a devil so you are, using the hack word again to wind me up. What you mean is, you can access the council tax database. Legitimately.'

'No, I have to hack it,' she repeated, unapologetic. *'I code an SQL injection string to return a valid set of log-in credentials. Then I use that to jump from her current account to her master data record where I can grab the details of any credit cards she has. It's super-easy, but only for someone like me.'*

He laughed again. 'Young Eleanor, modest in all things as always. But aye, I can see if you can get the sister's current and credit card details, then Maggie here will have a complete set of stuff to track them down. For example, as soon as either of the sisters spends anything, then bang, we've got them. Am I right in thinking that?'

'More or less,' she said, with a hint of truculence.

'That's great,' Maggie said. 'But there's one thing that struck me whilst we've been talking. What if they pay for everything in cash? Because then they won't leave a trail, will they?'

Eleanor shook her head and gave them a disparaging look. *'The list of hotels anywhere in the world who don't ask for your credit card details is like a big fat zero. As soon as they check in somewhere, you've got them. Unless they're sleeping on the street that is.'*

'Hardly likely I think,' Maggie said. 'But yes Eleanor, I take your point about the hotels.' She paused again, her brow furrowed as something else evidently came to mind. 'Actually, we've got a suspicion that Agnes might have been blackmailing one of the family in order to buy her silence. Mainly because she drives a new and very expensive car that we don't think she could afford on her wages as a housekeeper. I assume you could find out if she's getting these payments and if so, who it's from?' And then she answered her own question. 'But of *course*, I'll be able to do that myself once you train me on how to access the bank account stuff.'

'Or I could do it right now,' Eleanor said. They heard a clicking of a keyboard, then silence, then some more clicking. And then little more than a minute later, she came back with the answer.

'Agnes Napier was receiving fifteen hundred pounds a month from a joint account in the name of K. Bonnar and T. Harper. Until it stopped last month.'

***

Frank hadn't known what to make of Eleanor's startling discovery, given that the case was only just starting to appear on his radar. But for Maggie, who had thought of little else for the last seven or eight days, it had come like a bolt out of the blue, in the process blowing all her previous but admittedly half-formed ideas out of the water. As she walked back to the city centre, where she was planning to catch the Underground back to her Byres Road office, her mind was awash with swirling contradictions, each crazy idea negating the previous one until she didn't know *what* to believe. Unable to stand it any longer, she pulled her phone from her handbag and rang Lori, the words tumbling out at such a rate that they were barely understandable.

'Look Lori, the case has just gone mental, and my brain is *completely* fogged. I've just spotted a little tearoom, so I'm just going to dive in here and grab a seat, and then we'll get Jimmy on the line, and the three of us will try and thrash it all through, see if we can make even the slightest sense of it all. Because otherwise I'm going to go totally mad.'

'What's happened?' her assistant said, sounding alarmed. 'Obviously something big if it won't wait the fifteen minutes it'll take you to get back to the office.' Maggie told her what she had learned from Eleanor, garnering the reaction she had expected

'Flipping hell,' Lori exclaimed. 'Kirsty Bonnar and Tom Harper? I don't bloody believe it.'

'Me neither,' Maggie said, pulling out a chair of the nearest empty table, then absent-mindedly picking up a menu. 'But it's true, that's who was paying off Agnes Napier. Until last month, when the payments stopped.'

Just then, Jimmy joined them on the line. 'What's up? What's the big panic?'

'Your suspicion about how Agnes Napier could afford such a nice car was right,' Maggie said. 'She was getting hush money. But can you guess *who* was paying it?'

His reaction was identical to Lori when she told him. 'Bloody hell, I didn't see *that* coming. But what does this mean?'

'No bloody idea,' Maggie said, loud enough to cause the occupants of the table in front of hers to glance round. 'That's why I got you two on the line.'

'Well let's think about this,' Lori said, 'and apologies in advance, because I'm just going to say whatever comes into my head.' She paused. *'Right*. We think Agnes Napier saw something that meant she knew who the murderer was. She decided she could profit from it by indulging in a spot of blackmail. Now we find out Kirsty Bonnar and her husband are paying her fifteen hundred quid a month.' She paused again. 'So isn't the conclusion dead obvious? Kirsty and Tom killed Alasdair Macbeth, Agnes saw them do it, end of story.'

'But there's no bloody *motive*.' Maggie shot the words out, disturbing the neighbouring table enough for her this time to have to mouth an apology. She repeated it, but in a whisper. *'There's no motive*. Why would Kirsty and Tom want to kill their brother-in-law? Answer that question one of you, please.'

'I can't, and that's the bloody problem with this case,' Jimmy said gloomily. 'Motives are thin on the ground. And that's because Alasdair Macbeth seems to have been a thoroughly nice chap.'

'Maybe we're just overthinking this then,' Lori suggested. 'In murders, it's usually the significant other who does it, isn't it? And that's Eilish. How about she despised her husband because he was so hopeless and so poor whilst she wanted to be rich, so she killed him? Simple as that.'

Maggie nodded. 'Yes, that's certainly plausible, although Kirsty told me that Eilish really loved Alasdair, despite his supposed failings.'

'Aye, *Kirsty* said that, but now you can't trust her either,' Lori pointed out.

Jimmy laughed. 'Just what I was going to say. Although I accept it wouldn't have been exactly helpful.'

'It's the *motive*,' Maggie repeated for the third time, just managing to restrain herself from banging on the table. 'This case has always hinged on discovering the motive. And until we know what it was, we're going to be spinning round in circles for ever.'

'Maggie, I think you're being too hard on yourself, so I do,' Lori said. 'We've hardly been going a fortnight so *obviously* there's loads of stuff we still need to find out. You've always told us you can't get to the solution of a crime until you have every last piece of the jigsaw, so why should this one be any different? We just haven't got all the pieces yet, but we *will* get them. We always do. That's why Bainbridge Associates are so amazing and brilliant.'

Jimmy grinned. 'I'll tell you what wee Lori, see if being a detective doesn't work out for you, then you've got a sure-fire career as a motivational speaker. But you're right Maggie, it is all about the motive, as it has been in nearly every case we've ever been on.' He hesitated for a moment before continuing. 'Where's the passion, the anger, the bitterness, the seething resentment, the all-consuming hatred, the lust, the envy, the greed? Because it's emotions like these that drive someone to commit murder, we know that, yet right now, I don't see much evidence of them in our case. But someone was murdered, so these emotions must have been there, bubbling away under the surface until they exploded in that terrible act of violence. Maybe we've just not been looking hard enough, that's all.'

'That's very poetic Jimmy,' Maggie said admiringly, feeling her spirits rise, 'and you're totally right of course. There must have been a powerful hatred at work in this case, and it's that we must focus our minds on from now on.'

'Does the first one to work it out win a prize?' Lori said, laughing.

'How about a big night out at that dodgy place you like to go to on a Friday night?' Jimmy said, his tongue obviously in his cheek.

'Yes please,' she said. 'And if you're coming, Shania will want to come too.'

***

The Underground trip back to the office gave Maggie ten minutes to turn her mind to the bizarre flight of Agnes Napier. First up, she wished she shared Eleanor Campbell's confidence about how easy it would be to track down the Napier sisters, but all she could see when she thought about it some more were obstacles. Napier might not be very bright, but she was certainly cunning, and she wouldn't have put it past the woman to get her sister to deliberately lie to her neighbour about staying in a hotel for their Christmas getaway, hoping to send any nosey parkers down the wrong track. Sure, there was no doubting it would be difficult to book any sort of accommodation without leaving a digital trail, but it wouldn't be totally impossible. Perhaps they had found a quiet cottage advertised on a tourist information website and had then phoned the owner direct and said they would like to book their place for the Christmas period but that they would like to pay cash if that would be okay? And yes, they would be happy to pay the full amount on arrival to give the owner peace of mind, no problem with that at all. Maggie could imagine that working, the Napier sisters now holed up somewhere off the beaten track where they could be confident of escaping detection. But for how long could they hold out, that was the question? Even if they'd travelled with a suitcase full of the stuff, their cash would eventually run out, forcing a replenishment visit to a hole-in-the-wall machine, which would instantly reveal at least their geographical location, if not the precise address of their hideaway. They couldn't stay on the run for ever, and eventually they would have to come in from the cold, where Agnes Napier would be forced to tell the police all she knew, knowledge that somehow now implicated Kirsty Bonnar and her husband in the crime.

But it was impossible, surely it was impossible that this pair were involved? That was what she currently believed, but she recognised that it was nothing more than a gut feeling, and hadn't she'd been wrong about them before? Certainly, they fitted Jimmy's analysis of the modus operandi, which required a strong man to be part of the team. And if they were the killers, they would now surely be aware of Napier's disappearance and would surely be equally desperate to find her, to stop her revealing her incriminating secret. The trouble was, that was likely to prove impossible given that they didn't have access to the technology available to the police. It was hard to imagine what was going through their heads, as they awaited with fear and trepidation the inevitable reappearance of the housekeeper. But then, *would* they be fearing her return? For almost twelve months, the terrible crime had gone undetected, and in fact it hadn't even registered as a crime at all. It was true that Agnes Napier had made an unsubstantiated allegation to a private detective agency, but that allegation had not been backed up by evidence, and that was maybe because she didn't have any. And Harper was a lawyer, with an inside knowledge of the hurdles the prosecuting authorities must leap over before a case could go to court. Maybe he was confident Napier had nothing that could touch them. She shook her head in frustration, struggling to deal with the *utterly* incoherent nature of the situation. Kirsty Bonnar and Tom Harper had absolutely no motive to kill Alasdair Macbeth, and yet they were paying the housekeeper fifteen hundred pounds a month to keep her quiet. *Why why why?*

Looking up, she saw the train was about to pull into her station. In five minutes, she would be back at her desk, and a few minutes after that, Eleanor Campbell would be on the line, showing her how to operate the clever set of applications that might lead her to the whereabouts of Napier and her sister. That was what she must do, she realised. She must set aside all this fruitless speculation and theorising to concentrate one hundred percent on finding that bloody housekeeper.

Chapter 22

The text message from Lexy had been as brief as it had been exciting. *Suspects in town, black Range Rover (naturally).* So it seemed that the Midland-based hoods had taken the bait, presumably having caught sight of the provocative Shug Wilson video on the national news bulletins, to which it had been syndicated from Yash Patel's Chronicle newspaper. Frank had to admit that the ruse had given him some sleepless nights, such that he was now half-regretting placing the wee scumbag in such murderous danger. But if the next five minutes played out as he was expecting it would, then he could brush that regret aside. He turned to Patel who was sitting alongside him in the passenger seat of his police BMW.

'Now Yash my boy, this affair could get a bit tasty, so you need to keep your arse plonked firmly where it is throughout the whole proceedings, got that? Otherwise, it will be one of your sub-editor mates who'll be writing the article, not you, and the headline will be *star journalist shot dead in police raid.* And we don't want that, do we?'

Patel laughed. 'Star journalist I can take. The rest, not so much.'

'Good. We're just doing a wee detour to these pick-up lockers. Won't take long.'

A couple of minutes later, he pulled into the supermarket carpark, jumping out whilst barking a *wait here* instruction to Patel. As he walked to the bank of lockers, he swiped his phone, searching for the PIN code to the specific location of his item. *25- 12, very apt.* He punched it into the screen, then presented the QR code on his phone to the scanner, causing the door to pop open a fraction. He grabbed the handle and pulled it open to reveal its contents, which were exactly as he expected. *Nothing*. Once a low-life, always a low-life, Frank thought with some amusement. Wee Shug wouldn't have been able to resist. He'd probably sold the Aquanaut Island on to another scumbag, one with kids, for something derisory like a hundred quid or so. Or, more likely, he'd have swapped it for a bag of dodgy drugs, which he could then deal to the kids who attended the scheme's big comprehensive school.

'Okay Yash, that's done,' he said on his return to his vehicle. 'Let's go and find DC McDonald. She's parked just up the road.'

Lexy's car was parked on the street where Wilson lived, but about a hundred yards from his close. Frank pulled up behind and briefly flashed his headlights. She got out then sprinted to his car, getting into the back seat.

'What's happening then?' he asked.

'You probably can't quite see it from here, but there's a couple of guys in a Range Rover parked opposite Wilson's close. About half-an-hour ago, one of them went in but came out a few minutes later.'

'Shug's not in then I'm guessing. But what about his mother? He lives with her, I seem to remember.'

'The local bobby says she's a druggy who's out of her head half the time. She probably didn't even here them knocking on the door.'

Frank nodded. 'And how do you know about them going up the stairs? You can't see anything from here, unless you brought binoculars.'

'The Northamptonshire force has sent up a couple of officers, a DI Moore and a DC Newton. I had a quick chat with the DI earlier and we're in radio contact obviously. The two of them drove up early this morning in a van disguised with a builder's logo on the side, a Glasgow builder would you believe? They're parked fifty yards down the road, where they can see everything through the back door windows.'

'Impressive preparation,' Frank said. 'They must be smart guys. But not armed I assume?'

'No sir. I've told our ops centre to have a response team standing by, but we're keeping it low-key at the moment.'

'It makes you laugh though, doesn't it, that the hoods have turned up here in a blingy Range Rover,' he mused. 'You see, half the reason these bad guys do what they do is they're desperate to be someone, and not only that, they're also desperate to be *seen* to be someone. That's why it would never occur to them to come up in a clapped-out old Vauxhall. But come on, we need to get a bit closer so we can see what's going on. And so Yash here can get some pictures for his rag.'

He started the car again and edged it up the street, pulling into a vacant spot about a hundred feet from Wilson's residence and on the same side as the Range Rover which was parked with its back to them.

'They won't be able to see us, but we've got a reasonable view of the action from here,' he said, nodding out the windscreen.

'What are we going to do if and when Shug turns up?' Lexy asked. 'Are we letting the Northamptonshire boys deal with it?'

Frank laughed. 'Nah, they won't know how to work a close. They'll probably end up out the back amongst the middens before they realise, so they'll need us as guides. But we'll let them go first,' he added, only half-joking.

They sat for nearly half an hour before anything happened, Frank running the engine from time to time to keep the heater fan pumping out hot air. But then as he glanced in his door mirror, he observed a familiar figure coming towards him on a bicycle, dressed in a parka of indistinguishable colour and with a black woolly hat pulled down almost to his eyebrows.

'Lexy, look out the window quick, my side,' he shouted. 'Is that him?'

She peered out then shrugged. 'I'm not sure. It might be.'

'Nah, it's him alright,' Frank said. 'I recognised the glaikit expression.' He winked at Patel. 'That's a bit like vacant, since you're asking, but with a lot more nuance. Here Lexy, get your DI mate on the radio and let's make plans.'

She reached over and took the handset from him, then pressed the transmit button. 'DI Moore, we think we've just seen Wilson go by on his bike. Should be at his close any time now. I'm with my boss DCI Stewart and we need to figure out a plan.'

Frank stretched out and took back the handset. 'Aye, we want to know whether we're going in or whether we wait for the cavalry to arrive. We've got a squad on standby, and they can be here in fifteen minutes. And actually, I'm going to ask them to come here anyway, just to be on the safe side.'

'*No, I think we want to go in sir,*' the DI said. '*We don't want to take any chance that these bastards might get away, not after what they did to the lorry driver. But we thought we'd give it ten minutes, give them the time to get relaxed, so they're not expecting us.*'

'Oh aye, they'll be relaxed alright, once they've battered wee Shug's head in. And then think of all the paperwork that's going to generate for me. So no, we'll give them five minutes tops, and then we follow them in. Happy with that boys?'

With obvious reluctance, the Northamptonshire detectives gave their agreement. 'And let's just take a quick look inside the Range Rover once they've headed up the stair, just in case they've left a sentry behind,' Frank added, before replacing the handset in its holder.

'Okay Lexy let's go. And remember, you stay here,' he said, looking at Yash. 'I'll send you a text when it's safe for you to come and take pictures.'

They met up with their English colleagues at the entrance to the close, raising a hand in brief introduction.

'Any idea who they are?' Frank asked Moore.

The DI shook his head. 'No clue, and obviously we checked their motor.'

'False plates I suppose?'

'Afraid so. But our APNR guys tracked it leaving an industrial estate in Dudley. There's over a hundred businesses on the park, but obviously we can go door-to-door.'

Frank gave the DI a wry look. 'They'll probably have legged it before you can get round them all. But never mind, if we nab these guys today then all your problems disappear, don't they? Anyway, let's go in. What flat is it Lexy, do you know?'

'First floor, the one on the left,' she replied.

'Good, not too many stairs then. Now listen,' he said to Moore and his DC colleague, 'I'm the ranking officer here, and my orders are if there's any hint of firearms being deployed, we back off and wait until the experts turn up. Everybody understand? So come on, up we go.'

Frank and Lexy followed their English colleagues up the stair, and as they approached the landing, they began to make out raised voices coming from Wilson's flat.

'Naw, listen mate, I never touched the thing, honest. I put it in the locker just like you said, and I sent you a picture like you asked, so I did.' It seemed Wilson's defence was in vain, as a blood-curling scream of agony assailed their senses. *'No, don't,'* he pleaded. *'Don't. Please'*

'You're fucking dead pal,' a voice responded, the tone menacing, the accent West Midlands. *'Nobody messes with us and lives to tell the tale.'* There was a dull thump, followed by another scream, then laughter.

Frank placed a silencing finger on his lips, then nodded towards the door. 'Me first,' he whispered, 'but you boys can kick the door in, okay? After three.' He paused a moment to draw breath then began to count. 'One...two...three...'

Moore smashed his booted foot into the door, and it burst open and crashed against the wall of the hallway. 'Police!' Frank shouted, bounding along the hall and darting his head through each open door in turn. They found them in a blood-stained living room, Shug Wilson splayed on his back, blood gushing from his nose, with one of his assailants pinning him to the ground, the other kneeling alongside him. *With a pistol pointed at Wilson's temple.*

Taken by surprise, the gunman spun round and pointed his weapon at Frank, who involuntarily raised his arms in a gesture of surrender, instantly feeling raw fear envelop him. And then suddenly, there was a deafening crack of gunfire, and the man crumpled to the ground, face down, still clutching the automatic. Startled and dazed, Frank turned to see DI Moore crouching in the assault position, arms rigid, with the Glock automatic held out in front of him.

'Listen man, don't shoot,' the other hood was now pleading, his expression radiating shock and fear. With a half-smile, Moore rotated a couple of degrees and pointed the weapon straight at him. 'I just might,' he said. 'I'm tempted.' The man slumped to the ground, throwing up in the process. 'But it would be a waste of a bullet.'

'You're a frigging nutcase,' Frank shouted, seething with anger and jabbing a finger into the detective's chest. 'Who said you could bring bloody guns? It's not the bloody Wild West.'

Moore shrugged nonchalantly. 'My guv'nor said we needed to nail these villains and reckoned it would be better to ask for forgiveness rather than permission. And anyway, you're an ungrateful bastard, aren't you? 'Cos I've just saved your life.'

Frank shook his head in disbelief, his mind still in turmoil from the shock of what he had just been through. 'Lexy, get the paramedics out here as soon as we can,' he barked, 'and get this other hood in cuffs. And see if you can get Shug a drink of water whilst we're waiting for them.' Then turning to the two detectives he said, 'And you two get out of my bloody sight. This is going straight to the complaints commission, and you can say goodbye to your career and your pensions. Just sod off, the pair of you.'

As he gestured towards the door, he was startled to see Yash Patel standing just inside it, mouth wide open with horror, rigidly holding his phone up in front of him, the camera lens still pointing at the scene of carnage he had evidently just recorded on video.

Chapter 23

Eleanor's ten-minute on-line training session had in the event turned into nearly an hour, the forensic officer feeling compelled not only to explain how the law-enforcement applications should be used, but to comment on the efficiency of their underlying software architectural platforms – whatever that was – and the elegance or otherwise of their user interfaces. It wasn't that she was showing off - nothing could have been further from the truth - it was just she could not prevent herself from sharing her unbounded enthusiasm for the subject matter, no matter how hard she tried. Eventually though, Maggie gleaned what she needed to know, and armed with multiple user-codes and passwords, the latter thirty-two characters long at Eleanor's insistence, she set to work.

She started with the number plate recognition app, discovering that there had been multiple sightings on the southbound A9 as Agnes had driven down to Glasgow four days earlier. The final sighting had been on a slip road of the Clydeside Expressway, confirming that her destination had been the west end of the city where her sister Maisie resided. After that, there was nothing, proving they hadn't used the car to take them to their hiding place. She could have guessed that already, but it was good to have her assumption backed up by hard data.

Next, she checked the geolocation app, punching in Agnes's mobile number and selecting a time period covering the prior two weeks. As expected, there was plenty of time spent in Nethy Bridge, where Napier both lived and worked, but what was interesting was that in five successive days before she left for Glasgow, she had made a trip into Grantown-on-Spey, one of the nearest towns, and the trip had been made on each occasion at approximately the same time, twelve thirty in the early afternoon, which Maggie assumed coincided with the housekeeper's regular lunch break. Then finally, her phone location data tracked her down the A9 almost right to her sister's door, when the data abruptly stopped. That would have been when Agnes switched off her phone in preparation for her disappearance.

Finally, Maggie turned to the banking app, which gave her real-time access to Napier's bank statement. She selected the previous two weeks to peruse, studying it intently as the data popped up on her laptop screen. Besides the dull transactions of daily life such as utility direct debits and supermarket bills, five remarkable entries jumped out at her, entries that revealed the reason for her trips into Grantown and served to confirm what Maggie had suspected from the start. Because on five successive days, she had withdrawn three hundred pounds from a cashline machine located on the High Street, the daily limit her bank allowed.

So far so good, but after the last withdrawal, there had been no further entries, as Napier presumably began to pay for everything with cash. Now, it was time to look at the sister's data. Maggie didn't know if Maisie Napier had a car, but she assumed that with the woman's failing health and limited mobility – that information provided by Mr D. Prentice, her neighbour, so was uncorroborated – then she probably had given up driving. Nor did she have the woman's mobile phone number, but that probably was of no consequence since she was presumably travelling with her sister. But she did have her bank account details, courtesy of some Eleanor Campbell wizardry. She punched in the account number and sort code and waited for her screen to respond. Scrutinising it carefully, she saw the same mundane record of day-to-day life shared by everyone on the planet, but with rising excitement, Maggie saw that Maisie too had made successive trips to a cashline machine, this one in Byres Road, barely fifty feet from her own office. Each withdrawal had been three hundred pounds, meaning that Napier had amassed a total of three thousand pounds in cash to support them whilst they were on the run. But then, to her astonishment, her attention was grabbed by something even more significant. *A transaction from just two days earlier.* It was for the princely sum of three pounds forty pence, the recipient IL Catering Limited, not a name she recognised. Hurriedly, she punched the name into her search engine, the result appearing almost instantly. *IL Catering is the catering arm of Island Link Ferries, who operate a daily service from Aberdeen to Lerwick, Shetland.*

Yes, she shouted at the top of her voice. *Got you. Got you both.*

***

It was the second time in as many days that Jimmy had received an almost incomprehensible phone call from Maggie, but eventually he was able to glean that one of the Napier sisters had made a purchase in a restaurant on the Aberdeen to Lerwick ferry, and accordingly they must be holed up in Shetland somewhere. Her assumption was that Maisie had gone to get some light refreshment and when presented with a contactless payment machine, had automatically proffered her debit card, not realising what she had done until it was too late. Acceding to Maggie's urgent request, he had gone home, thrown some clothes in a bag, kissed Frida goodbye and half an hour later, was making the near sixty-mile journey from Braemar to Aberdeen airport. Two hours after that, he was touching down at

Sumburgh, twenty-five miles south of the main town of Lerwick where he was staying, before making the onward journey to his hotel in what he considered had to be the world's most expensive taxi. The hotel wasn't cheap either, but it turned out it had a nice location on a street called the Esplanade, with a view across an expanse of water to what he assumed was one of the other islands that earned the Shetland Islands its collective title.

'Where's this?' he asked the pleasant young receptionist as he was checking in. 'Island-wise I mean.'

She smiled. 'This is Mainland. And across the water is Bressay. You're staying with us two nights, is that correct?'

He nodded. 'Aye, that's right. I'm a private detective, and I'm here looking for a couple of missing persons. Folks are anxious to find them as you can imagine.'

'I haven't seen anything in the paper,' she said.

'No, you won't have. The thing is, they don't want to be found. We're keeping it low-key for now, so we don't scare them away.'

And it was true, the low-key bit. With the Alasdair Macbeth murder not yet an official case, Frank was limited in terms of what help he could request from the local force. He'd promised he make a call in the morning to Lerwick police station to see if they were willing or able to allocate at least one officer to the search, but according to Maggie, he wasn't holding out much hope. For the time being, Jimmy was on his own.

'Will you be having dinner with us this evening?' the receptionist asked as she handed him his keycard. 'Just to let you know, we've got an office party booked in for their Christmas do. Twenty covers I think. Should be lively.'

She made no further comment, evidently leaving it for Jimmy to decide whether this was a good thing or a bad thing. He shook his head. 'No, I'll just grab a sandwich in a bit and then maybe find a wee pub later on to have a pint or two.'

'I'll be in the Breiwick Arms later, once I'm finished here,' she said. 'It's just down the road. They have folk music, it's always a great wee night. I'll be there with my girlfriend and a few of my other pals, if you fancy popping in,' she added. Grateful that she had clarified the benign nature of the invitation, he said, 'Yeah, I might just do that. Thanks.' He peered at the badge pinned to her waistcoat. 'It's Fiona I take it? I'm Jimmy. Maybe see you later.'

His room was on the first floor, small but perfectly comfortable, with a view that took in a small harbour and the expanse of water he had noticed earlier. There was a kettle and a mug on a tray, the former already filled with water. He switched it on, tore the top off an instant coffee sachet and poured it into the mug, then flopped down on the bed whilst he waited for the kettle to boil. Where to start, that was the question? He already made the assumption that the two sisters would be staying in Lerwick somewhere, if only for practicality. It was mid-December, the middle of the off-season, when the choice of accommodation anywhere on the islands would likely be limited, and more so if you didn't want to use a credit card, which ruled out probably every hotel and definitely all the on-line booking sites. You'd want to be in the town too if you were relying on cash to buy your essential provisions – no on-line supermarket deliveries for the Napiers, which would surely prevent them taking a quiet little cottage out in the wilds. To get a feel for the size of his task, he took out his phone and punched *Lerwick accommodation* into the search engine. He watched as his screen filled up, then smiled as he did a quick count. Around thirty or forty entries, some of them hotels and quite a few from house-rental sites, each of which would demand a credit or debit card to make a booking. This was encouraging, he thought. Lerwick was a compact wee place, and he could easily scoot round the couple of dozen properties left on the list in the two days he was here.

Not all accommodation options would be online of course. Another search revealed the existence of a tourist information centre, located in Market Cross in the centre of town, and pleasingly, open all year round according to their website. In the morning, he would pop round there and ask for their accommodation list, which might be a better place to start. And then it occurred to him that it might very well have been the centre that found the Napiers a place to stay, and given that it could only have been booked a week earlier at the most, the chances were one of the staff might remember the transaction and be able to provide him with an address.

Next, he considered how the pair would have been transported from the ferry terminal to their accommodation. Since they presumably travelled with luggage, it was more likely they would have taken a taxi rather than stagger onto a bus, but had the taxi been pre-booked or had they just grabbed one from the rank, assuming there was one? Another quick search revealed that indeed there was a rank. Earlier he had discovered that the ferry from Aberdeen sailed overnight, a twelve-hour crossing that docked in the Lerwick terminal at around seven-thirty in the morning. With a mild groan he realised he'd have to get up early if he wanted to talk to some of the drivers on the rank, to ask if any of them remembered picking up the Napiers. The terminal was apparently about two miles from the town centre, so maybe he would just stick on some running kit and scoot up there before breakfast. He had photographs of the pair, Agnes's taken from the 'meet our staff' section on the Christmas Lodge website, Maisie's from the bowling club's site where she was some sort of official. He would get Fiona at reception to photocopy a few of them to leave with the drivers.

So that was probably all he could do for now. He'd have his coffee then go and have a mooch around town, perhaps pick up a burger and fries, then find a pub to while away an hour or so before he took in that folk evening the receptionist had mentioned. Being the time of year it was, he hoped the town had put on a bit of a light show, and maybe there would be a big decorated tree to get him into the Christmas spirit. Or he might just have a few mulled wines, which always had the same effect.

***

His one or two pints had somehow turned into four or five, causing him to curse his phone alarm when it chirped into life at six o'clock the next morning. It had been a good night though, the music thoroughly entertaining and Fiona and her group of folky friends making him most welcome. Overnight, there had been a hard frost so running at any pace had been a hazardous proposition, but in the event, it took little more than half an hour to reach the taxi rank. There were about a dozen cabs waiting in the line, most of the cabbies sitting in the driving seat with their engines running, but a couple had braved the freezing cold, standing on the pavement smoking cigarettes. He had a chat with them and gave them each the photocopy of the Napiers' photograph, on to which he'd scribbled his mobile phone number, but none could recall taking the pair into town. He'd then walked down the row of parked vehicles, waiting until the drivers wound down their windows before handing them a flyer, accompanied by a quick explanation. None of the others remembered the pair either, but everyone agreed to mention it to other drivers in their acquaintance. Disappointing, but he would have been surprised if he'd made the breakthrough so soon into his visit. Perhaps once the word got round the taxi community, that would change.

After a hearty breakfast he headed along to the tourist information bureau, or the iCentre as it now was branded. A woman of about fifty appeared to be replenishing the rack of information leaflets but paused her activity then turned to greet him on hearing the alerting ring that accompanied the opening of the door.

'Good morning sir, how can I help?' she said brightly as she walked back to the reception counter. 'I'm Julie by the way.'

'I need some information about accommodation please,' he said.

'Certainly, that's what we do. How long are you planning to stay in Shetland?'

He smiled. 'Thanks Julie, but I'm booked in at the Queen's Hotel already. What it is, I'm a private investigator, and I'm working on behalf of the Chronicle newspaper. They're trying to find two sisters who have been staying in Lerwick since about two days ago.' It wasn't exactly the truth, but it was close enough.

'The Chronicle, did you say?' she said, evidently intrigued. 'What, have they won a competition or something?'

He shook his head. 'No, not exactly. They're called Agnes and Maisie Napier, and the younger sister is around mid-fifties, the other a few years older. I just wondered if you or anyone else who works here might have arranged accommodation for anyone fitting that description? Their visit was planned at the last minute, so the accommodation request would have only been seven to ten days ago at the most.'

'You'll appreciate I wouldn't be able to give out information like that, even if we had,' she said. 'Even to the Chronicle. But no, I don't think we have. We get so few bookings at this time of year, so I'm sure we would have remembered.'

'Fair enough,' he said. 'Just one more question for you. We're certain the Napier would have paid for their accommodation in cash, for reasons I won't bore you with. Are there any places on your books who would accept a booking on that basis? Because I know most places nowadays require a credit or debit card.'

She was silent for a moment as she considered his question. 'Well, most do insist on one, for the obvious reason that if there's any damage or theft, then they can take financial compensation by retaining some or all of the security deposit or making a one-off charge.' She paused again. 'But there's a couple of local holiday-let owners who are prepared to take that risk in return for let's call it the tax advantages. Or rather, the tax-avoidance advantages,' she added acerbically. 'Not many by the way, just a few. I wouldn't like you to think we're an island of lawbreakers.'

He smiled. 'I didn't think that for a moment. But it would be great if you could give me a list. Anyone who you think might take a cash booking.'

She hesitated for a moment, then reached under the counter to retrieve a leaflet. She spread it out, then taking a pen, ran down the list, marking an occasional entry with a tick.

'There you go. There's only a small handful.' She paused then asked, 'Should I want you to find these mysterious sisters? Or would it be better if you failed?'

He gave her a rueful look. 'It would be better if I found them, believe you me. Because the other folks who're looking for them won't be sticking them on the ferry back to Aberdeen.'

***

Just nine addresses. Jimmy could hardly believe his luck, as he saw Agnes Napier's flawed strategy unravel in front of his eyes. On paper, it must have made perfect sense to choose one of the remotest parts of the UK to flee to, but now the holes in the plan were only too plain to see. The fact is, she would have been a million times more undetectable if she'd gone to London, or even if she stayed in Glasgow. In either of those cases, it would have been like looking for the needle in the proverbial haystack, whereas in this wee place, it seemed you could be tracked down in little more than a day, or at least, that's what he hoped. Checking the map on his phone, it looked like five of the addresses were in the heart of the town, each within easy walking distance of his hotel, to where he had returned to take stock. The others were dotted on either side of the main road on which he had arrived yesterday, in an area called Sound, a mile or two from the town centre. There was one that particularly intrigued him, the map telling him it was located in what looked like a quiet street, but only a couple of hundred yards from a large supermarket. *Just the sort of place you might choose if you didn't have a car and your mobility was limited.* He reckoned a brisk walk would get him there in thirty minutes maximum, and if that drew a blank, he could tick off the other nearby properties within another hour or so.

Twenty-seven minutes later, he was standing outside the door of the property, a modest whitewashed mid-terrace home on a modern estate. He paused for a moment to compose himself, then rang the bell, giving it a long and insistent push before taking a step back and folding his arms expectantly. Eventually, the door was opened, and a figure poked her head around the slim gap she had left, scrutinising him with narrowed eyes.

He smiled at her. 'Afternoon Agnes. Mind if I come in for a wee cup of tea and a chat?'

Chapter 24

The news from Shetland, relayed by Jimmy in disbelieving tones, could not be described as anything less than sensational. *It wasn't evidence of murder that Agnes Napier had observed, it was sex. Dirty, forbidden sex*, as she had described it, *and nothing more than you would expect from that filthy little trollop Christabelle.* Now Maggie and Lori had convened once more in the Bikini Barista cafe, this time to try and work out what the *hell* it meant for their case. Jimmy was still in Lerwick, and with a few hours to kill before his flight back to Aberdeen, had joined them from the lounge bar of his hotel, where he seemed to be the only patron.

'Who was it she was shagging then?' Lori said, wide-eyed. 'Would Agnes not tell you?'

He shook his head. 'She really is a stupid foolish woman. All she would say was that she saw one of the men going into Christabelle's room and that she heard them *doing* it, as she put it.' He paused for a moment and grinned. 'And guess what?'

'What?' Maggie and Lori said in unison.

'She recorded it. On her phone. She stood outside the door and listened, so she said.'

'God, she really is a piece of work, isn't she?' Maggie said, shaking her head. 'This woman is evil in so many ways.'

'She certainly is,' Jimmy said. 'And as to the who, obviously there are only two possibilities, Drew Henderson and Tom Harper.'

'Three,' Lori said. 'There's three possibilities. There were three guys staying at that lodge.'

'That's *sick*,' Jimmy said. 'You don't think she could have been doing it with her stepfather? Yuk.'

Maggie shrugged. 'It's unsavoury, but it's not impossible I suppose. And you can't get away from how incredibly serious this is. Because Christabelle was only fifteen, and having sex with a minor is a very serious offence, for which you get years in prison and an entry on the sex offenders register. It ruins your life, as well it should,' she added.

'There's been a massive cover-up then?' Lori said. 'And that's what stupid Agnes has been profiting from. She knew who it was, and she knew who was covering it up too.'

'Exactly,' Maggie said. 'Did you ask her to explain the payments she was getting from Kirsty and her husband?'

He laughed. 'Well at first, she denied she was getting any payments at all, until I told her we had been to the police and that they had given us access to her bank records.'

'Cover-up money,' Lori said. 'Got to be. And by the way, just because the payment was coming from their joint account, it doesn't mean they both knew about it. Because they're both so filthy rich I bet they never ever look at their bank statements. See, what if it was Tom Harper that sneaked into sexy wee Christabelle's room, and then a few days later, an audio file pops into his inbox? That would scare the shit out of him, so it would.'

'That's true,' Maggie said. 'So how did Agnes try to explain it.'

Jimmy shrugged. 'She said Kirsty and Tom have a holiday let in the village, and they were paying her to look after it for them.'

Maggie smiled. 'Did you believe her?'

'No,' he shot back. 'I find it hard to believe *anything* she says. But at least that one can be easily proved or disproved if we talk to Kirsty or her husband.'

'And what about the linen cupboard? Did you ask her about it and if she saw anyone taking out the sheets?'

'I did and she's still lying to us. She said she didn't have a clue what I was talking about. She claimed she often forgot to reset the lock, and anyone could have taken the sheets, and it wasn't a big deal anyway because they had hundreds of pairs in the estate's storage warehouse.'

'And then you told her that you knew Alasdair had asked the cleaner for the combination and that the cleaner had left her a note to that effect,' Maggie said.

He nodded. 'I did, and as you might expect, she denied ever seeing any note.'

'Bloody hell, this is all getting *completely* ridiculous,' she said, allowing her frustration to bubble up to the surface. 'So why the *hell* did she come up with her stupid murder allegation for God's sake?'

Jimmy sighed. 'I asked her that of course. She said she was getting fed up seeing Eilish and Christabelle lording it on the television and wanted them taken down a peg or two. She said she knew Eilish would be the prime suspect because the wife always is.'

'And that's *it*?' Maggie said, incredulously.

He shrugged. 'That's what she said. And perhaps I even half-believed her. But only half.'

'Sorry, but that's total bollocks,' Lori said. 'Harper shagged Christabelle then was paying Napier to keep quiet and then he decided he didn't want to be blackmailed any more. Maybe he decided to confess to Kirsty and let Agnes do her worst.'

'And face going to prison?' Maggie said, shaking her head. 'I don't believe he would do that. In fact, I don't believe *any* of this. None of it. Agnes Napier is the very definition of the unreliable witness, and so we have to take anything she's told us with a massive pinch of salt.'

'About Christabelle and the sex too?' Lori asked.

'No, I believe *that*. But the tale that's being woven around it, I don't believe.' She paused for a moment. 'It's back to the drawing board for us, I fear. We need to rip up everything we thought we knew and start afresh.'

***

Providing corroborating evidence for the truth of the old adage *tomorrow is always another day,* the crushing disappointment of the news from Shetland had been soothed to some extent by two interesting developments that emerged the following morning. The first, conveyed to her via text from Frank, was that Eleanor Campbell's facial recognition search for the two girls suspected of being involved in the Drew Henderson murder case had been successful. A grandmother had posted a photograph evidently taken at the end of a school hockey match, the perspiring participants wildly celebrating a victory with sticks held aloft and arms wrapped around their teammates. Conveniently, the photograph featured both girls, and equally conveniently, the proud grandmother had mentioned the name of the school in her post. DS Andy McColl was on his way there to speak to the head teacher, who of course would be able to identify them.

The second development was that Maggie had received a reply to her email to Claudette Barbour, Isla Bonnar's literary agent, informing her she was back in the UK for the Christmas period and would be happy to take a call with the proviso that Maggie send her mobile number in advance so that it would be recognised. Having complied with that request half-an-hour earlier, and with a growing sense of excitement, she picked up her phone and punched in the number she had been given. After a few seconds, it was answered.

'The Barbour Agency, Claudette speaking.'

'Good morning Claudette, it's Maggie Bainbridge. Thanks for taking my call.'

'No that's fine. I was intrigued by your email, and even more so now in the light of what has happened. I just read it in the paper yesterday.'

Maggie nodded. 'You're referring to the death of Isla's partner Drew Henderson I assume? Yes, he was murdered about ten days ago, but the police only recently released his name to the media. I've had no reason to speak to Isla since it happened, but I did speak briefly to Kirsty, and the whole family is devastated as you can imagine.' Or they *claim* to be devastated, Maggie reflected, which is a whole different thing all together.

'If you don't mind,' she continued, 'could you tell me a little about your business relationship with Isla? As I said in my email, it was Kate Strong at The Clarkstone Press who put me in touch with you, and I should tell you in advance, she has a very jaundiced view about my knowledge of the publishing business. One that is well-earned I should say.'

She heard the woman laugh. *'Yes, everyone says it's the darkest of dark arts. As to Isla, I took her on as a client for two reasons. The first was that she has an insane drive to be a successful author, a drive that's as intense as any I've ever seen, and that is something you need if you want to make it. You must possess the resilience to forget about the constant rejections and criticism you will face and plough on regardless. And luckily, Isla has that in spades.'* She hesitated before continuing. *'The second reason I took her on, I'm slightly ashamed to admit, was because of who her sister is. Kirsty Bonnar is box-office, and if she ever decided to tell the story of her life, or even better, decided to try her hand as a novelist, well I would want to be first in the queue to represent her. I thought if I continued to represent Isla, then I would be in a good position should that happen.'*

'And how long have you represented her?'

'Three years, perhaps four, I'm not exactly sure.'

'But no success for Isla in that time,' Maggie mused. 'Why is that, do you think?'

'She's quite a nice writer,' Barbour said, *'but she isn't much of a storyteller I'm afraid, even within the limited confines of the genre she's chosen to write in. And of course, these books must have sex,*

and she's particularly bad at writing that. She once told me she doesn't actually like sex herself, which isn't a great recipe for a writer of steamy romance. She also told me it had been months since she'd made love with her partner.'

Maggie laughed. 'That sounds like the definition of too much information to me. But why does she persist, if she is so terribly bad at it?'

'Haven't you heard of Fifty Shades of Grey?' Barbour asked. *'One hundred million copies sold and counting. It was and still is a massive seller, and it made its author both famous and seriously rich. Despite it being utter rubbish in my opinion.'*

'Is that what it is? Is that what drives her?'

'No question,' the agent said, *'because you see, she wants to be as rich and famous as her big sister, and she sees writing as the only way she can hope to achieve that, however deluded that belief is. But given the general poor quality of the writing in the genre, I've kept her on as a bit of a long shot, just in case by some miracle she does come up with a work with commercial potential.'* She paused. *'And I don't think she will give up, and I suppose I'm helping to keep her hopes alive. It costs me nothing to keep her on my client list, save for an occasional encouraging phone call.'*

'But now her other sister is a best-selling author and never off the television. That must be gutting for her surely, having two famous sisters, after she's spent years slogging away to no avail?'

To Maggie's surprise, Barbour replied, *'Yes, I expect so, but perhaps I was responsible for that success in some little way.'*

'Really?' she said, startled. 'In what way?'

'It goes back about eighteen months ago. I decided to invite her down to London for lunch, at my expense of course, to have what you might call a gentle heart-to-heart. Over the course of that lunch, I told her what I told you, that she was quite a nice writer, but that there were a lot of authors in her genre who were rather better storytellers, which was why she was struggling to get published. To cut a long story short, I suggested that she might find more success if she moved into writing non-fiction. It was completely shameless on my part I know, because I was hoping she might choose to write about Kirsty and all the troubles she was having with her relationship. But the fact remains, there are any number of authors making a fortune writing what I call tabloid biographies. You pick a soap star or a pop idol and you chronicle the pathetic little dramas of their pathetic little lives. And every few weeks or so you leak some other little vignette to the newspapers to keep sales booming. You know, I slept with my sister's gay boyfriend, or my mother thinks she's a werewolf. Nonsense like that. And with the Bonnar name on her side, I thought Isla might make quite a good fist of that.'

Maggie hesitated for a moment, struggling to take in what Charlotte Barbour had just told her. She said, 'You recommended all this to Isla Bonnar? And are you now thinking she encouraged Eilish to use it? To exploit her terrible tragedy? Forgive me for saying this Charlotte, but that sounds bonkers.'

'Bonkers or not, it's worked, hasn't it?' the agent said wryly. *'As you said yourself, Eilish Macbeth and her daughter are never off the morning TV couches. And the last time I looked, they'd sold one*

and a half million of their little comic books. But I should stress, I've no evidence that Isla had anything to do with it.'

'But there was something else you said,' Maggie said, her mind struggling to focus. 'About the troubles Kirsty was having with her relationship? I'm sorry, but that's not something I've picked up on.'

Barbour laughed. *'You obviously don't read the tabloid newspapers dear, do you? Her husband had an affair with an intern at his law firm, about three years ago. And when I say intern, I really mean a work experience girl. She was only seventeen. Nothing illegal of course but he was very lucky not to lose his job. It generated plenty of headlines at the time. Brave Kirsty sticks by love-cheat husband, you can imagine the kind of thing. I'm surprised it passed you by.'*

'Let's just say I was having some issues back then,' Maggie said. 'I barely knew what day of the week it was, let alone what was going on in the news.' With a wry smile, she reflected that back then, she *was* the news, and she would have had no problem in pushing Kirsty Bonnar off the front page. 'But what you say about Kirsty and her husband...that's just more craziness to add to this already crazy affair,' she added, shaking her head in disbelief.

Barbour made no direct comment, simply saying, *'I hope what I've told you has been helpful. Off the top of my head, I can't think of anything else that might be useful. Unless you have any other questions?'*

'No, I can't think of any. And thank you, you've been enormously helpful.'

***

Maggie ended the call with her head spinning even more than it had been after yesterday's incredible developments, an outcome that before the call she would have considered barely possible. For once she was glad Lori wasn't seated at the desk next to her, her assistant having popped down to the Bikini Barista cafe for a late-morning injection of caffeine. Right now, more than anything, she had to be on her own to *think*, to try and make sense of the continuing madness surrounding the case. And then her phone rang. It was Frank.

'My *darling*, so *lovely* to hear from you. It must be what, two and a half hours since we sat across the breakfast table having a lovely chat? But I can understand you missing me already. Many people have told me I have that effect on men.'

He laughed. *'Well you do on this man, that's for sure. But really what it is, I'm just bouncing up and down with excitement after Eleanor's big breakthrough and I was desperate to share with you how it's all going. If you're not too busy that is?'*

'Nope, nothing going on here, nothing at all,' she said, deadpan. 'But seriously, it's amazing news. Well done to Eleanor and I assume we should also raise a glass to grandmas everywhere?'

'Exactly, we should. Anyway, my new DS Andy McColl blue-lighted it down to the school and locked the head teacher in her office until she told him who the two girls were. We've got their names now and we're just waiting on their parents to arrive before we take them down the station for questioning. They're both seventeen so they can be charged with adult crimes but there are certain safeguards still in place because of their age. I'll be making sure

Andy's familiar with these before we ask the lassies anything. We don't want any screw-ups over procedure.'

'That's fantastic Frank. And where is this school exactly?'

'It's called Blair Park School,' he said. *'I looked it up on the internet. It's a posh place on the south side, somewhere near Shawlands. And get this, it costs nearly twenty grand a year to send your little darlings there.'*

'Wait, did you say Blair Park?' Maggie said incredulously. 'Because that's the place that Christabelle Macbeth got sent to, after the incident with the teacher. The place that her auntie Kirsty is paying the fees for.' Suddenly she had a thought. 'Can you send me the photograph that Eleanor matched with please? Quick as you can.'

'Aye, nae bother. You'll have it in ten seconds.' He was silent for a moment. *'There, you should have it now.'*

Simultaneously, she heard the corresponding ping as it landed in her inbox. She wanted to see the photograph for herself, of course she did, but she also knew without looking at it precisely what it would portray. Exactly as Frank's text had described, it captured a sports team's post-match victory celebration, and there they were, all three of them, hogging the limelight in the centre of the shot, their expressions a mixture of pride and arrogance. And in the middle of the trio, even on the hockey field radiating a precocious sexuality, was Christabelle Macbeth.

And at that moment, she realised what she must do. She had often used the jigsaw metaphor to describe the process of solving a complex crime, where each piece eventually locked together to reveal the complete picture. But now she recognised that this case was *so* different from all the others she had worked on. On previous investigations, as each clue was revealed, you could see where it fitted with the others, the picture gradually building up until you only needed one or two final pieces to click into place to reveal the solution to the crime. By contrast, this one was a mess. It was like that moment right at the start when you opened the box and tipped all the pieces on to the table. As you looked at the pile in front of you, you knew of course every piece required to solve the puzzle was in there somewhere, but when you examined any individual one, you had no idea where it fitted. And sometimes, you picked up a piece and were absolutely convinced that the manufacturers had made a mistake, that this one surely belonged in a totally different puzzle altogether. This was exactly where Maggie was with this investigation. A pile of clues had been tipped out onto the table but there was no guidance as to how each one fitted with any other. But they *would* fit, she knew they would, just like always.

'Frank darling,' she said quickly. 'I hate to be rude, but I need to go. I need to go for a walk, in the park. My head's exploding, or at least it will if I don't get some air.'

He laughed. *'You've reached that moment, haven't you, when your giant brain turns itself up to eleven and starts whirring away like a supercomputer? Off you go then, and wrap up well, because it's bloody freezing out there. And give me a wee call when you've worked everything out. Then I'll nip round to wherever we have to go to and make the necessary arrests.'*

She threw on her coat, feeling around in the pockets to make sure her hat and gloves were in them. Pulling them on, she tossed her handbag over her shoulder and stepped out into the street. Her route would be both pleasant and interesting, first traversing the full length of University Avenue and then down into beautiful Kelvingrove Park, before perhaps heading out onto Sauchiehall Street and following that iconically named thoroughfare until the point it was cut in half by the urban motorway system. Or maybe she would climb up to the top of the hill and find a quiet bench somewhere, assuming it wasn't too cold to sit for the hour or more she would need. No, that was plain daft, she would freeze to death if she did that. Instead, she would keep walking, circling the perimeter of the park as many times as required until she had finally worked it all out, or at the very least, worked out what it was she still didn't know.

So now it was time to mentally tip all the pieces out of the box and sift through them one by one, making an audit of everything she knew or thought she knew, not worrying at this stage whether any of them fitted with any other. Starting with the sixty-four-thousand-dollar question. Was Alasdair Macbeth's death a murder, or wasn't it? Agnes Napier had told them the victim's feet had been dangling three feet off the ground, but she was a liar, so that had to be treated with something more than caution. But Kirsty Bonnar, who had discovered the hanging at eight o'clock or thereabouts on Christmas morning, had recalled looking up into his face as he hung there, a much more reliable statement. That was the one that clinched it. Yes, it had been a murder, and everything else had to be evaluated in that context. Next, there was the extraordinary statement by the housekeeper that one of the men had gone into Christabelle's room and had sex with her, an act that, twelve months ago, would have been illegal due to her being just fifteen years of age. There were just three possible suspects for that crime, but only one of those,

Tom Harper, was paying Napier fifteen hundred pounds a month, apparently to buy the housekeeper's silence. Quite extraordinary, but how was that morally reprehensible sex act connected to Alasdair Macbeth's murder, as Maggie knew it must surely be? Then there was the bizarre business of Eilish Macbeth's best-selling book and the connection or otherwise to her sister Isla, the aspiring author who had been advised by her agent to give up fiction and try her hand at non-fiction instead. There was the murder of Isla Bonnar's partner Drew Henderson, a death that was surely one hundred percent connected to the killing of Alasdair Macbeth. Now it had emerged that the young vixens who had seemingly lured him to his death were school friends of Christabelle.

As she walked along Kelvin Way, treading carefully to avoid patches of slippery ice underfoot, seemingly unconnected facts pertaining to the case leapt into her head. *It was Tom Harper who had cut down Alasdair's hanging body, before the police and paramedics had a chance to examine it. A man must have been involved in the murder because Alasdair Macbeth was six foot tall and weighed sixteen stone. Stupid Agnes Napier is refusing to say who it was who had sex with Christabelle in her room. Eilish hadn't been sleeping with her husband because she had seen her hopes of wealth and status dashed through the business ineptitude of her father-in-law. Kirsty, the woman with seemingly everything, was jealous of her sisters because they had children, and she didn't. Isla and Drew had put their house up for sale. Someone had engineered access to the Christmas Lodge linen cupboard in order to fashion a rope from the spare sheets.*

Halfway along, in a sudden change of plan, she turned sharp right to cross the road, intending to take one of the paths that headed in the direction of the city's beautiful Art Gallery and Museum. That would be a smarter idea, she decided. She would find a quiet corner of the lovely cafe, take out a ballpoint and start to scribble everything down on a napkin, laid out in a random pattern but in such a way that connections might be more easily visualised. It would need to be a bloody big napkin mind you, given the explosion of facts that were now filling her head, but she could always lay a couple alongside each other if she needed to.

Ten minutes later, she had set up camp, essential fortification provided by a large americano and an iced gingerbread square, the latter a delicacy that had become an essential part of her life since she moved to Glasgow. Mischievously, she took a close-up photograph of the cake and sent it on to Frank with three grinning emojis. Then she got to work, and after a couple of minutes of scribbling, it was all laid out in front of her, each piece of the jigsaw metaphorically tipped up on the table. Taking a sip of her coffee, she examined the collage, her head darting from side to side as she drew imaginary connecting lines between two disparate facts then erased them just as quickly when it became apparent that a particular connection was a dead end. Occasionally she would pick up her pen and draw an actual line on the napkin when a connection seemed irrefutable, but with growing annoyance, she realised there weren't too many of them. Gradually, it became apparent what the problem was. As had been the case in so many of her previous investigations, there was something missing, some small but critical fact that could very well shine a light on everything. But what was it, that was the question? She put down her pen and stared hard at the napkin, her brow furrowed as she struggled to make sense of it.

And then she saw it. A fact, written on the napkin in black ink, but a fact that until that moment she had not realised the critical significance of. She rammed her hand into her handbag and snatched out her phone, feverishly sliding her finger down to Lori's number and prodding it hard.

The girl answered promptly. *'Hi Maggie, how you doing? I'm just having a wee sneaky pie and beans at the Barista...'*

'Sorry Lori, no time for that,' Maggie barked. 'Listen, do you know what school Isla Bonnar's kids go to? It'll be a primary somewhere, they're only young still.'

If her assistant was surprised by the question, she disguised it well. *'Well, they live on that new estate that's spread out past Summerston,'* she said. *'The builders had to put up two new schools on it, a Protestant one and a Catholic one as well. Hang on, I'm just trying to remember what they were called. No, I'll have to look it up on my phone, hang on.'* She was silent for a second then said, *'Oh aye, that's it. Dawsholm Rise Primary is the Protestant one and the other one is called St Francis of Assisi. They're right next to one another according to this wee map I'm looking at.'*

'So which one would the Bonnar kids go to?' Maggie asked. 'Quickly, please.'

'Just hold your horses, because I'm way ahead of you there,' Lori said. *'I'm looking at Kirsty Bonnar's Wikipedia entry right now. And nah, there's nothing about the Bonnar family being brought up as Catholics, so it must be the Dawsholm Rise one.'*

'Okay, I think I've left my car keys on my desk, so can you go and grab it from my usual parking spot and meet me in the Art Gallery carpark. Quick as you can. I'll explain everything on the way. On the way to the school I mean.'

Next, she called Frank, launching into her speech before he even had time to say *hello*. 'Darling, I've not much time to explain, but I've got two things to ask you. Firstly, can you get a uniformed female PC and meet me at Dawsholm Rise Primary School? It's on that new estate on the north-west of the city, where Isla Bonnar lives. And by the way, it's a kind of low-key family liaison matter, so it would be better if the PC didn't turn up wearing her stab jacket with a baton and a taser hanging off it.'

'Message understood,' he said. *'Keep it low-key. Got that.'*

'Exactly,' Maggie said, 'And you need to get there in time for school coming-out time. It's really important, trust me.'

'I know better than to ask why you need the uniformed PC,' he said, half-laughing, half-serious.

'It'll be obvious when you get there,' she said hurriedly. 'The second thing is, can you send someone round to Isla's house before she gets back from the school pick-up, then go in and seize her laptop before she can wipe anything. I know you should have paperwork and the like, but it's vitally important she doesn't get the chance to wipe anything.'

He laughed. *'Will do, and I'm sure we can sort out the paperwork afterwards. But just one question. Is this it? I mean, does this mean you've solved it? Everything?'*

'I think so,' she said. 'But if you don't mind me saying, I think you'll find that was actually three questions.'

Chapter 25

For the first ten minutes of the journey, they travelled in silence, as Maggie wrestled with the rightness or otherwise of her planned course of action. It was a plan not without risks and perhaps morally questionable too, but the problem was, she could see no other way of getting the vital answer she needed. But what the hell, in just a few seconds she was going to have to let Lori in on it and that wise young head would no doubt give her opinion and give it *fortissimo* at that. The girl probably wasn't going to like it – no, scratch that, she *definitely* wasn't going to like it – but Maggie would pull rank if need be, unless of course Lori had a better idea, which was not outside the bounds of possibility, given how smart she was.

'So what the hell's this all about Maggie?' her assistant asked suddenly, evidently unable to put up with the silence any longer, 'and why are we racing to that school at a hundred miles an hour? Because you've not said a word since we left the Art Galleries, not a single word. Except for telling me to drive like a flipping bampot, that is. And just so you know, I can't go any faster than I'm going. It's a thirty mile an hour speed limit along here, in case you haven't noticed.'

'Yes, I'm really sorry,' Maggie said. 'My brain's been in a total spin, and I've been trying to calm it down, without much success I'm afraid. And mad things still keep popping into my head, even though I'm trying so hard to shut the door to anything new.' She wondered for a second whether she should tell Lori about one particular mad thing that had appeared out of nowhere just a minute ago, about the taxi that had turned up outside Isla Bonnar's door just as they were leaving after their interview with the woman. But since she had no idea yet if it had any significance for their case, she decided to stick to the matter in hand. 'But yes, what the hell is this all about, that's a good question. To try to answer that, let me ask you a question instead.' She hesitated then said, 'Can you remember what time it was that Kirsty Bonnar discovered Alasdair Macbeth hanging in the big living room?'

Lori nodded. 'Of course. It was eight o'clock or thereabouts, that's what she said. And Agnes Napier said the same.'

'Exactly. And can you remember when you were a kid, what it was like on Christmas morning? I can, and that's a longer time ago for me than it is for you.' Not waiting for Lori to respond, she continued, 'You hardly slept a wink, and when you woke up you kept shouting to your mum and dad *has Santa been yet?* And then eventually they would let you get up and that was normally at half past six or some ridiculous time like that.' She paused for a moment. 'Don't you see Lori, don't you see?'

'Where were the wee kids?' Lori said, open mouthed. 'That's what you mean, isn't it? Why weren't they up and running around like crazy, like they should have been?'

'Got it in one. And that's the question I'm going to ask one of the Bonnar kids in about ten minutes' time, whilst you distract the mother. Why weren't they up at the crack of dawn, opening their presents?'

'What?' Lori said, astonished. 'No way Maggie, you can't do that. The oldest one's only about six or seven, for God's sake, and the poor wee things have just lost their daddy. Or had you forgotten that too?'

'No, I hadn't forgotten. That just makes it ten times more difficult,' she said, the question raising even more doubts in her mind about the saneness of her plan.

Lori shook her head. 'But you're still going to go through with it, aren't you? I can tell.' The girl paused for a second. 'If you ask me, you've taken complete leave of your senses. Don't you realise that if we do this, we'll probably get arrested for child abuse or abduction or something like that. And what do you mean, whilst I distract the mother?' she added acerbically.

Maggie laughed. 'We won't get arrested, honestly. Frank will be there, and he's bringing a woman PC with him, or at least I hope he is. It'll all be official. All I want is for you to buttonhole Isla Bonnar at the school gate and keep her in conversation for a minute or two, just so that I have a minute to talk to the little kid.'

Lori looked distressed. 'Bloody hell Maggie, I'm not happy with this at all. What am I going to say to her for a start?'

'Anything. Just tell her we've got a couple of follow-up questions that we thought of after our visit to her home.' And then a thought came to her. 'No actually, ask her this. Who was it that the taxi dropped off at her house just after we left that time? Don't you remember, there was all that kerfuffle with our driver when he was trying to set off?'

She nodded. 'Oh aye, I remember that now. Do you think it's important?'

Maggie shrugged. 'I don't know. But perhaps we'll find out once you've asked her.'

'Fair enough,' Lori said, then added in a suspicious tone, 'And you've told Frank all about this plan of yours? And he said it was all okay, did he?'

Her boss gave her a sheepish look. 'Well, not *exactly.*'

Lori frowned. 'What, you've not exactly told him, or he's not exactly said it would be okay?'

'Both,' Maggie admitted. 'But he *will* be okay with it, once I've explained it to him. Anyway,' she said, anxious to change the subject, 'you've got that family photo on your phone, haven't you? The one that Agnes Napier sent us. Can you remember the kids' names? Because I think she did tell us.'

'Aye, I remember them. Isla's two are called Daniel and Hope. The wee girl's seven I think, the wee boy a couple of years younger. I'm not sure if he's at school yet.'

'And do you think you'll be able to recognise little Hope from that photograph? Because we need to look for her as she comes through the school gate.'

'Bloody hell Maggie, you're asking a lot,' Lori said, shaking her head. 'All these wee ones look exactly the same in their blue sweatshirt uniforms. I don't know if I could tell one from the other. Not unless I got really close, and that would be seriously weird.'

Maggie sighed. 'Yes, I thought that too. Maybe we just have to wait until she sees her mummy and then we make our move.'

'Do you not hear how that sounds?' Lori said incredulously. 'We're going to make our *move* outside a primary school, pushing away a tiny wee lassie's mummy so that we can ask the kid a few questions? With the greatest of respect Maggie, you've gone a little bit nutty. No offence, but you have.'

She laughed. 'I know, you're right, it is a bit crazy. But I only want to ask Hope one question, that's all, and I'll have a nice woman police officer standing alongside me when I do it. And you too of course,' she added. 'You'll have your phone out to record what the wee one tells us.'

Lori frowned again. 'Is this to gather evidence? Because I don't think you would be able to use the statement of a seven-year-old in court. And anyway, how can I do that and distract the mother at the same time?'

Maggie sighed. 'Hadn't thought of that, but I'm sure you'll work something out. And for your peace of mind, we won't be calling little Hope as a witness. All I'm trying to do is get corroboration for my own crazy theory of what happened, and I'm very well aware that the police will still have their work cut out to make any charges stick. Because believe me, when I say my theory is crazy, I mean *really* crazy. But I also happen to believe it's true.'

'Well anyway, we're here now,' Lori said, nodding towards the school sign that had just appeared on their left. 'And look, there's Frank across the road. I'll see if I can get a parking space and we can join him.'

Maggie glanced at her watch. 'We've got five minutes before the wee ones are let out, so time is tight. I'll give him a little wave, so he knows we're here.' And then suddenly, she gasped as she recognised the figure standing next to him. 'Wow, it's Lexy McDonald. In *uniform*.' She leant over and parped the horn, then made a broad smile as Frank and his colleague recognised who it was who had startled them. A few minutes later, she and Lori were standing beside the two police officers, watching their consternation grow as Maggie explained her plan to them. As she had expected, it didn't go down well.

'That's bloody madder than the maddest thing in the world,' Frank said, shaking his head. 'We've got safeguarding protocols in place when it comes to dealing with very young children, and they're there for very good reason.'

'I know that,' she said, feeling herself becoming agitated. 'And believe me, I've already changed my mind about a hundred times as to whether I should do this or not. But I need to know if my theory is correct or not, before I tell you all about it. It's so crazy, I'm worried you'll just laugh you see. That's why I need to ask little Hope the question. It's for me, no-one else. You see, I think my explanation as to what happened is right, but this will make me one hundred percent sure.'

'Why can't we just ask the mother your bloody question?' he said, uncharacteristically irritated. 'What's wrong with doing that?'

Maggie shrugged. 'Because she'll lie, just like they all have been lying all through this. And that'll get us nowhere. I'm sorry, but that's the truth.'

Lexy wrinkled her nose. 'I can kind of see where Maggie is coming from sir,' she said tentatively. 'But I can also see how it could get difficult. But isn't it worth the risk? If it helps us with our two murder cases I mean? And if the wee girl gets distressed in any way, then of course we would stop immediately.'

He shook his head vigorously. 'No, it bloody well isn't worth the risk, since you're asking. And you're a barrister Maggie,' he continued, jabbing a finger in her direction. 'You more than anyone should see what would happen if this ever turned up in a court of law. I can just see the smirk on the face of the defence brief when he or she tells the jury that the prosecution is relying on the testimony of a wee six or seven year old lassie.'

'But it's precisely because I'm a barrister that I know what the law is on this subject,' Maggie responded, feeling uneasy that she was going to have to disagree with him. 'There's nothing in the law that says you can't question a child in connection with a crime, and there's nothing that says the child must have a parent or a guardian alongside them either. I'm certain of this because the exact same situation arose on a case I worked on a few years ago.' Not only a few years ago, she thought ruefully, but a whole lifetime ago too. 'That's why I wanted you to bring along a uniformed female officer. Because obviously if anyone saw some random adult approaching a child outside the school gates, it would quite rightly raise alarm bells, whereas with a police officer present, they would be curious, but they would be unlikely to intervene. And it means the interview will be properly documented in the case files and not just the word of a private investigator.' She turned and smiled at Lexy. 'And I'm so pleased he chose you Lexy. It's fantastic. And you look amazing in your uniform by the way.'

Lexy laughed. 'I've always kept it hanging up in the station. I quite like wearing it from time to time. Makes me feel like a real police officer.'

'Alright, can we just break up the love-in, please?' Frank said. Then he grinned. 'Maggie flipping Bainbridge, you've got this all worked out, haven't you?'

She smiled. 'Well, not really, it's just that I had to investigate the law on this for that previous case. And it's stuck in my mind ever since.' She paused. 'And just to reinforce the point I made earlier, I'm not suggesting for a moment that we use the child's evidence in any court case. But it's important we get to hear what she has to say to help us get to the truth.'

He sighed. 'Aye, well fair enough. But I can't imagine the mother is just going to stand around and let it happen. If there's a scene, we call it off immediately, okay? There's no way we're going in heavy-handed, because that *would* screw up the case, big time. Police harassment is never a good look in court.'

She hesitated for a moment. 'Lori's got a few questions to ask Isla. We're hoping that'll distract her whilst we're talking to the child.'

He sighed again. 'Bloody hell, I'm liking this less and less with every moment that passes.'

'And I don't like it any more than you do,' she said ruefully. 'It seems very sneaky I admit, but I can't see any other way to get the information we need.'

'It wouldn't be sneaky if *you* did the questioning,' Lori piped up, looking directly at Frank. 'Of the mother I mean. You could just stick your wee warrant card in her face and say *Isla Bonnar, I wish to question you in connection with the murder of Drew Henderson and the murder of Alasdair Macbeth. You do not have to say anything, but anything you do say....*'

He laughed. 'Just so you know, we only say all that stuff if we're arresting someone.' He paused for a moment, evidently considering the matter. Then, to Maggie's surprise, he said, 'Okay then, she's obviously a person of interest in the murder of her partner, the case on which I am the senior investigating officer, so I will on this occasion accede to your request. Although I don't bloody know why. I must be going soft in my old age.'

She grinned. 'You're not old, just slightly rusting. But that would be amazing if you would do that. Though it won't get you into any trouble, will it?' she added, suddenly concerned.

He shrugged. 'Trouble's my middle name, you know that. No, it'll be fine. I *suppose.*'

Just then, she became aware of a rising tide of excited little voices coming from behind her, and as the sweet music reached a crescendo, Maggie spun round to view the scene. Eyes narrowed, she craned her neck forwards and focussed on the untidy scrum of parents and kids gathering around the gate, then nudged Lori.

'Can you spot either of them?' she asked.

'There's Isla, just left of the gate,' her assistant said, pointing. 'Hang on, she's on the move.' They watched Bonnar edging her way through the crowd, and a second or so later the purpose became clear. 'That must be the teacher,' Lori continued. 'She's got a lanyard around her neck. And look, there's the wee daughter grabbing hold of her coat.'

Bonnar smiled down at her daughter and said something, at which point the little girl let go of the coat and skipped away to join a group of friends who were chatting animatedly a few feet away.

'Right, let's go,' Maggie said. 'Lexy, are you ready?'

The DC gave a thumbs up. 'Yep, I'm ready.'

Frank nodded towards Isla, who was still in conversation with the teacher. 'I'm just going to let this play out before I dive in with my big hobnailed boots. I might not even be needed if you're quick with your question.'

Maggie gave him a wry smile, knowing from her own experience with her lovely son Ollie that whilst the question might be short, with a small child, the chances were the answer would be anything but. Delightful, true, but brevity wasn't normally a skill treasured by a wee one. 'Don't count on it,' she said, 'and we can hardly ask the little girl to hurry up, can we?'

'Too true,' he conceded. 'But anyway, best of luck.'

Maggie and Lexy took the few steps over to where Hope Bonnar had convened with her little schoolmates. 'Good afternoon Hope,' she said brightly. 'I'm Maggie, and this nice police lady is Lexy.'

'Hello,' the little girl said, smiling. She was a strikingly beautiful child, hardly surprising given the attractiveness of her mother and her two aunts.

'Are you looking forward to Santa coming?' Lexy asked her.

'Yes, I am,' she replied earnestly, 'because last year he forgot we were staying in a special Christmas house, and we didn't get our presents until we got back to Glasgow and that made me and my brother very sad. Although it was okay in the end because I got a lovely doll's house and my brother got a Hotwheels garage set.'

Annoyed, Maggie realised she hadn't properly thought through the aftermath of Alasdair Macbeth's body being discovered. Presumably the parents must have gathered up the presents and loaded them into their cars before they raced back to Glasgow, struggling to maintain some semblance of normality for the young children.

'And we've sent Santa a map to our house,' the little girl continued, 'so that he doesn't make a mistake *this* year.' She gave a heart-melting frown as she said it, at the same time placing her hands on her hips.

'No, I'm sure he'll be able to find it without any problem if you've done that,' Maggie said. 'That's very clever of you and your mummy.' Then she hesitated, steeling herself for the question she was about to ask.

'And last year, can you remember what happened when you were at that lovely house? The house that silly Santa and his silly reindeers forgot about?'

The girl nodded. 'Yes, they were very silly, weren't they? But he is very busy on Christmas Eve, so I suppose sometimes he makes mistakes.' Maggie smiled, recognising the voice of an adult in Hope's response.

'Me and my cousins were very excited when we woke up, but we were told that Santa hadn't been and so we had to stay in our beds and not go downstairs because he never delivers presents if he sees that children are awake, and that's because he would always want to chat to them and introduce us to Rudolph and his friends, but he's too busy to do all of that on Christmas Eve, isn't he?' She gave a sad smile. 'But he didn't come at all.'

Maggie gave DC McDonald a knowing look, took a breath, then said quietly, 'And who was it that told you you couldn't go downstairs to open your presents? Can you tell me and Lexy please? If it's okay with you?'

'It's okay with me,' she said. 'It was my mummy and my auntie Eilish and my big cousin Christabelle. That's who told me.'

Chapter 26

Things moved at lightning pace after the Dawsholm school interview, but Maggie felt bad for several days afterwards, regretting she had put Frank in the horrible position of having to choose between his love for her and his duty as a policeman. But she consoled herself with the fact that without her intervention, the two murder cases would probably still have been floundering in a sea of confusion. Now, three arrests had been made and the Procurator Fiscal was drawing up charges, a complicated affair given the crazy mechanics of this most convoluted of murder plots. A paucity of hard evidence meant that much of the case was circumstantial, which was never a totally satisfactory state of affairs. But the Fiscal could see that Maggie's theory of how it was done answered every question that an aggressive defence barrister might ask, and so, after some soul-searching, decided it was safe to put the outcome in the hands of a jury.

For Yash Patel of the Chronicle, Christmas had come early, with this juiciest of juicy stories slipping down his chimney beautifully wrapped and set to dominate the media narrative for weeks and weeks to come. It had everything: the gorgeous award-winning writer of *My Daddy's Dead* exposed as a murderess and a fraud, an underage sex scandal covered up by an Oscar-nominated actress, and three evil women shown to be the architects of a premeditated murder plot breathtaking in both its planning and its execution. The paper's lawyers had moved fast, as was their normal *modus operandi,* and had secured an exclusive on the story by placing Maggie and her little company under contract. Now any media company who wished to speak to Miss Bainbridge or any of her associates was required to pay a substantial syndication fee. As part of that arrangement, the Christmas get-together she had planned for their little teams had been seriously upscaled, courtesy of the Chronicle, and now they were gathered in one of the biggest function rooms of one of Glasgow's swankiest hotels, enjoying a delicious and belt-busting lunch, accompanied by some seriously expensive wines from a seriously expensive wine-list. Soon Maggie was to present her astonishing theory to the world's media, who were seated at a dozen or so extravagantly decorated circular tables each able to seat a dozen hacks, but right now she was just so happy to have the whole gang together for the first time in a while. They had their own table of course, and with Eleanor Campbell and Jimmy's lovely girlfriend Frida both present, there was naturally much talk of babies. Lorilynn Logan and Lexy McDonald, seated alongside each other and newly established as best friends, were giggling away at a private item of amusement. Maggie speculated from their regular but furtive looks in his direction that Patel, notably good-looking and somewhat of a peacock when it came to attire, was the object of their mirth and perhaps their desire too. Jimmy, Frank and Ronnie French were talking football as was their want, although the Stewart brothers appeared to be mainly in listening mode as the Cockney detective eulogised about various Scottish footballers - Jocks, as he insisted on calling them - who had played for his beloved West Ham United over the years. It was such a lovely occasion, and for about the eighteen-millionth time in the last three years, she rejoiced in how lucky she had been that Frank and Jimmy Stewart had entered her life.

But now, on an adjacent table, Patel was on his feet, holding an empty champagne glass in one hand – a glass which he had himself emptied several times that afternoon – and a spoon in the other. With a discreet clink and a clearing of the throat, he waited until the hubbub of conversation died down before speaking.

'Ladies and Gentlemen, welcome to the Glasgow Grampian Hotel, and Merry Christmas to all of you. I hope you've enjoyed this amazing lunch and the superb service from the excellent staff.' He paused whilst his audience applauded in approval. 'Thank you,' he continued, 'it really was wonderful. And if I can just say something before I hand you over to Maggie Bainbridge and Jimmy Stewart of Bainbridge Associates...' He paused again and smiled. 'Which is, don't forget to pick up your bills before you all scoot off back to your news desks. Especially your bar bills,' he added sardonically, getting the roar of laughter he was expecting. 'But without further ado, let me introduce Maggie and Jimmy.' The pair got to their feet amid further enthusiastic applause from the gathered media representatives, acknowledged by Maggie with a self-deprecating wave.

'If I was in a rock band I'd shout *hello Glasgow* at this point,' she began, 'but I'm not, so I'll just say good afternoon instead.' She hesitated for a moment before continuing. 'So yes, what can I tell you about the astonishing Bonnar affair, or the Christmas Lodge murders as Yash's paper likes to call them, even though only one of the murders actually took place there? This, I have to say, is both one of the most difficult and at the same time most crazy affairs we've ever been involved in. And much of the reason for the difficulty was that it was *so* difficult to work out a credible motive for the killing of Alasdair Macbeth or indeed of Drew Henderson either. That's right Jimmy, isn't it? Until you put our motive dilemma firmly in focus, that was.'

'Did I?' he said modestly. 'It was a team effort I think.'

'No no, I remember your exact words,' Maggie said. 'You said *where's the passion, the anger, the bitterness, the seething resentment, the all-consuming hatred, the lust, the envy, the greed?* There didn't seem to be any of that directed at either of our victims. And that's when I finally realised.' She paused. 'That's when I realised the deaths of Alasdair Macbeth and Drew Henderson were nothing more than collateral damage in a much wider plot.'

The room responded with a sharp gasp. 'Yes, exactly, it is very hard to grasp,' Maggie said, giving a wry smile. 'But when we looked more closely for the anger and the bitterness and the resentment, and yes, the pure hatred too, it was there, right in front of us, staring us in the face. These and more were the emotions Eilish Macbeth and Isla Bonnar felt towards their sister Kirsty.'

Jimmy nodded. 'Yes, what they hated with an all-consuming passion was the fame and attention her talent had brought her, and more than anything in the world, they wanted to have the same for themselves.'

'That's exactly right,' Maggie agreed. 'And it all could be traced back to their childhood and their parents failed marriage. Kirsty was older than her two sisters when the split happened, and the family court was prepared to support her driving desire to live with her dad rather than her mother. Eilish and Isla, being so young, were not given the same opportunity. We heard from the housekeeper at Christmas Lodge that their mother Nan Bonnar was not a nice woman, and we might speculate that it was this which caused her husband to break up the marriage. Whatever the case, Kirsty went on to have a gilded childhood, with her adoring father supporting her in every way he could in her desire to become an actress, whereas the younger sisters were brought up in an atmosphere of bitterness and recrimination. I think we can assume it was not a happy home, and it was that which sowed the seeds for the terrible events that followed twenty-five years later.'

'Yes, there's no doubt the younger Bonnar sisters were seriously starved of love and attention as kids,' Jimmy said, 'and so as adults it was what they craved more than anything. Quite simply, they wanted to *be* someone, just like their sister.'

Maggie nodded. 'Exactly. In Eilish's case, she thought she had found the route to the status she craved through her marriage to Alasdair Macbeth. One day his father would die, and his son would inherit the estate and his title, and Eilish would become Lady Macbeth.'

Jimmy laughed. 'How apt is that title? And with her great beauty, she would be a big name in the society magazines, which is what she wanted so much. She had it all worked out. So much so, she was prepared to sit and wait for the inevitable death of her father-in-law.'

'And as for Isla, she dreamed of being a famous author, selling millions and millions of books,' Maggie said, 'but unfortunately her talent as a novelist did not match her ambition.'

'But then, eighteen months ago the landscape changed dramatically,' Jimmy said. 'Firstly, the death of old Robert Macbeth revealed that his estate was bankrupt and, in that moment, Eilish's dreams went up in smoke. She could still have called herself Lady Macbeth of course, but without the money and land to go with it, she would soon become a figure of ridicule. But conversely and at about the same time, Isla Bonnar had had an epiphany after her literary agent Claudette Barbour had attempted to give her some career advice. Barbour suggested she should turn her hand to non-fiction instead of the soft-porn rubbish she'd been writing, and had even told her that stories of family tragedy were often big sellers. The only problem was that the Bonnar family didn't have a family tragedy to write about.'

'Which is when Isla had her crazy idea,' Maggie interjected. 'Suddenly, she could see how her dreams and those of her sister could be fulfilled. And so, a dastardly scheme was meticulously conceived and planned, a scheme that was to be executed over a period of two years or more, and a scheme that would involve Eilish's precocious daughter Christabelle too, who already shared the same driving desire for fame and recognition as her mother and her aunt. But for the plan to work, there had to be a family tragedy, and what better tragedy could there be than the suicide of a father of two on a Christmas Eve?'

'Coldly and cynically, Isla and Eilish plotted it all out,' Jimmy continued. 'Eilish had never loved her husband, having only married him for his expected inheritance, so she was delighted to go along with the scheme. Alasdair was to be murdered, with his death staged to look like a suicide driven by his family and marriage troubles. But they needed a man to help string him up, which meant that Isla's partner Drew Henderson had to be ensnared. She had come to hate him for his cruelness and infidelity and saw that his predilection for very young women presented an opportunity for him to be coerced into assisting them. So the young Lolita

Christabelle was recruited to seduce her uncle. And that's what she did, on the Sunday night before Christmas.'

'That's disgusting,' someone shouted from the audience.

'It is,' Maggie agreed. 'The police have subsequently discovered through interviews that no actual intercourse took place, but that Drew was pleasured, if that's the right term. It's very unsavoury, and very embarrassing for me to say it too,' she added, reddening. 'But nonetheless, Henderson had now committed a sex act with a minor and so was under their control.'

Jimmy nodded. 'Although unknown to any of the killers, an obstacle was about to present itself.'

'Yes, because the nosey busybody housekeeper Agnes Napier had seen Henderson sneaking into Christabelle's room and had made an audio recording of the encounter. But more of that later.' Maggie paused for a moment. 'On Christmas Eve, everything was in place. Wine had been flowing at dinner, and Alasdair was very drunk, having had his glass filled at every opportunity by the killers. By eleven o'clock, everyone had gone to bed, and the victim, who was sleeping alone, was out cold in his room. Eilish Macbeth stayed in her room where she was sleeping with the three youngest children, whilst Isla, Drew and Christabelle went into Alasdair's room and killed him by smothering him with his pillow. He was a strong guy, but so was Drew, who was a muscled builder, and there were three of them too. There may have been a struggle, we don't know that for sure, but eventually the evil deed was done.'

'The next part was probably the hardest bit,' Jimmy said, 'and that was getting him downstairs without disturbing Kirsty and Tom and the old mother Nan and the housekeeper Agnes Napier, all of whom were sleeping on the same floor. Whilst Isla and Drew dragged the body downstairs as quietly as they could, Christabelle went back to her room to collect the rope she had been making over the previous two days. Meanwhile, Eilish stationed herself just outside the nursery door, where she could intercept and delay anyone who might have heard something and had got up to investigate. But in the event, that wasn't needed. It all went completely smoothly.'

Maggie nodded. 'At this point, it's worth saying something about the rope, because it was very important in the murder scheme, obviously. It was made from sheets, and to do that, the murderers needed to gain access to the linen cupboard in which they were stored, which was secured by a combination lock. And this fact is one of many that shows how coldly premeditated these murders were. The Macbeth family had arrived early at Christmas Lodge, about an hour before the cleaners were due to finish, but they were allowed in because of how cold it was outside. Not long afterwards, Alasdair Macbeth asked Jana, one of the cleaners, for the combination so that he could retrieve an extra pillow for his stepdaughter Christabelle. But of course this was just an excuse so that Alasdair was witnessed by an independent party asking for access, which would support the premise that it was he who had fashioned the rope with which he hung himself.'

'When in fact it was Christabelle who needed to know the combination, so that *she* could take the sheets and make the rope,' Jimmy explained. 'But it turned out the cleaner wasn't allowed to give out the combination to guests, that was the sole preserve of the housekeeper. So she left a note in the kitchen letting Agnes Napier know of Alasdair's request.'

Maggie laughed. 'And we've plenty left to say about that evil old devil. But suffice to say she must have acted on Jana's message whilst deliberately hiding the fact from us, and that made us question whether it really was murder. It was very confusing. Anyway, to get back to the murder itself, Isla and Drew carried the body to the lounge, where they were joined by Christabelle with the rope. It was slung over the beam and secured, and then two chairs were fetched from the dining room, on which Isla and Drew stood in order to hoist Alasdair up several feet above the ground. His head was placed through the noose and then they let him drop, breaking his neck in the process. One chair was left lying on its side, the other was returned to the dining room, and the deception was complete.'

Jimmy nodded. 'The only problem was, Alasdair was left dangling too high for him to have killed himself by stepping off that chair, a critical mistake that the murderers evidently didn't notice at the time. They wouldn't have hung about the scene of course, if you forgive the terrible pun. As soon as it was done, they would have rushed upstairs and gone back to bed.' He paused. 'And then eight hours later, Kirsty Bonnar came downstairs and discovered the body, whilst Eilish and Isla made sure that the wee kids were kept in their bedroom.'

'That's right,' Maggie said, 'and now, with Alasdair's death accepted as suicide, the next part of Isla Bonnar's evil plan could kick into action. Because now they had a real family tragedy to write about, and she already had a killer title for the book, ready and waiting. *My Daddy's Dead but He Still Loves Me.*' Maggie paused, took a breath, then looked straight at the audience, eyebrow raised in wonder. 'I mean, you've got to admit it, it was a work of total genius, perfectly designed to tug at the heart strings. And it worked, just like her agent Claudette Barbour had predicted. Overnight, the book, ghost written for her sister Eilish, became a sensation, and the photogenic Macbeths were everywhere on the media. And just occasionally, so as not to be accused of over-exploiting the grief of a child, little Mirabelle would join her mother and big sister on the sofa and look into the camera and say *my daddy's dead but he still loves me,* and a million viewers would burst into tears then go out and buy the book. As I said, it was bloody genius.'

'But we told you of a wee snag, you'll recall,' Jimmy said. 'That Agnes Napier had made an audio recording of Drew Henderson and Christabelle Macbeth engaged in a sex act. Well, she decided it would be smart to use it to indulge in a spot of blackmail. She told Drew and Isla she knew what had happened, and if they didn't play ball she would go straight to the police and tell them what Drew had done.'

'Isla Bonnar of course didn't give two figs about what happened to her partner,' Maggie said, 'but she didn't want the police poking their noses into the family affairs. She told her sister Kirsty what had happened and pleaded for her to pay Napier what she wanted to stop her beloved Drew going to prison. Kirsty of course didn't want the adverse publicity either, even although she had nothing to do with the affair, and fifteen hundred quid a month was nothing to her anyway, so she agreed. Which, to be fair, sent us down a blind alley for quite a while, because it made us suspect it was her husband Tom Harper who'd had a sexual encounter with Christabelle.'

'Meanwhile, Isla's plan was ticking along beautifully,' Jimmy said. 'The book was selling by the truckload and she and her sister were sharing the massive royalties, so much so that Isla was in a position to sell her modest house and move to somewhere altogether grander.'

'Yes, that's something I missed when my associate Lori and I visited her in her home,' Maggie said. 'We saw the for-sale sign outside and asked her about it, and she said something like *I might get a flat down by the river, they're really nice.* Not, *we* might get a flat, but a definite *I*. It was a slip on her part, knowing as we now do the fate of her partner, but it escaped me at the time. But as Jimmy says, their plan was ticking along beautifully and twelve months on, they were ready to move on to the next stage.'

'That's right,' Jimmy said. 'They knew that eventually the sales of Eilish's book would start to drop off, but they had a Plan B waiting in the wings. And that plan meant that Drew Henderson had to be killed too. So Christabelle recruited a couple of her minxy schoolfriends whose job was to latch up with Drew at his favoured Burns Tavern and leave him with no doubt that they were up for sex. Afterwards, one of them lured him into a secluded lane off Mitchell Street, where Isla was waiting to stab him to death. But luckily, Maggie and Lori remembered something that put the police onto that.'

She nodded. 'Just as we were leaving Isla's house on the night of the murder, another taxi arrived which happened to be from the same firm as our driver's. The police have followed it up with the taxi firm and have been told that the driver dropped off a young girl who had said she was going to be babysitting for her aunt. That was

Christabelle, who was supposedly at a sleepover with one of her schoolfriends, who had been persuaded to provide her with an alibi. The driver was then asked if he would come back an hour and a half later to take a woman into town, dropping her off near the Central Station. CCTV subsequently spotted a hooded woman walking down Gordon Street in the direction of Mitchell Street. The cameras couldn't identify her of course, but the police do have a capture of the moment she got out of the taxi, and the capture naturally includes its registration number. There's no doubt that woman is Isla Bonnar, and I'm sure a jury will have no difficulty in working out why she took that late-night trip into town.'

'Yeah, they're all locked up now awaiting trial, so their carefully worked-out plan is now dead in the water, thank goodness,' Jimmy said. 'But that didn't make it any less audacious.' He paused and smiled at the gathered journalists. 'You'll remember the headlines you guys wrote after the identity of the Glasgow victim was revealed as Drew Henderson? *Second Bonnar Sister Suffers Death Tragedy,* or something like that, wasn't it? Just as they had planned, the sisters were back on the front pages again, and ready to launch phase two. Firstly, there would be the sensational revelation that it was in fact Isla who had written the first book, not Eilish. Secondly, there would be the announcement that a follow-up book was planned, focusing on the terrible loss that Isla's young children were now having to deal with. Then thirdly, Christabelle Macbeth would reveal that she had been raped by her murdered uncle, and that she was now struggling with the mental health fall-out but wanted to share her pain, firstly on her social media channels, and then in a book that her auntie Isla was planning to write. We talked to their publishers,' he added, 'and they stood to make millions.

They'd be richer than their sister Kirsty, and probably more famous too. Which, of course, was the point of it all.'

'That's right,' Maggie said, then paused. 'I just wanted to mention one final point to put a seal on this, and that's the matter of Isla Bonnar's laptop, the one she used to write *My Daddy's Dead*. It was seized by the police, and as I expected, it proved she had started to write the book at least a month before Alasdair Macbeth died. And that, ladies and gentlemen, is a fact that's going to take some explaining when she's standing in the dock.'

***

Afterwards, there were a few media interviews for Maggie to take care of, organised by Yash Patel and strictly policed to a maximum of five minutes per journalist. But soon she was done, and she was able to join her friends back in the main room. Returning, she was surprised to find a large and garish object taking centre stage on their table.

'Wow, is that an *actual* Aquanaut Island?' she said, surprised.

'It is indeed,' Frank said. 'Thanks to the slightly dodgy efforts of the excellent DC Ronnie French, our friend and colleague.'

'How come?' Lori asked.

'That gal from Suffolk Police who was leaking the details of the shipments to the gangsters had three in her garage,' French explained. 'I relieved her of one of them in case we needed it for evidence.'

Lexy laughed. 'But in the end, the Northamptonshire boys recovered about five hundred of them from a warehouse in Dudley.

And the distributors claimed on their insurance, so they don't want them back.'

'So this one's going spare,' Frank said. 'Except, we've been thinking. Me, Jimmy and Ronnie that is. And Eleanor too, who in fact came up with the suggestion in the first place.'

'Aye, that's right,' Jimmy said, looking strangely uneasy. 'But we don't know how you'll feel about it Maggie, given how much Ollie wants one for Christmas.'

'Okay...' she said slowly, then smiled as she began to work out where the conversation might be going. In fact, *praying* it might be going in that direction.

'You see, it's the season of goodwill to all men, and I suppose that includes women and, above all, kids too,' Frank said tentatively. 'And so we thought that we should really donate this to a children's ward at a local hospital. The poor wee things will be having such a horrible time, and it would really cheer them up. And the thing is, there's loads of them coming into the country soon and we could get Ollie one later, couldn't we? So he wouldn't really be missing out for long.'

Maggie burst out laughing. 'Thank *God* for that, because I was so worried about telling you after all the effort you had been going to. Here, let me show you something.'

Frank gave her a puzzled look as she rummaged in her clutch-bag then took out a folded sheet of paper and handed it to him. 'It's Ollie's letter to Santa. He doesn't really believe any more, but he still likes to write the letter.'

He took it from her and started to read. And then let out a loud guffaw. 'What, he doesn't want an Aquanaut Island after all? He wants an *England* shirt instead, with his favourite Arsenal player's name on the back? An *England* shirt?' he repeated in mock disgust.

Jimmy laughed. 'But he is English after all. Why wouldn't he want that?'

Frank frowned. 'I know, I know. But he's a brilliant wee player and he's qualified to play for Scotland too and we don't want him getting any wrong ideas about this in his formative years. And have you heard him recently anyway? The wee boy's got a perfect Glasgow accent now, a better one than me in fact. But of course, I'd be just as proud if he played for England,' he added. 'But let me tell you something now. See our new wee baby? The first thing we're getting him after he's born is a Scotland shirt.'

'But we're rubbish at sport,' Jimmy said, laughing, 'except for Andy Murray of course. And don't forget the new wee guy will be qualified to play for England too, through his lovely mum.'

'You're right about all of that,' his brother conceded. 'So maybe we'll get him a wee tennis racket instead then.'

Maggie laughed. 'And you're so sure it's a boy we're having? Because we'll find out soon enough.'

Frank leaned over her and kissed her. 'I don't mind which we have. Because boy or girl, it'll be perfect. Like you.'

A BIG THANK YOU FROM AUTHOR ROB WYLLIE

Dear Reader,

A huge thank you for reading *Murder at Christmas Lodge* and I do hope you enjoyed it! For indie authors like me, star ratings are our lifeblood, so it would be great if you could take the trouble to post a star rating on Amazon when prompted.

If you did enjoy this book, I'm sure you would also like the other books in the series -you can find them all (at very reasonable prices!) on Amazon. Search for 'Rob Wyllie' or 'Maggie Bainbridge'

Also, take a look at my webpage - that's **robwyllie.com** - where you can download a free Maggie Bainbridge mystery for your Kindle.

Thank you for your support!

Regards

Rob

Printed in Great Britain
by Amazon